# SKATING WITH THE STATUE OF LIBERTY

★ ★ ★

## ALSO BY SUSAN LYNN MEYER

*Black Radishes*

# SKATING
## ✦ WITH ✦
# THE STATUE
### ✦✦ OF ✦✦
# LIBERTY

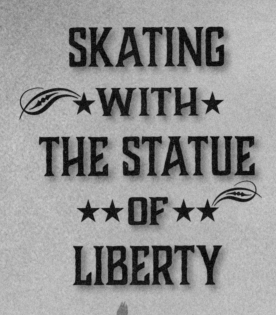

## SUSAN LYNN MEYER

DELACORTE PRESS

Text copyright © 2016 by Susan Lynn Meyer
Jacket art copyright © 2016 by Tim Jessell

All rights reserved. Published in the United States by Delacorte Press,
an imprint of Random House Children's Books,
a division of Penguin Random House LLC, New York.

Delacorte Press is a registered trademark and the colophon is a trademark of
Penguin Random House LLC.

Visit us on the Web! randomhousekids.com

Educators and librarians, for a variety of teaching tools, visit us at
RHTeachersLibrarians.com

Library of Congress Cataloging-in-Publication Data
Meyer, Susan
Skating with the Statue of Liberty / Susan Lynn Meyer.—First edition.
pages ; cm
Summary: After having escaped with his family from Nazi-occupied France,
Gustave finds a home in New York City, still worried about Marcel, his good friend
who he left behind, and surprised to find bigotry in America, too.
ISBN 978-0-385-74155-2 (hc) — ISBN 978-0-375-98576-8 (ebk) —
ISBN 978-0-375-99010-6 (glb) [1. Refugees—Fiction. 2. Immigrants—Fiction.
3. Jews—United States—Fiction. 4. French—United States—Fiction. 5. Family
life—New York (State)—New York—Fiction. 6. Race relations—Fiction.
7. New York (N.Y.)—History—20th century—Fiction.] I. Title.
PZ7.M571752Sk 2016
[Fic]—dc23
2015004686

The text of this book is set in 12.25-point Caslon.
Jacket design by Sarah Hock
Interior design by Trish Parcell

Printed in the United States of America
10 9 8 7 6 5 4 3 2 1
First Edition

*In memory of my father,*
*Jean-Pierre Meyer*

# ★ 1 ★

*On the Atlantic Ocean*
*January 1942*

**G**ustave had the dream again the last night on board the ship. The Nazi soldier was shoving his friend, Marcel, forcing him farther and farther away down a long, dark Paris street. As they turned the corner, Marcel stumbled and looked back, his eyes glistening. This time Marcel raised his arm, and before the soldier yanked it down, Gustave saw a flash of something yellow.

*"Au secours!" Help!* Marcel called. In the dream, Gustave tried to run toward his friend, but the air was heavy, and then Gustave was swimming, doing the breaststroke, frog-kicking his way across the Atlantic to France, yet the waves kept pushing him backward, pushing him toward America. He was struggling to keep his head above the waves, but when he tried to shout, salt water rushed at him, filling his mouth and lungs.

Gustave cried out, waking himself with a jerk when he heard his own strangled voice. He lay in the dark, gasping, his heart pounding, feeling the ship, the *Carvalho Araujo,* heaving up and down. His mind, half-asleep still, churned like the rough sea. What was that yellow thing in Marcel's hand? A feather, he suddenly realized. That yellow feather he and Marcel hadn't been able to find in a Boy Scout scavenger hunt one day back when they all lived in Paris. Marcel was trying to pass the feather to him. It felt desperately important.

But the ship rocked and creaked, and now Gustave was waking up all the way, his mind clearing. That scavenger hunt was long over. Gustave was on his way to America, and Marcel was still somewhere in Europe, no one knew where, far away now. No matter how much Marcel cried out, Gustave couldn't help him.

Gustave was shaking and drenched with sweat. He could feel the others still sleeping thickly around him. Papa was in the bunk below him, breathing evenly. An unpleasant stranger, Monsieur Lambert, who was their temporary cabinmate, snored loudly across from him on the other lower bunk. In the upper bunk across from Gustave, his cousin, Jean-Paul, turned over, the blankets rustling. Just a year and a half ago, in Paris, it had been the three of them against the world, Gustave, Jean-Paul, and Marcel. In Boy Scouts together, in school, hanging out in the afternoons, it was all for one and one for all, the Three Musketeers. Now there were only two of them, Gustave and Jean-Paul, sailing away from Europe and the

Nazis and heading, with their families, toward an inconceivable new life in America.

Gustave stretched his leg across the space between the bunks and nudged his cousin with his foot.

*"Qu'est-ce qui t'arrive?"* *What's going on?* Jean-Paul was instantly awake. He sat up abruptly and whacked his head on the low ceiling. "Ow!"

The men below were awake now.

"Shut *up!*" Even half-asleep, Monsieur Lambert sounded as if he wanted to strangle someone.

"Boys?" Papa's voice was weary. "What's the matter?"

Through the dirty porthole, Gustave could see a dim light in the sky. "I just . . . I wanted to be up early. Let's all go up on deck and be the first to see America."

"We won't be there for hours!" Papa said groggily. He turned over and went back to sleep. But across the aisle, Jean-Paul pushed off his blankets.

Gustave reached for his clothes at the end of his bed and wiggled into them, then scrambled down and fumbled in the darkness under Papa's bunk for his shoes.

"Don't you dare come back until we're awake!" Monsieur Lambert grunted as Jean-Paul pushed the cabin door closed behind them.

"Race you to the top deck!" Jean-Paul whispered, starting to run before he finished saying it.

"No fair!" Gustave sprinted after him down the corridor, up the winding stairway to the first deck, and across the inside of the ship. He squeezed past Jean-Paul on the first set of stairs, but he couldn't help hesitating for a split second at the captain's news board outside the salon, and Jean-Paul pushed ahead of him and raced up the second flight of stairs.

"Beat you!" Jean-Paul shouted triumphantly as he shoved open the door to the top deck. A bitterly cold wind slammed into them. Gustave hurriedly buttoned his flapping coat and turned up his collar. The sun was rising behind the ship, a cold, distant yellow ball in the eastern sky. No other passengers were on deck yet, just one yawning sailor on watch.

"We're the first people awake," Jean-Paul exulted, panting and leaning forward over the railing. "We're going to see America first!"

The company of his cousin and the daylight sparkling on the waves were chasing away Gustave's dream. A thick band stretched across the horizon. "There!" Gustave pointed. "I see land!"

"That's fog."

Jean-Paul was right. A few minutes later, the gray band dissolved into nothingness.

"I wish we were sailing right into New York, not Baltimore." Jean-Paul yawned widely. "I want to see the Statue of Liberty."

New York. At the name, Gustave's brain belatedly processed the headline he had seen on the captain's news board. NAZI U-BOATS TORPEDO SHIP OFF MONTAUK POINT, NEW YORK. Images of people struggling in the cold, dark waves flashed into Gustave's head, images of a ship in flames. No wonder the New York harbor was closed.

Gustave scanned the ocean apprehensively, something he did every few minutes whenever he was on deck. Nothing visible at the ship's stern. No signs of a Nazi U-boat on the port side. No air tubes or periscopes from a submarine sticking above the waves to starboard. None beyond the prow.

Jean-Paul stamped his feet to warm them. "Do you think you'll like the United States when we get there?" he asked abruptly.

"Well, it'll be safer than France is right now."

"But what if they don't like people like us there either?"

"We'll be far away from the Nazis. They won't hate Jews." Gustave stopped, unpleasant memories floating up in his mind. Could that really be true?

"Far away from my father too, though." Jean-Paul's face clouded. His father, a French soldier, was in a German camp for French prisoners of war.

"But he'll come join you when he gets released. He knows where we're going."

"I guess. You're lucky you started learning English already. We hardly learned anything in Paris after the Nazis took over."

"Yeah, well, I can't say that much."

"Remember that Tintin book you had about America, where he gets captured by that Blackfoot chief?" Jean-Paul laughed. "Did you bring it?"

Gustave hesitated. "That one was Marcel's."

Jean-Paul fell silent, and his eyes went blank. Gustave was starting to recognize that look. It meant that Jean-Paul had gone off in his head, somewhere far away. These days, he sometimes stayed like that for a long time, not answering if anyone talked to him. He hadn't been like that before the war. The change had happened sometime in the year and a half that they had been apart, Jean-Paul still in Paris with his mother and sister while Gustave and his parents were hiding in Saint-Georges, a tiny village in the countryside.

Gustave frowned at his unseeing cousin and then looked back at the sea. Jean-Paul wouldn't be any help in watching for U-boats now.

"I'm starving," Jean-Paul burst out suddenly. "Let's go get breakfast."

"You go. I'll keep watch."

"All right." Jean-Paul ran off.

Gustave watched him go and then turned his eyes away, over the port side of the ship. He glimpsed movement, and his muscles tensed. But it was something wonderful. A porpoise leapt out of the water and crested. Then another emerged from the sea right behind it, and the two of them raced the ship, flashing up over the waves, slipping down into the dark water, and leaping up again, joyfully, into the sunlight.

As the porpoises moved away, getting smaller and smaller against the horizon, Gustave realized that he had stopped scanning the sea. He shifted his eyes to starboard, and his heart jolted in alarm. There, jutting up from the glittering water, was a dark tube with a funny-shaped top.

*Periscope.* The word flashed through his mind as if he

were hearing someone say it. It was the periscope from a Nazi submarine. He tried to shout, but his voice wasn't working. For a long moment his feet wouldn't unstick from the deck. Then he was running, slipping once and righting himself.

"Help! Germans!" he managed to cry out, but the deck was empty now, and the wind swallowed his words. He darted to the stairs, glancing back at the periscope. It had shifted and was changing shape. A pair of wings stretched out, the periscope became the long neck of a cormorant, and the dark bird lifted up and flapped away over the water.

Gustave collapsed into embarrassed laughter, feeling it going on and on, strangely out of his control. When the laughter finally stopped, he drew in a few shuddering breaths. Luckily, the deck was still empty. No one had heard him shouting or seen him laughing like a crazy person. He rubbed his eyes with shaky fingers.

After a half hour or so, Jean-Paul thudded against the railing to Gustave's left, holding a partly eaten pastry.

"*Salut!*" he said, cheerful again. "Your turn for breakfast. Hey, while you're there, get me another one of these."

"Are our parents awake yet?"

"They're in the dining room with the other French passengers. When I left, everyone was talking about how they snuck extra money out of Europe and complaining about how you could starve on the little you're allowed to bring to America. Monsieur Benoit announced that 'the best hiding place is in plain sight.' He *is* pretty smart. Nobody but a jeweler would have thought of prying off his old suitcase corners, making new ones out of gold, and painting them black. That's a neat trick!"

Gustave shifted nervously. "Papa didn't tell . . ."

"No. Your mother elbowed him when he opened his mouth. My fingers are still sore from rolling those bills around the corset bones."

"Mine too." Their family had several black market American bills, sewn into Maman's corset. Those and the two uncut diamonds buried deep in the sawdust of her pincushion were enough to keep them alive for about six months.

"*Dépêche-toi! Hurry!* They only serve breakfast for another half hour."

Gustave hesitated. "You'll watch for U-boats while I'm gone?"

"Of course! Go! And don't forget my pastry!"

Gustave's parents were just getting up from breakfast. He gobbled down some bread with plum compote, grabbed a sweet roll, and ran back up to the top deck. He handed the pastry to Jean-Paul, who stuck it into his coat pocket. Several sailors were now on deck, keeping watch. The ocean was calm, and light sparkled on the water. Finally, there was something that looked like land, a thick, dark strip bobbing above the horizon, disappearing, then bobbing up again, growing more and more solid.

"*That's* America!" Gustave shouted.

"Where?" Jean-Paul searched the horizon frantically. "Yes! That must be it!"

Soon the other passengers were gathering on both decks, squinting in the cold sunshine, dressed in their best clothes for the arrival. Gustave's parents and Aunt Geraldine made their way through the crowd and joined him and Jean-Paul at their spot by the railing. Elderly Monsieur Benoit, the friendly jeweler from Lyon, who had been to the United States before, was with them. As a wave surged against the ship, Papa clutched Gustave's shoulder for support. His left leg was shorter than his right and slightly twisted, the lingering result of childhood polio. His bad leg had made it hard for him to balance during the sea voyage, but it had also kept him out of the French army. So he was here now, not in a German prisoner-of-war camp like Jean-Paul's father. Gustave flushed, glad that Papa was here, but also ashamed of being glad that Papa was free when Uncle David wasn't. He squeezed to the side to let Papa grip the railing. As he did, Giselle, Jean-Paul's little sister, slipped in next to Papa.

"Not so near the edge!" Aunt Geraldine gasped, clutching Giselle's dress and pulling her back. The shapes of buildings were starting to form on the horizon. No Statue of Liberty holding up her torch to welcome them, but it was definitely a city, definitely the United States.

"There it is," Maman said in a choked voice. "America."

"The land of freedom!" exclaimed Monsieur Benoit. "Where 'all men are created equal.'"

"No more laws making trouble for Jews," murmured Aunt Geraldine. "No Nazis."

"Finally!" Papa said, his deep voice cracking. "We're safe."

9

It was hard to believe, after they had barely escaped from Europe with their lives. Gustave watched as if America might disappear, might turn out to be a mirage, might sprout wings and fly away like the cormorant. But it was real.

Where all men are created equal, Gustave thought. His heart swelled in his chest. At least Jean-Paul was here now, even though he was different from the way he used to be. At least he was here and safe. If only Marcel were on the ship and could see this too, Gustave thought, sharp grief piercing him and mingling with his excitement.

A man standing by the railing was crying, quietly but openly, dabbing at his face with a white handkerchief. Crackly music boomed over the ship's loudspeaker. "O say, can you see . . ."

The few Americans on the ship began to sing their national anthem, and then several foreign voices picked up the tune, the different accents blending. Other passengers murmured prayers. After nineteen months of Nazi persecution, after travelling from France through Spain and Portugal, after the long, cramped, seasick weeks aboard the ship from Lisbon, they had made it safely across the Atlantic, untouched by U-boats. They really were leaving Europe and the Nazis behind. They really were coming to a land of freedom, of equality. Blinking the blurriness out of his eyes, Gustave stared at the skyline of the city coming more and more sharply into view, as their ship, the *Carvalho Araujo,* steamed forward into Baltimore harbor, forward to America.

# ★ 2 ★

A discarded customs form drifted across the sunny upper deck. "There's one!" Jean-Paul shouted, but Gustave darted behind two women sitting on suitcases and grabbed it first.

He folded it into a paper airplane and tossed it into the air. "It's a British Spitfire! Coming your way!"

Jean-Paul jumped up, trying to catch it, but the sea breeze suddenly shifted, and the plane zoomed sharply down in front of a man's nose.

"Hey!" the man shouted.

"It's too crowded here for that, boys," Papa said wearily.

Their arrival in America was turning into something of an anticlimax. They had been waiting on board for two days now. All foreigners had to be interrogated and their papers inspected, one at a time, by FBI officials.

"Mine!" Giselle whined, running to her brother. Jean-Paul ignored her and retrieved the crumpled Spitfire, which had lodged between a large trunk and a violin case. Unfolding it, he sat down cross-legged on the deck next to Gustave and added it to the pile of scrap paper they had weighed down with the corner of Maman's handbag.

"Remember in Paris when we learned how to make folded paper animals from that book?" Gustave asked Jean-Paul, folding rapidly. "Look—a bird!"

"Does it fly?" Jean-Paul tossed it up, and a gust of wind carried it sideways, overboard.

"Hey! No!"

"Sorry. Tic-tac-toe?" Jean-Paul scooped up a pen and another discarded form.

"Bird!" Giselle whined. She reached out for the pile, but Jean-Paul tucked it under his foot. "That's *our* paper, Giselle," he said. "We found it."

Giselle wailed.

"Aren't they *ever* going to call our names?" Aunt Geraldine muttered to Maman.

Gustave and Jean-Paul had nearly used up the pile of paper when finally their names were called and they filed down the gangplank of the ship and into a building where they waited again, in a windowless, low-ceilinged room. Customs inspectors rummaged through each of their bags. Then a stern-looking man examined the forms and asked the adults even more questions, which were translated into strange-sounding French by the bored-looking man next to him. Gustave's attention wandered but snapped back when he heard, "Your family may now enter the country."

Papa kissed Maman joyfully. Aunt Geraldine lifted

Giselle high into the air. "We made it!" Gustave said, grinning at Jean-Paul. "We're in America!"

Outside, the sky had clouded over, and an early dusk was falling, but the clash of metal and the shouts of dock-workers still rang out. Papa tapped Gustave on the shoulder. "Get ready—you tell the cabdriver where to take us."

"Me?"

"Sure. Your English is the best."

When a yellow taxi pulled up, the driver leaned over and rolled down the window.

"Where to?" he shouted.

"We go to . . . to trrren stah-syohn," Gustave said shakily in English, climbing in.

The driver scowled at Gustave in the rearview mirror. "Which train station?"

Gustave looked at him blankly.

The cabdriver barked something else that Gustave didn't understand. Then he looked at Papa and repeated the question, sounding irritated. Papa nodded at Gustave.

"Trrren stah-syohn . . ." Gustave hesitated. "New York?" The driver sighed breathily and pulled into the street, honking at a truck in front of them and muttering to himself. Gustave caught the word "stupid," but he still felt a rush of pride. He had spoken English in America to a complete stranger—and it had worked!

He watched the streets of Baltimore blur by the windows of the cab. White marble steps gleamed through the dusk.

After a few miles, the driver pulled into a taxi line in front of an imposing white building. An illuminated clock on the front of the station spilled golden light out onto the street. In front of the building, an American flag waved proudly against the darkening blue of the sky. At the bottom of the flagpole, two men were working the pulley to bring it down for the night.

As soon as the taxi came to a stop, Jean-Paul and Gustave jumped out and started unloading bags, and Papa paid the taxi driver. A freezing drizzle was starting to come down. Behind them, another cab pulled up, and Gustave saw that Monsieur Benoit and some of the other French refugees his family had met on the ship had squeezed in together. Gustave tapped Papa and whispered urgently, "I need to find the toilets."

"Run on ahead," Papa said. "We can manage with the bags."

Shielding his face from the rapidly intensifying rain, Gustave ran toward the station doors. On the side of the building, he saw a sign with some words he didn't know, but also an arrow and the English word REST-ROOMS. He ran down the cement stairs and through a door marked MEN.

He was hit by a smell so strong that it made his eyes sting. The room was cold and lit by a single bare light-bulb. An overflowing trash can stood in the corner next to a chipped sink with an empty soap dish. As Gustave washed his hands with water afterward, he noticed that two men, both of them *africains*, had come in. He had only ever seen Africans in France once—a group with instrument cases in front of a theater in Paris. Gustave glanced curiously at their dark skin for a moment, until he noticed that they were both looking at him strangely. He rubbed his hands dry on his shirt and hurried out, glad to be breathing the fresh air.

At the top of the cement stairs, two women with elegantly coiffed blond hair were stepping out of a cab, holding umbrellas in their white-gloved hands. Both of them stared at Gustave. The taller one murmured something inaudible to her companion, then shot Gustave an unmistakable look of disgust. Gustave sidled past. Just beyond them a broad-shouldered young man with his collar turned up muttered something that sounded like a curse and spat onto the sidewalk in front of Gustave's feet.

A flash of memory hit Gustave. A French street and a shouting woman with a snarling face. Marcel and Jean-Paul running ahead of him through the rain. Spit dripping down his bare leg. *"Sale juif." Dirty Jew.*

But he couldn't understand why that would be happening here. Feeling bewildered, he ran toward the front of the building, where his family was standing with the other French refugees, surrounded by suitcases and trunks. Monsieur Benoit watched Gustave approach. Jean-Paul, who was squatting down to talk to a sleepy Giselle, straightened up.

"Where are the toilets?" he asked. "I need them too."

Gustave turned to point, but Monsieur Benoit interrupted. "Not there. Did you use those? They're the wrong ones."

"No, it was the men's room, I'm sure."

"Gustave, you went into the women's room?" Maman asked, amused. "I know English is hard to understand, but it isn't *that* hard, when you see women there!"

"No!" exclaimed Gustave. "I didn't!"

"But didn't you notice that people were looking at you in a funny way?" Monsieur Benoit asked.

"The sign said MEN," Gustave insisted. "There were other men in there." He looked down the dark side of the building. One of the African men was just coming up the steps.

"See?" said Gustave.

"Look at the sign again," said Monsieur Benoit.

Gustave peered through the dusk at the sign above the cement stairs. It *did* say MEN. But above that was a word that Gustave had ignored because he didn't know it. In crude, block print, the sign read COLORED.

# ★ 3 ★

"Colored?" Gustave sounded out the English word. "What does that mean?"

Monsieur Benoit cleared his throat. "The Americans have separate toilets for 'whites' and 'coloreds.'"

"Which are we?"

"We're . . . In America, Jews are considered 'white.' You should use the other toilets. 'Colored' is what the Americans call Africans. Or 'Negro'—I believe that's the more polite word."

"Why are there different toilets?"

"It's just the custom here, in the South. On one of my trips here before the war, someone told me about it," Monsieur Benoit said. "You won't see it farther north, when you're in New York."

"But . . ."

Papa flipped the timetable shut. "Gustave, we need to hurry! The train leaves in twenty minutes. Help bring the bags in and see if you and Jean-Paul can find the right toilets."

The men's room off the waiting room was heated and larger than the one outside the building. As Gustave waited for Jean-Paul, he washed his hands with soap, studying the brilliant white basins and shiny mirrors gleaming under bright lights. It was a lot cleaner than the bad-smelling room where he had been a few minutes ago.

When the boys left the men's room, the grand, high-ceilinged train station lobby was filled with echoing sound. It had gotten crowded and was now full of soldiers wearing khaki-colored military uniforms. He felt a surge of panic. They're American soldiers, Gustave told himself, as he and Jean-Paul hurried across the vast room to join their parents and they all went down the stairs to the track. They're on our side. But his breath came fast.

The train was packed. Sweating in their winter coats, squeezing their bags between the full seats, they made their way to the back of the train. Finally, they came to a car with a few empty seats and watched as the other French passengers ahead of them stowed their bags and sat down.

Papa and Monsieur Benoit took two seats together, and Aunt Geraldine and Maman sat in the two behind them. The seats across the aisle were empty. Gustave heaved the suitcase he was carrying onto the luggage rack.

Jean-Paul pushed ahead. "I call the window seat!" he said. "Want to play cards?" He pulled a deck out of the small bag by his feet.

"Me play!" Giselle whined, wiggling down from Aunt

Geraldine's lap and crawling over Maman so that she could squeeze in between the boys.

"You're too little," said Jean-Paul.

Giselle climbed onto Jean-Paul's lap and grabbed at the cards, knocking some to the floor.

"Giselle!" Jean-Paul cried out.

"Maman!" Gustave said, nudging his mother across the aisle. "Tell Aunt Geraldine that Giselle is annoying us!"

Maman groaned. "Can't you boys tell her a story? Then maybe she'll go to sleep. She's cranky because she's tired."

"No way. Not me. You do it, Gustave."

"She's *your* sister."

"Forget it."

Aunt Geraldine was already asleep in the corner, leaning against the window, her head tilted back and her mouth slightly open. Gustave looked reluctantly at Giselle, who was sucking her curled index finger. She was a decent sort of kid when she was in a good mood, but she was being aggravating right now, and he couldn't think of any fairy tales. Then he grinned, remembering the way Marcel had once narrated "The Three Little Pigs" for a skit at Boy Scouts.

"Once there were three stupid little pigs and a very smart, hungry wolf," Gustave started. "But one of the pigs wasn't *quite* as dumb as the others."

Giselle took her finger out of her mouth and looked at him with big, dark eyes. *"Les maisons?"*

"Yep, you know this story? They made houses."

By the time he had gotten to the part of the story where the wolf tries to blow down the brick house, Giselle had fallen asleep. Gustave finished the story out loud anyway, murmuring it to himself. He wasn't going to stop before telling the best part—the part where the wolf slides down the chimney, lands in the boiling water, screams his way back up the chimney, and runs away forever. Giselle's curly head was heavy, warm, and damp on his arm. Gustave shoved her upright several times, trying to get her to lean on Jean-Paul instead, but she kept flopping back against him, and finally he let her stay there. Across the aisle, Maman's eyes were closed. Jean-Paul seemed to have fallen asleep too, with his head leaning against the rain-spattered window. Gustave let his head fall back on the seat, listening to the wheels of the train, the chuff of the engine, and the intermittent, lonesome wail of the whistle.

In the darkness, behind his closed eyes, Gustave could be almost anywhere. His mind drifted along with the rhythm of the train wheels. Gradually, the wheels started to sound like the ticking of the clock in their old apartment in Paris, where they had lived before the war. In his mind, Gustave could see the way the sunlight fell across the wooden floor. It was Sunday morning, and he was running with Marcel and Jean-Paul down the steps of the apartment building and over to the bakery at the corner. For a moment, Gustave could almost smell fresh French bread, could feel it, warm and crusty, in his hand.

He pulled himself awake, focusing his eyes on the cold American night outside and the rain running down the train window. He wouldn't think about Paris again. That world was gone. Misery twisted inside him. The Nazis were in Paris now, their soldiers on the streets in ugly green uniforms, their banners draped arrogantly over French buildings. Although Gustave and his parents had fled Paris just before the Germans came, he had seen photos in the newspaper. Sometimes Jean-Paul talked about what it had been like, but he usually wouldn't say much.

Gustave pushed his memories of Paris away fiercely. If he wanted to think about France, he might as well think about the tiny village of Saint-Georges-sur-Cher, where he and his parents had been living until recently. Things were better there because, unlike Paris, it wasn't in the part of France occupied by the Germans. But even in Unoccupied France, the Germans still told the French leaders what to do.

Gustave should look to the future, his parents said. Think about America, about the good new life they would have here.

*A-me-ri-ca*, the train wheels started to sing in his ears. *A-me-ri-ca, A-me-ri-ca*. Gustave remembered the way the American flag had looked, waving in the deep blue sky over the train station. The darkness behind his eyes closed in from all sides, and he drifted into sleep.


Gustave's head snapped forward, waking him, as the train stopped with a jolt.

"Where are we?" murmured Maman's voice. "Not Philadelphia already?"

"It must be a checkpoint," Papa said.

"A border?" asked Aunt Geraldine nervously. "They're going to check our papers again?"

"Oh, no. No borders—it's all one big country," said Monsieur Benoit. "There must be some mechanical problem with the train."

Jean-Paul was awake too, rubbing his eyes. Giselle still flopped, heavily asleep, against Gustave's side. Beyond the French voices, Gustave heard the Americans talking, sounding indignant at this unplanned stop. In the blackness outside the window, he could see only that they were at a small, dimly lit station.

The door at the front of the train car opened, letting in a gust of cold air. The conductor stepped in, and behind him came two men with stern faces, one tall and broad-shouldered, the other much more slightly built. All conversation ceased abruptly.

"Who is Mister Ben-oyt? Mister Arn-owd Ben-oyt?" the bigger of the two men demanded.

The man's accent was so strange that it took Gustave a moment to realize that he was saying Monsieur Benoit's name. A chill ran over him as the conductor pointed toward the French passengers.

Monsieur Benoit stood up slowly and stepped past Papa into the aisle. Both men walked toward him. The bigger one said something and gestured. Monsieur Benoit held his arms out to his sides. The man examined the flaps of his coat, then patted his hands over Monsieur Benoit's chest and arms and even down his legs.

The burly man straightened, his face red, and barked

something again. Monsieur Benoit reached up and took down his bags from the rack over the seat. The man examined their exteriors, rubbed at their metal corners, then shook his head and handed them to the thinner man behind him.

The front door of the car opened again. Two railway men staggered in, carrying Monsieur Benoit's trunk.

"Ah!" The burly man squeezed past the thin man and strode toward it. He leaned over.

"Arn-owd Ben-oyt!" he read out, pointing at the label on the trunk. "Yours?" he demanded.

"Yes." Monsieur Benoit spoke the English words quietly. "I am Arnaud Benoit."

Huffing, the big man leaned down and scratched at one of the corners of the trunk. The dark paint flaked off. Gustave gasped. Even from his seat, he could see the soft gleam of the trunk's corner.

"Gold!" the thinner man said triumphantly. "There it is!"

Gustave's heart thudded. Were they all going to be searched?

The man with the big belly unclasped something from his waist and held it out toward Monsieur Benoit. Light glinted on dull metal. The elderly jeweler held his arms out, and the handcuffs clanked shut around his wrists. He stumbled slightly as the big man pushed him to the side and strode toward the other French passengers, shouting.

They looked at one another, bewildered. Monsieur Benoit turned around. His face was pale, his hands were shackled awkwardly in front of him, and Gustave saw sweat on his forehead below the brim of his hat. His voice was shaky but still courteous as he translated the command.

"These gentlemen are from the government, from the FBI. They say that all foreign passengers must get out their papers and bags for inspection. One row at a time. Starting here."

A low, panicked murmur ran through the railroad car. People began to stand and pull at their bags. The thinner of the two FBI agents started patting down another Frenchman from the ship. He ripped open the lining of the man's coat, pulled something out, shouted, and pushed the man forward. Gustave's pulse pounded in his temples. What if Maman's corset with the hidden money crackled? Or what if they felt around carefully and noticed that the stays of the corset were bulkier than they should be?

Across the aisle Maman sat still, as if frozen, her eyes on the floor. Giselle was still sleeping against Gustave. His thoughts raced. They wouldn't disturb a woman and a sleeping baby, would they? He slid his hands underneath his baby cousin. Keep sleeping, Giselle! he thought, as if he could will her to stay asleep if he thought it forcefully enough. Don't wake up!

Maman lifted her head, and a look flashed between

her and Gustave as she opened her arms to hold the little girl. Amazingly, Giselle remained asleep as Maman took her onto her lap and pressed her against her waist where the money was hidden. Giselle's feet, in tiny, scuffed buckle shoes, dangled in the aisle.

The FBI agents were opening bags, rifling through them, and patting down people two rows ahead. The big-bellied one looked at Gustave and Jean-Paul.

"Stand up, boys!" he said wearily, as if he were getting bored. Then he looked at Maman and Aunt Geraldine and gestured. "Stand!"

Maman looked up and smiled, dimpling. She pointed helplessly at Giselle on her lap. *"Le bébé,"* she murmured, closing her eyes and tilting her head to act out sleeping.

The agent began to pat down Jean-Paul and then Gustave. Gustave felt big, sweaty hands, too close, too personal, on his chest, his legs. Then the agent stood up, sighing, his knees creaking.

"Oh, fine," he said to Maman and Aunt Geraldine, nodding. "You ladies stay seated."

There were no more passengers from the *Carvalho Araujo* in the seats behind them, only Americans with suspicious eyes, silently staring.

The big-bellied man made his way back to the front of the train car. He and the other FBI agent took Monsieur Benoit and the second Frenchman by the elbows and steered them, wrists shackled, toward the door of the train. Monsieur Benoit's hat slipped as he stumbled through the door, and the agent shoved it back onto his gray head, perching it at an odd angle. Gustave clenched his fists until his fingernails bit into his palms. He watched through the window as the FBI agents led the two men across the platform to an automobile waiting in the shadows.

Nobody spoke until the train started forward again and American voices—loud, startled, curious—rose around them, creating a screen of noise.

"Papa!" Gustave whispered, leaning forward. "Where are they taking him?"

"To jail, I think, then back to France," Papa murmured. "For breaking the law by bringing in the gold."

"Back to the Nazis?" Jean-Paul's voice cracked.

"They must have found something on the other man too," Aunt Geraldine whispered.

"Someone must have informed on him," Gustave said.

"I bet it was Monsieur Lambert, from our cabin," Jean-Paul said indignantly. "No one else would be mean enough to do that."

Maman looked at Gustave. "That was quick thinking," she whispered, glancing down at Giselle on her lap.

Gustave felt a momentary throb of relief. But what if the FBI searched them when they got off the train in New York?

"Monsieur Benoit was planning to stay with his nephew in Philadelphia, who's a lawyer," Papa said. "He gave me the phone number so we could stay in touch. I'll call his nephew when we get to New York and let him know what happened. Maybe he can help."

Gustave's family fell silent. Around them, the Americans were still talking loudly.

"Refugees," Gustave heard a man say. Then from behind him, he heard a woman utter a one-syllable word. It was the first time he had heard the word in English, yet somehow he knew what it meant. He knew that tone of voice. It was the same tone of voice in which he had heard certain people in France hiss "*juifs*," the same tone of voice in which Germans spat out "*Juden*." He hadn't thought he would hear that particular mixture of repulsion and smug superiority here in America. But he had. The woman had muttered "Jews."

Nausea rose in Gustave's throat. Jean-Paul was staring out the window. Across the aisle, Maman and Aunt Geraldine were soothing Giselle, who had woken up cranky. Either they hadn't heard or they hadn't understood.

The train rumbled onward, through the night. The wheels clacked rhythmically, energetically in the darkness. Gradually Gustave's eyes closed, but for hours he wasn't quite sure whether he was asleep or awake, until the loudspeaker crackled.

"Ne-e-e-e-e-w Yawk!" the conductor roared. "Penn Station!"

Lugging his two heavy bags, feeling exhausted and grimy, Gustave stumbled out behind the grown-ups into the vast, crowded brilliance of the train station. It was warmly lit and echoing, a blur of light and noise, even in the middle of the night. He glanced around, but he saw no sign of any further baggage checks. No sign of the FBI. Everyone seemed to be travelling somewhere or waiting for someone.

Papa's voice rang out joyfully. "Cousin Henri! Cousine

Thérèse!" He hurried toward an elderly couple. Gustave paused at a newsstand, trying to decipher the English headlines of the newspapers on display—something about ships, something about Japan—but the others were getting too far ahead. He hurried to catch up with them, the suitcases he was carrying banging painfully against his legs.

The tall, stout man and slight, gnarled woman Papa was embracing looked almost like Americans, Gustave thought, but there was still something French about them. Maybe it was the pattern of the silk scarf Cousine Thérèse had knotted around her neck. He had a flash of memory from a day long ago. He was much younger and eating ice cream with some of Papa's visiting relatives at a café in France by a blindingly blue sea. Deep purple ice cream, he remembered suddenly. It had dripped and stained his shirt. *Cassis* ice cream. Black currant. His favorite. He hung back now, watching the adults embrace.

"And this tall young man must be Gustave!" Cousin Henri's voice boomed. Gustave felt his hand in the elderly man's large, warm grip and looked up into his friendly face. "*Bienvenue!* Welcome to the United States!"

In the morning, at Cousin Henri's apartment, the adults made plans over breakfast. Cousine Thérèse was going to take Papa, Maman, and Aunt Geraldine to meet with some people at HIAS, the Hebrew Immigrant Aid Society, to get help with apartments and jobs and to find out about night school. Cousin Henri offered to take charge of Jean-Paul and Gustave.

"What do you say, boys?" Cousin Henri asked. "While your parents deal with the boring stuff, do you want to go up the Empire State Building with me? See how your new city looks from the top of the tallest building in the world?"

"Sure!" said Gustave and Jean-Paul together.

"You're lucky!" Papa said. "First things first for the grown-ups."

As everyone got ready to leave, Gustave caught Papa in the hall, where he was waiting for a turn in the bathroom. "Will you ask those HIAS people if they can help find Marcel and get him and his mother out of France?" he whispered urgently.

Papa hesitated. "I'll see what I can do. It depends on what the organization is like. Go—have a good time with your cousin."

Jean-Paul and Cousin Henri were in the kitchen with their coats on.

"Look at this, boys." Cousin Henri poured pills from a medicine bottle into his palm. "You know what these are made of? Gold! I take them for my arthritis." He winked and took a pill with a big swig of water as the boys stared.

"I can't believe they make pills out of gold in this country!" Gustave whispered to Jean-Paul as he put on his coat. "People here must be so rich!"

Outside, a dusting of snow covered the sidewalks. "It's freezing!" Jean-Paul said, pulling his hat down over his ears. "It was a lot warmer yesterday."

"In Baltimore? You were a lot farther south there," Cousin Henri explained. "New York winters are bitterly cold."

But the bus was steamy, hot, and crowded. They got seats in the back.

"Watch out the window," Cousin Henri said from the seat behind the two of them as the bus turned. "There. That's the east side of Central Park. We'll go there another day when it's warmer. There are playing fields, a lake, a zoo, and statues and fountains. You'll love my favorite statue, Balto."

"Who's he? An American general?" Jean-Paul asked.

Cousin Henri laughed. "He's a sled dog. He pulled a

sled carrying medicine through a blizzard to some sick children in Alaska. He reminds me of a dog I had when I was a child in France."

"Why don't you have a dog now?" asked Gustave.

"Oh, in an apartment—I just don't think it is right. Dogs need space to run free. In the French countryside, when I was a child," Cousin Henri said wistfully, "there were meadows and woods to run in."

After a while the bus left the park behind and entered an area with tall buildings. "Now we're going to make a quick stop," Cousin Henri said, pulling the cord. "I want you to see the New York Public Library."

As they got out, they saw a parade going up Fifth Avenue, a large group of people with placards and banners. The marchers were all *africains*, Gustave noticed, or—what was the American word? *"Negroes."* He said the word silently to himself, looking at the signs the marchers were carrying. Some words that were almost the same in French leapt out at him: LIBERTY, JUSTICE, VICTORY, DEMOCRACY.

"What's going on, Cousin Henri?" he asked, jumping to look over the shoulders of the people standing in front of him. "Why are they marching?"

"Did something happen with the war?" Jean-Paul asked nervously.

"No, no," Cousin Henri said, glancing at the parade over his shoulder and turning away. "It's some sort of Negro protest. Nothing to do with us. Now look, isn't this a beautiful building?"

On each side of the library steps, massive stone lions

guarded the entrance. Jean-Paul ran up. Cousin Henri put his hand on Gustave's shoulder for support and started up slowly.

"I always liked those lions," he said. "That one on the right looks a bit like Charles de Gaulle to me."

Gustave laughed. With his long face and serious expression, the stone lion did look a little like the French general.

When they got to the top of the steps, Gustave looked back at the parade. From up here, he could see that there were quite a lot of people marching.

"As soon as you get an address, you can get a library card," Cousin Henri said, breathing heavily, as the three of them went in. "There are also smaller branches all around the city. We'll just peek inside for a moment." He led the way to the main reading room, and they peered in. Bronze lamps shone on massive oak tables surrounded by readers, and overhead, ornate gilding framed panels painted with rosy summer skies. The hush of the room seemed to vibrate with energy.

"Are you sure we can use the library? Even though we aren't American citizens?" Gustave whispered as they went back out. Clouds had gathered while they were inside, and the day had turned gray and even colder than before.

"Sure. You're going to find out that America is a big and generous country." Cousin Henri stopped with his hand on the railing. "At least, it is for the people who get in," he added after a moment, in an undertone.

Gustave's mind flashed back to Lisbon, in Portugal, to

the interminable lines of desperate Jews at the consulates. If his family hadn't had a relative in America, they never would have been given papers to enter the United States. Most of those people were stuck in Europe.

As the three of them waited at the bus stop, Gustave's dream about Marcel and the yellow feather washed back over him, leaving him dizzy and sick.

The second bus trip was short, but the line for the elevator to the Empire State Building observation deck was agonizingly slow. Jean-Paul pulled a blue yo-yo out of his pocket and rewound the string.

"Is the line always this long?" he asked.

"I've only been up to the top once before," Cousin Henri said. "It was one of the first things I wanted to see when we got to New York. Actually"—he looked at the boys solemnly—"are you sure you really want to go up? Maybe that would be a bit too much for you—maybe you'd rather just look around the lobby."

"What?" Jean-Paul protested, letting his yo-yo stall at the bottom of its run. "We have to go up now that we're here!"

Cousin Henri laughed. "Gotcha! Did you really think I wouldn't take you up?"

Jean-Paul grinned and rewound his yo-yo. "It would be cool to have a yo-yo long enough to go all the way down to the ground from the observation deck," he said to Gustave. "You'd have to jerk it really hard to get it to come back up."

Gustave had been examining the picture of the building on the lobby wall. "You couldn't, though," he said. "You couldn't reach out far enough. The building gets narrower and narrower as it goes up, see?"

When it was their turn, the elevator lurched and started upward. Gustave watched floor after floor speeding by through the accordion gate. When the doors opened onto the observation deck, Gustave and Jean-Paul squeezed through the crowd. Gustave gasped, transfixed, while Jean-Paul darted around, trying the view from different spots. The sun had come back out, and building after building rose up, far below them, the gleaming snow on their roofs making them look clean and untouched.

Gustave peered down, searching for the Negro protest parade, but from this height he could only see the snow-topped buildings. Between them, here and there, light glinted on a moving taxi or a bus. Through the iron railings and beyond the buildings, Gustave saw rivers feeding into the blue of the harbor. So there it was, the Atlantic, sparkling and vast, part of the great distance they had crossed.

Cousin Henri put a warm hand on Gustave's shoulder. "Well, there it is," he said. "Your new home. America."

Gustave turned his gaze downward. Far below, an American flag fluttered from a building. New York City spread out around him, its windows catching the light, fracturing it into rainbow colors. Under the slanting light of the January sun, the city beckoned to him, a place for a new life, a place of infinite promise and possibility.

Late the following afternoon, Cousin Henri, Gustave, and his parents entered a small apartment. The rental agent, a brisk young blond woman wearing heavy makeup, waited in the doorway, jingling her keys. That morning, Jean-Paul and his mother and sister had gone off to stay with an elderly aunt of Jean-Paul's father in the Bronx. She had a big apartment, and she needed help with the house-keeping, she had written. It was a job for Aunt Geraldine and a place to live. But Gustave and his parents had been looking at apartments all day, with Cousin Henri coming along to translate, using a list given to them by HIAS. Now Cousin Henri leaned wearily against the wall, and Gustave's parents looked discouraged.

"This is the last one on the list," Cousin Henri said. "What do you think?"

It was a single room with a rudimentary kitchen. An old sofa sagged next to the wall, and in the corner was a stained, bare mattress.

"It's furnished!" the rental agent announced cheerily. "It has steam heat! And hot water from seven a.m. to seven p.m."

"Where are we now?" Maman asked Cousin Henri. "I'm all turned around."

"West Ninety-First Street, in Manhattan."

"Is it anywhere near the Grand Concourse, where Geraldine is staying?"

"No, I'm afraid not. The Bronx is much farther north. But you can get there by subway."

Maman sighed. "New York is *so* big."

"This apartment isn't," Gustave muttered.

Maman bit her lip and looked around, gesturing. "This is the whole thing?"

"It's small, true, but this is a good neighborhood," the rental agent said briskly. "You aren't going to do any better in your price range. There are other Jews nearby. I know *you people* like to live close together."

A grimace flickered over Cousin Henri's face before he translated, leaving out the last sentence, Gustave noticed.

Maman pushed down on the mattress, testing its springiness, then opened the door of the oven and looked inside.

"It's a cozy space, isn't it?" the rental agent said after a moment. "It's true that a few Negroes are moving into the area too, these days. But not too many. And there aren't any in this building," she added in a reassuring voice, adjusting the ends of her scarf. "Don't worry."

"What do you think, Lili?" Papa asked Maman in French.

37

"I suppose we could use the mattress and Gustave could sleep on the sofa," Maman murmured. "But ask her where the bathroom is please, Henri."

"At the end of the hall," the rental agent answered, when he translated. "You wouldn't expect your own bathroom at *this* price."

"Would you prefer to wait and keep looking?" Cousin Henri asked apprehensively.

Maman and Papa consulted in the corner. Gustave squeezed past the others to the window and looked out. There was no view. He could almost have reached out and touched the brick wall across the way. Faded red-checked curtains hung limply inside the grimy window opposite.

Papa cleared his throat. "We'll take it."

*"Formidable!"* Cousin Henri beamed. *Wonderful!*

The rental agent pulled out the papers and set them down at a small table in the hallway. Papa and Maman signed. Cousin Henri reached for the pen.

"I have to cosign, as your sponsor," he explained quietly, in French. "In case one month you can't pay the rent." Papa's face turned a mottled red.

"This is what American apartments are like? Shared bathrooms?" Maman murmured to Papa as they went out the door. The rental agent clicked briskly down the hall ahead of them in her elegant shoes. Something in the set of her shoulders made it evident she was relieved to be done with this unpleasant task.

"We'll move somewhere nicer as soon as I find a good

job," Papa said. "Don't worry, *chérie*. We'll get along in this country. It'll just take a little time."

Gustave took a last look at the dingy room. It was nothing like the apartment they had lived in back in Paris, with its high ceilings and tall windows, where light fell quietly on elegant furniture handed down through the generations. Somehow, they had become poor.

# ★ 7 ★

"Which would you rather do?" Papa asked. "Paint with me, or help Maman clean the shared bathroom?"

"Paint," Gustave answered quickly. "That bathroom is disgusting!" Whenever he had to go in, roaches scuttled all over the place when he switched on the light, scrambling into cracks and holes. He spent as little time there as possible.

"Well, somebody has to clean it," Maman said grimly, rolling up her sleeves.

When the paint was dry, Gustave and Papa put up shelves. Gustave got his French Boy Scout manual and his two favorite novels, *The Three Musketeers* and *Around the World in Eighty Days,* out of the bottom of his suitcase. He set them on the shelf next to the brown Berlitz book of English phrases and the new, red-leather-bound French–English dictionary that Cousin Henri had given them and stepped back to look around. Maman's hand-embroidered tablecloth lay on a small table that Gustave and Papa had bought at a secondhand store. His parents' familiar bedspread covered the mattress that had come with the apartment. With fresh white walls and the books up, the small room was starting to feel a bit less depressing and a bit more like home.

Gustave took a piece of onionskin paper out of the box of airmail stationery and sat down at the table.

"Who are you writing to?" asked Papa.

"Nicole Morin in Saint-Georges. She said she'd keep trying to find information about Marcel Landau and his mother."

Papa sighed. "I think you're being too optimistic. Even the people at HIAS thought there was nothing that could be done. I doubt we'll find out anything more about the Landaus until the end of the war."

"But Nicole's father is in the Resistance," Gustave insisted. "They helped us, so why couldn't they help Marcel? Anyway, I want her to have our address."

"Airmail is expensive, but I suppose you can send one letter. Hurry, though—I want you to help me wash the windows."

Gustave picked up a pen and started to write.

*18 January, 1942*

*Chère Nicole,*

*We're in America! I know you wanted to hear about movie stars, but I haven't seen any yet, sorry. I've seen some ladies on the streets wearing fur coats, though.*

*New York is enormous and crowded. They have dog statues*

*in the park and lion statues at the library. At night, there are neon signs in all different colors in Times Square. There's so much food here, but Jean-Paul always keeps a piece of bread in his pocket. He and I went up the Empire State Building with Papa's cousin when we first got here. We could see the whole city. It was amazing!*

*We found an apartment last week. Our address is 165 West 91st Street, New York, USA. I wrote it on the envelope too.*

*What's happening in Saint-Georges? Please write as soon as there is any news about M. I haven't started school here yet. Jean-Paul is living far away, so we won't be going to the same one. He's living with his father's aunt. I wish I could spend some time learning English better before starting school, but my parents say they don't want me to get behind the other kids my age, so I'm going soon.*

Gustave hesitated at the signature. Should he write, *"Je t'embrasse,"* Kisses, "Gustave"? That was the usual ending in France if you knew someone well, but . . . maybe she'd take it the wrong way. Finally, he wrote:

> *Bien à toi,*
> *Gustave*

*Best wishes.* That sounded better. He folded up the delicate paper and slid it into the thin blue envelope.

\*   \*   \*

After Gustave finished washing the windows, Papa handed him two quarters. "That should be plenty to pay for one stamp, I hope," he said. "Be careful with the change."

Gustave walked around outside for a while instead of going straight to the post office. Maman or Papa would surely give him another job to do the moment he came back, so there wasn't any point in rushing home. In front of a building on 92nd Street, a group of girls wearing fingerless gloves sat on crates in a patch of pale, wintry sunshine, knitting and laughing together. At the corner of 91st and Amsterdam, inside a window marked QUONG'S HAND LAUNDRY, a cat was curled up on a red-and-gold blanket. Gustave tapped on the window. *"Salut, le chat!"* he said. The cat picked up her head and meowed at him.

By the time he got to the post office, Gustave had worked out what to say in English.

"Goes to the France?" he asked nervously, pushing the envelope forward.

The clerk nodded. "Forty-five cents."

That was an awful lot of money, enough to buy five loaves of bread. Gustave handed over the quarters, hoping Papa wouldn't mind.

It was cold outside, but at least it wasn't windy, and Gustave still didn't feel like going straight home. The apartment lease listed the school he would be going to as P.S. 118 on 93rd Street. He headed over to find it. There it was, a new-looking building, eight stories high. A name was carved into the stone front: JOAN OF ARC JUNIOR HIGH.

How odd to travel so far from France and end up at a school in America named after a French heroine! It was a school day, but it was after four o'clock, so the building was quiet. The afternoon light reflected blankly off the windows. After a while, Gustave wandered idly down 93rd Street, west toward the Hudson River. He came to a small flight of steps leading up to a park. At the top he stopped in surprise, looking at the back of a statue of a figure on a horse. Was that who it looked like? He ran around to the front. Yes! It was Joan of Arc.

Gustave felt a rush of excitement. What was Joan of Arc, a French heroine, doing here in Manhattan, with New York apartment buildings all around her? People in France loved Joan of Arc, especially now. She had fought to free France from the English, so now the French Resistance fighters were using Joan of Arc's double-barred Cross of Lorraine as a symbol of the French fight against the Nazi occupation. Gustave searched carefully on all sides of the statue, but to his disappointment, the double-barred cross wasn't on it. It was nearly dusk now, and there was nobody else around. A half-frozen puddle stood near the base of the statue. Gustave dipped his finger in it and drew a Cross of Lorraine on the granite base. It shimmered on the stone, drying quickly but leaving a faint mark behind, like a secret.

Gustave turned over and over on the sofa, trying to get comfortable. It was Sunday night, and tomorrow he was going to school. He could hear the sounds of traffic far below in the street and his father snoring across the room. When Gustave finally fell asleep, he kept startling awake, imagining kids laughing at him, or not being able to find the bathroom in time, or having to take a test and not understanding a single word on the page.

"Good luck today, Gustave," Papa said in the morning before leaving for the employment office. He looked a little bit nervous too, Gustave noticed.

So did Maman, who came to the school with Gustave to show his papers and register him. Gustave's heart beat so rapidly he could feel it pulsing in his throat. All of his senses felt on hyper-alert, as if by watching and listening as intently as possible, he would somehow be able to make sense of the ocean of alien language swirling around him.

Mrs. Hale, the principal, was a tall woman about

Maman's age, with a serious but kind face. "Hello," she said, smiling.

"From ze France," Maman got out, in a thick accent. "Lili Becker, Gustave Becker." She gestured toward herself and then toward him.

The principal nodded and began to talk. Gustave caught some of the words here and there, but he could tell that Maman didn't understand anything at all. She sat wordlessly next to him, her mouth twitching in an awkward smile, making embarrassing little humming noises and playing nervously with the fringes of her scarf.

After Mrs. Hale had asked Maman several questions and watched her shrug helplessly, her patience seemed to be wearing a bit thin. She turned to Gustave and spoke slowly and loudly.

"Do . . . you . . . understand . . . English?"

"A little bit," Gustave said. "I study in the school."

"How . . . old . . . are . . . you?"

"I have twelve years." Gustave's head hurt with the effort of listening and answering.

"We'll put you in Seven A." She stood up and led them into the outer office, saying more words that he did not catch.

Maman looked immensely relieved that the conversation was over. "Have a good day, *mon petit chouchou*," she said to Gustave, too loudly, in French. *Sweetie pie!* Gustave winced. Maman leaned forward to kiss him. Just as she did, a girl his age pushed open the office door, and Gustave jerked back, bumping into a bookcase behind him. Maman nodded to the principal and the secretaries and hurried away.

The girl looked at Gustave curiously as the secretary handed him a schedule card. She was tall, maybe two inches taller than he was, and dark skinned, with alert, intelligent eyes. The American word floated into Gustave's head. Negro, he thought, practicing the word silently. The secretary said something to the girl, wrote a few words on a piece of paper, folded it up, and handed it to her.

The girl took it, nodded, and turned to Gustave, her face neutral, neither friendly nor unfriendly. "Come with me," she said, gesturing for him to follow.

She walked quickly up two flights of stairs, glancing over her shoulder to be sure he was still there. On the third floor, she left the stairwell and headed down the corridor, staying several steps ahead. The hallway was quiet except for the murmur of voices coming from some of the classrooms. The girl stopped suddenly and turned around, her hands on her hips. Her face still unsmiling, she said something so abruptly it seemed as if she had been trying not to talk to him but couldn't stay quiet a moment longer.

Gustave had no idea what she had asked him, only that it had been a question because her voice had gone up at the end. Guessing at what she had probably asked, he held out his hand.

"My name is Gustave Becker," he articulated carefully in English.

The girl's blank expression shifted into a crooked smile. He realized he must have guessed wrong. After a moment, she took his hand in her fingertips, gave it a quick shake up and down, and then dropped it. "Hello, Gustave. My . . . name . . . is . . . September Rose," she said slowly and clearly.

"Septembarrrrose." Gustave tried to pronounce the difficult name.

The girl giggled. "No! Sep . . . tem . . . ber Rose," she said again, sounding out each syllable separately. She repeated the last part and bent over, pretending to smell something. Her name meant "flower" then? Oh—*rose!* It was almost the same as in French, but the "r" sounded different.

Gustave repeated her name, better this time.

"Where . . . are . . . you . . . from?" she asked loudly.

In his head Gustave shaped another sentence he'd learned in school. "I am from France."

"Really?" Excitement flickered over her face, and she started talking rapidly. All he could understand were the words "France? Really?" and "Wow!" He nodded again.

"Where in France? Paris?" she asked.

He didn't know enough English to explain that he had lived in Paris most of his life but that his family had moved to Saint-Georges in the countryside to hide from the Nazis, so he just nodded. "Yes. Paris."

"Paris!" She exploded into incomprehensibly rapid, excited speech again.

A door opened, and a teacher's head poked out.

"Shhh!" The teacher frowned at the two of them, putting a finger to his lips.

September Rose gestured to Gustave to come and hurried around the corner to another classroom.

She said a few words, pointed at the door, then went in.

This was it. A whole room full of kids who only spoke this strange, fast, difficult language. Gustave took a deep breath and went through the door.

September Rose handed the teacher a note and then went to her desk. The teacher, a frizzy-haired middle-aged woman, looked at Gustave. She seemed flustered.

"I . . . AM . . . MRS. . . . . MC . . . A . . . DAMS!" she boomed at the top of her lungs, pointing at herself. She hurried out of the room, and Gustave stood there awkwardly, aware of all the staring eyes and the whispers and grins. A few minutes later, Mrs. McAdams came back, followed by a janitor lugging an extra desk.

Gustave sat down. The girl sitting in front of him, who had a green ribbon in her golden-brown curls, turned around and stared, then winked, smiling.

Mrs. McAdams began talking to the class. Gustave felt the cascade of rapid sentences crashing into him like rough surf. Only a word or two glimmered, intelligible, and his brain grabbed at them, but by the time he had made sense of one sentence, another wave of words from

Mrs. McAdams was crashing into him, followed by another and then another.

Then there was silence. A tall, thin boy got up, opened a cupboard, and walked around the classroom handing out a stack of green books.

The boy didn't give Gustave one. As the other students started to read, Gustave examined them. Most of the kids were pale and tall, and there was more blond hair in the classroom than he was used to seeing in France. Not many of the people in this school were Negroes. None of the adults were, and only one other girl in the class was as dark as September Rose. The girls in this class were curvier and the boys had more muscles than the kids his age in France did. Their clothes all looked brand new. Gustave was suddenly aware that his clothes were old and faded. And his pants were wrong. The other boys all had pants that went down to their ankles. His were the French style, *un pantalon de golf.* They were wide and short, ending just below his knee, showing his thin legs. A flush of shame rushed over him, and he pulled his feet as far as he could under his desk.

Mrs. McAdams dropped a book meant for a small child on Gustave's desk.

"READ . . . THIS!" she boomed at him, opening it and running her finger over the words under the pictures. She smelled of sickly-sweet perfume. Gustave leaned away.

I know what a book is for! I'm not a moron—I just don't speak English! he thought. But he didn't know how to say that, not that he should anyway, so he just nodded, set his elbows on either side of the book, trying to hide it, and bent his head low over the page, the large-print words blurring in front of him.

A bell rang. Everything instantly became chaotic as the students jumped up, gathered their books, and crowded into the hallway. Gustave was confused. Where were they going? Was it recess already, or lunch? September Rose had gotten up with the others, but she looked back at him and pointed to the schedule card on his desk before going out the door. Gustave looked at it, and then he realized that things must work differently here. In France, when it was time for a new subject, a new teacher came into the room. Here it seemed the students switched rooms. He was the last one left in the room, so he must already be late. He scanned his schedule card nervously. In the block with his next class, geography, he saw the number 611. That must mean it was on the sixth floor. Hurrying through the empty halls, he found the classroom after the bell rang and slid into a vacant seat.

"Hello. Are you Gustave Becker?" the teacher said slowly and clearly.

Gustave's palms and armpits prickled with sweat. "Yes."

"I am Mr. Coolidge. I teach geography and history. Come!" Gustave stood up, shoving his pants down as far as they would go, trying to make them look longer. His socks still showed. He shuffled to the front of the room with his hands jammed in his pockets to keep his pants from riding up. Two girls whispered and giggled as he went by. He noticed September Rose scowling in their direction.

Mr. Coolidge pulled down a world map and spoke to the class. In the blur of sound, Gustave heard his name, and the words "welcome," "new," and "friend." Then Mr. Coolidge turned back to Gustave and spoke slowly.

"You are here . . . war?" Gustave heard. "Refugee . . . from France?"

It sounded like a question, and what he was saying seemed to be true. Gustave nodded.

Mr. Coolidge smiled. "Welcome to America!" He gestured to the class, and they echoed his last words. Some of the voices were enthusiastic, but underneath the cheerful ones, a few were singsongy and mocking.

"So," said Mr. Coolidge, and then came another stream of words.

The teacher seemed to be asking him to tell them about what it was like living in France now, with the war going on. Gustave swallowed. All at once, there were no English words in his head. His eyes swept over the other students, all staring at him. He knew he had to say something. September Rose was sitting in the third row with her brown eyes fixed intently on his face. She held his gaze and then moved her chin slightly, indicating the wall behind him. Gustave looked over his shoulder desperately. There was the map. He felt a few English words rising up in his head. He took a step back and pointed at Germany. Then, feeling heartsick, he traced a route through Belgium, slipping over and around the Maginot

Line, the line of forts meant to defend the French against the Germans, and down into France.

"Germans come," he choked out. "Nazis. Very bad. Not food. Not heat. Bad for the France. Bad . . ." Gustave paused. He wanted to say that it was bad in Europe for the Jews. Did Americans know about that? They should be letting more Jews come here. But was it really safe to let people know that his family was Jewish? Gustave hesitated, the opportunity passed, and then he felt ashamed of having missed it.

"Well done, Gustave," said Mr. Coolidge, patting him on the shoulder, and he made his way back to his seat.

By lunchtime, Gustave was exhausted, and the roar of noise in the cafeteria didn't help. He spotted September Rose sitting with a small group of Negro students at the end of a long table, and he started toward her. When he got there, she had her head down and was busily unwrapping her sandwich, smoothing out every crease in the wax paper until it made a perfect flat square.

The girl across from September Rose looked at him warily. He extended his hand. "Hello. I'm Gustave."

"Lisa," she said, looking startled.

She didn't take his hand, so he pulled it back, flushing. "Hello, September Rose."

September Rose finally looked up, and he could tell from her face that she had known he was there all along.

"Hi," she said quietly. She glanced at him with a dark,

intense gaze, as if she were trying to tell him something, shook her head slightly, and looked down.

"Gus—tuv! *Gus—tuv!*" At the next table over, two boys from geography class were standing and waving. "Leo," one athletic-looking boy introduced himself curtly. He kept running his hand through his blond hair as his eyes roved around the lunchroom.

"I'm Frank," said the tall, dark-haired boy with big ears who had passed out the literature textbooks. "What were you doing over there? Sit here with us." Frank patted the bench next to him.

Gustave reached out to shake hands. "I am called Gustave," he said. The boys grinned at him in a friendly way. At the next table, September Rose was giggling with Lisa as they shared a package of thin, crispy crackers.

The noise in the cafeteria was overwhelming. So many voices were talking, shouting out their strange words, and laughing all at the same time that it was like the roar of a storm, and Gustave could hardly understand anything at all. He unwrapped the sandwich Maman had made for him, weirdly orange cheese between pieces of too-pale, too-soft bread.

Leo and Frank made a few attempts to talk with Gustave, but when he couldn't answer, Leo turned away and yelled something else at a boy down the table, then hooted with laughter. The boy had bitten holes into a piece of bread for eyes and a mouth and then smashed it over his face, shaping it over his nose and letting his tongue stick through.

When a group of girls appeared next to their table, the

boy with the bread on his face wiggled his tongue, and the girls shrieked. The two in front pushed forward a very pretty girl with creamy skin, pink cheeks, hazel eyes, and golden-brown curls. It was the girl with the green hair ribbon from Mrs. McAdams's class.

"Gustave!" the girl called in a teasing voice. She put one hand on her hip and sashayed around the end of the table. When she got close, she flipped her hair back and pursed her lips.

"Geef me a French keeess!" she murmured, in a fake French accent.

*"Comment?"* Gustave leaned back instinctively. Then he blushed when he realized he had spoken French.

The girl wiggled her shoulders. "Come on, Frrrenchie!" she murmured again, winking, her voice low and throaty. She pursed her lips, making a kissy mouth. "Geef me a Frrrrench keeess!"

Gustave felt all the grinning faces pushing in at him. He had no idea what to do.

"Geez!" Disappointment flickered over her face. She half sauntered, half ran back to the other girls as they screamed with laughter, throwing flirtatious glances at Gustave. The boys at Gustave's table were laughing too, and one of them reached across and poked his shoulder. Gustave heard the name "Martha" several times. Leo was scowling. He shoved the boy next to him, a bottle fell over, and milk poured across the table. Gustave jumped up, but some of the milk had already splashed onto his pants. Now he had to go through the rest of the school day with his pants wet and smelling like sour milk.

At the next table over, September Rose and her friend Lisa were the only people in the whole cafeteria who didn't seem to be laughing at him. September Rose flashed him a sympathetic glance. Then, almost as if she hadn't meant to do it, she dropped her eyes back down to her lunch, picked up a hard-boiled egg, dipped it carefully in a small pile of salt, and started eating again.

# ★ 10 ★

The air outside the school building was cold, and it smelled as if it might snow again soon. Gustave walked home slowly, climbing over grimy mounds of ice at the curb and looking in the shop windows. A five-and-dime he had passed on the way to school that morning now had a red, white, and blue poster in the window with an American flag on it. Next door was a candy store. A few buildings over, the warm smell of spicy tomato sauce drifted out of Mama Regina's Italian restaurant. And beside Mama Regina's was a clothing store. Gustave stopped and studied the gray pants, crisp white shirt, and dark tie and jacket on the boy mannequin standing in the window. He had never cared about clothes before, but it wouldn't be so obvious that he was a refugee if he had clothes like that.

As he approached the corner of Amsterdam and West 91st Street, Gustave smelled the familiar aroma of Quong's Hand Laundry, a mixture of steam and perfumed soap. He glanced in to see if Mr. Quong's cat was in her usual spot on the blanket in the corner of the store window. Yes, there she was. Beyond her he saw a sign he hadn't noticed before. BARGAIN: ABANDONED CLOTHES. He had figured out the word "bargain" already from seeing it everywhere in stores. And "clothes" he knew. Hesitantly, Gustave pushed open the door. A bell tinkled. Inside, it was warm, and a radio on the shelf was playing jaunty piano music as a woman's voice sang a lilting song. The cat in the window meowed, stretched luxuriously, and then jumped up and ran over to him. Gustave squatted and petted her for a moment, then walked over to the small rack of clothing in the corner. She followed him, rubbing against his ankles.

The clothing on the "bargain" rack was an odd assortment: some men's shirts in different sizes; a few little girls' dresses, one with a duck embroidered on the front pocket; and a pale yellow woman's blouse with the shadow of a stain on the collar. The clothes weren't new. They must be washing that people had never picked up. Between the blouse and a large gray pair of men's trousers, Gustave saw one pair of boys' pants, navy blue, sturdy, and about his size. They were definitely long enough to go down over his ankles, and suddenly he wanted them badly. He found the price tag. Two dollars. Not as expensive as new pants, surely, but still, it was too much money. He couldn't ask his parents. Papa hadn't even found a job yet. Reluctantly, Gustave slid the pants back onto the rack.

"Can I help you?" A short, elderly Chinese man had come out of the back of the laundry and was peering at him curiously.

"No." Gustave felt like an imposter. There wasn't so much as a penny in his pockets. What was that American sentence? He had heard it a few times while shopping with Papa. "I'm just seeing."

Mr. Quong squinted at him, puzzled, then smiled, a warm smile that went all the way up to his eyes. "Oh, just *looking*! Sure, go ahead." He opened up a notebook on the counter in front of him. The cat leaped up and sat down exactly in the middle of Mr. Quong's page, meowing. Mr. Quong laughed and lifted her off, dropping her gently to the floor and saying some words that Gustave couldn't understand. Even the cat knew more English than he did.

Gustave mumbled a quick thank-you to Mr. Quong, then pushed open the glass door of the laundry, hearing the bell jingle again as a blast of wintry air hit him full in the face. Snow was falling now, small flakes driving down hard and slanted in the cold wind. When Gustave got back to the apartment, Maman was out. He flopped down on the shabby sofa and looked up at the cracked ceiling, wishing that Jean-Paul lived nearby so that they could go to school together. Maybe he'd be able to help Gustave figure it all out. Why had Martha come over to him at lunch? Had she been teasing him or flirting? It sort of seemed like both. And why had September Rose talked to him when they were walking to his first class but been so unfriendly at lunch? Gustave sighed. It was difficult enough to understand what was going on in girls' heads in France. In Saint-Georges, Nicole Morin had been his friend. Even though she was a girl, she had acted just like a normal person. Here in America, though, it might be completely impossible to understand what girls were thinking.

Maman's key turned in the lock. "Hello!" she said. "How was your first day of school?"

"All right, I guess."

"Do you have homework?"

"Yeah, but I'm tired. I'm resting before I do it."

"Fine, then!" She smiled at him. *"Allons-y,* lazybones! You need to help me go shopping. Some fresh air would be good for you."

"Now? It's freezing outside!"

"You'll be hungry soon, and then you'll want to eat. Come on. I need you to help me talk to the shopkeepers."

Not *more* speaking in English. Gustave groaned and sat up.

Outside the wind was howling, and snowflakes drove into their faces. Maman walked briskly down Amsterdam Avenue to a small store a few blocks off. It was filled with fruits and vegetables as well as bottles of milk, eggs, and canned goods. "The food in this store looks good," she said. "But the prices are too high. You need to help me bargain."

While Maman was selecting vegetables, the shop door jingled, and two boys Gustave recognized from geography class came in. "Hey, that's Gus-tuv," he heard one of the boys say as they went down the canned-vegetables aisle.

Maman's basket was full. "Come on," she said, striding toward the register. "Time to negotiate!"

"Maman!" Gustave hissed. "No one else is bargaining. I don't think they do that in America."

"Nonsense!" Maman held up a head of lettuce. *"C'est trop cher!" It's too expensive!* she said to the cashier loudly in French. "Gustave, tell her. Some of the leaves have bad spots. I'll pay half price."

"It is old, a little," Gustave stuttered miserably in English. "She say she pay half."

"Huh?" The cashier stared at Maman, uncomprehending. "The price is ten cents!"

Maman held up five fingers. "Five!" She fingered the darkened spot on the leaf. "See? No good!" she said loudly in English.

The cashier rolled her eyes. "Then get another one."

Gustave wished he could disappear. "Maman," he hissed in French. "Just pay what it says."

Maman shook her head. *"Nous n'avons pas assez d'argent,"* she said loudly, looking into her wallet. *We don't have enough money.*

"Then come on!" Gustave muttered. On his way out the door, he looked over his shoulder. One of the boys from school was standing next to a display of canned tomatoes, watching them. Outside, tiny, hard pellets of ice were coming down. Gustave turned to Maman angrily. "I *told* you Americans don't bargain! You just pay what it says."

Maman shook her head stubbornly. "We'll try another store." She grabbed his arm to keep him from running away. Gustave shrugged her off, slipping and nearly falling on a patch of ice. He walked angrily behind her as she threaded her way through the streets as if she had always lived there to another store seven or eight blocks north. DEROSA'S, said a large red sign. A row of brightly colored snow shovels stood to the right of the door, a stand piled high with apples and potatoes to the left. "Here!" Maman announced triumphantly. "We'll try this one."

The narrow aisles were stacked high with fruits and vegetables, and the market had a fresh, earthy smell. Maman scrutinized the food, selecting three small red potatoes from one barrel and reaching on tiptoe to get the best carrots from the top of a display. A burly man in a green apron who had been singing snippets of Italian opera in the back headed toward her, still humming.

"Ah! A lady who knows a good potato! I am Mr. DeRosa." He was stout and not much taller than Gustave, with curly black hair and a jovial face. He held out his hand.

Maman shifted her basket to the other arm and held out her own hand. "I em Madame—Meeseez Becker."

They shook hands. Maman held up a parsnip. "Zees," she said loudly in a strong accent. "How much zees?"

Gustave cringed. "It says right *there*, Maman," he muttered in French, pointing at the sign. But Maman ignored him.

"How much?" she demanded, waving the parsnip.

The Italian grocer looked pleased and amused. "For you, Madame Becker," he said, gesturing toward her basket, "all this—ten cents?"

"Ten cent." Maman nodded happily. "Ten cent ees good! And zees?" She held up an onion.

Mr. DeRosa laughed. "Just like in the old country!" he said. "Three for a nickel?"

Maman reached for two more. Then she turned to the eggs and opened a carton on top of one pile, with brown eggs in it, marked forty-three cents, then a carton on top of another, marked fifty cents. The eggs in the second carton were white. "More cheap," she said suspiciously, pointing to the brown eggs. "Bad?"

Mr. DeRosa shook his head. In the protesting flood of words that followed, Gustave heard "eggs" several times and "fresh, very fresh."

Maman took a carton from the cheaper pile. Gustave walked away to look at a display of unfamiliar curved, greenish-yellow fruit near the front window. He picked one up and sniffed it absentmindedly, watching the people going by outside the window.

Two Negro boys who looked high-school aged meandered by, tossing a small pink rubber ball back and forth between them. The taller one stopped and threw the ball straight up, watching it rise through the snowflakes. He held up his hands and took two steps backward, ready to catch it. But as he did, he crashed into one of the snow shovels on display outside Mr. DeRosa's shop. It clattered to the sidewalk, taking several other shovels with it. As the boy picked them up and set them back in place, Mr. DeRosa hurried to the front door of the store, frowning.

"Go away! Go on!" he shouted, making shooing gestures.

"Sorry, sir," called the boy, adjusting the last of the shovels.

"Hoodlums," Mr. DeRosa muttered. He looked over at Gustave. "Aren't those beauts?" he asked. "You like bananas?"

Gustave quickly put it back on the display, shrugging.

Mr. DeRosa waddled over and broke off two of the curved fruits, beaming, and dropped them onto the counter. "For you and your mother," he said. "No charge!" Gustave caught the word "yellow" as Mr. DeRosa pantomimed ripping off the skin. It was obvious what he meant: wait until it is yellow, then peel it before eating it.

Humming once more, the grocer rang up Maman's purchases at the cash register.

"See?" she said triumphantly to Gustave as they went out. "I told you I know what I'm doing! Shopping is the same all around the world."

# ★ 11 ★

Gustave woke up the next morning confused about where he was. He blinked at the cracked, unfamiliar ceiling above him. When he turned his head and saw the two green bananas on the windowsill where he had put them to ripen, he remembered, with a sickening feeling of dread. He was in New York, and today was his second day of school.

In homeroom, Mrs. McAdams stopped taking roll when she came to Gustave's name. "Too foreign," she said. "YOU NEED AN AMERICAN NAME! WE'LL CALL YOU GUS!" she boomed at him.

Gustave shook his head. But around him, the kids in the class were nodding.

"Sure, Gus!" said Pete, who sat to his right. "That's a good name! And easy to say!"

"Yeah, hi, Gus!" said Elsie, a delicate-looking girl with short blond hair.

Everyone seemed to have decided that would be his new name. But it was so unfair. His name was two syllables long. He had to learn their whole language!

Gustave was exhausted again by the end of the day, so he was glad to see that on Tuesdays the last period on his schedule card was music. At least that probably wouldn't involve very much talking. He glanced at the placard by the door to be sure he was in the right place. It read: MUSIC. HEINE. He felt sick to his stomach. Heine was a German name.

But he had to go in. He opened the door slowly.

"Move it, Frenchie!" Three boys pushed past. The classroom was huge, with a piano and chairs arranged in three groups, all facing the center of the room. As he had done in all his other classes, Gustave stood waiting until the other kids were sitting down. Then, as the bell rang, he slipped into the nearest empty seat. But this time a slender young woman in a close-fitting blue dress marched toward him, her heels clicking emphatically along the floor. She spoke to him, shaking her head. This must be Mrs. Heine, and obviously he wasn't supposed to sit there. Gustave gathered up his things awkwardly and stood.

The teacher folded her arms and watched. Her short pale hair curved elegantly along her cheek, ending just below her ear. "What's your name?" she demanded.

"Gustave Becker."

Mrs. Heine frowned slightly.

"What kind of name is *that*?"

"I come from France." He didn't like her, but that was two questions in a row that he had answered in perfectly correct English, he was pretty sure. For a moment, he felt proud of himself.

"Come here," Mrs. Heine commanded, gesturing toward the center of the room, and Gustave's confidence left him. He stumbled forward, feeling the eyes of all the students on him, hotly aware of his shabby sweater and short pants.

Mrs. Heine fired out a series of words that Gustave couldn't follow. Then she barked, "Sing!" and slid onto the piano bench.

Gustave stared. Did she want him to sing all by himself, in front of all these kids? But he hated singing in front of people. She struck a few notes on the piano.

"What songs do you know?" she demanded. "O say, can you see?" She sang the first words to the American national anthem, her fingers moving over the keyboard. Gustave shook his head, looking at the floor. No. He remembered the American national anthem a little, from hearing it on the ship, but he didn't know it yet.

"What about 'Lili Marlene'?"

Gustave shook his head again, miserably.

Mrs. Heine sighed. "Then sing 'La Marseillaise,'" she said, her tone mocking as she uttered the name of the French national anthem. "You *must* know that." She turned to the keyboard and played the opening of the song.

Gustave listened to the beautiful, forbidden notes in this strange, foreign schoolroom, and pain flooded over him. He hadn't heard the song since the German victory. Now that France was occupied by the Nazis, the national anthem was illegal. Anyone caught singing it was shot. The last time Gustave had sung it must have been at a Boy Scout meeting in Paris, just before his family had fled to the countryside. Marcel had hammed up the anthem. With his hand on his chest, he had warbled out the high parts like an opera singer, making Jean-Paul snort with laughter in the middle of the song.

"Let's go!" Mrs. Heine snapped Gustave back to the present. "Sing."

She played, and although his throat felt swollen shut, Gustave lifted up his head, tried to ignore the watching students, and, his voice choking, he sang for wounded, shamed France.

*"Allons, enfants de la patrie,*
*Le jour de gloire est arrivé!*
*Contre nous de la tyrannie,*
*L'étendard sanglant est levé!"*

Gustave had never felt the meaning of the words more keenly, even though some of them felt painfully ironic now. *Arise, children of the fatherland/The day of glory has arrived.* Not glory for us, thought Gustave as pain twisted in him. *Against us the bloody flag of tyranny is raised.* That felt like a stab in his chest. The French flag no longer flew over France. The Nazi flag, red with a black swastika on a white circle, whipped arrogantly in the French wind. It was a bloody flag, too, soaked red with French blood.

The flag line was repeated again, higher. *"L'étend-ah-ard sanglant est levé."* Gustave's voice cracked. He couldn't sing any longer. He stood with his head down, desperately squeezing back the tears in his eyes.

Mrs. Heine played a few more bars, then stopped. "The French!" she said to the room at large. "Can't even sing their own national anthem!"

Somehow Gustave understood *that* comment perfectly well.

"Sit there." She gestured to the center section, to the row in the very back of the classroom. "You're an alto. More or less," she added in an undertone. Gustave glanced up just long enough to see, blurrily, where she was pointing.

He made his way to the back and slid into a seat at the end of the row while Mrs. Heine spoke to the class, her voice rapid and sharp and unintelligible. By now he wasn't even trying to listen.

"Gustave!" a voice whispered from his right. "Don't let her get to you." September Rose, a few seats away, was leaning over to get his attention. He didn't understand the words, but he could tell that she was saying something friendly.

Mrs. Heine put a record on the record player. When the music ended, Mrs. Heine talked for a few minutes and then class was over. Gustave waited while September Rose gathered up her things.

"What means 'get to you'?" He quoted her words back to her in a whisper.

September Rose glanced around. The two of them

were screened from view by the chaos of many people talking and gathering books. She spoke slowly and clearly, and he understood most of it. "I meant, don't let Mrs. Heine make you feel bad. It's not just you. She used to be mean to this other Jewish boy too. You're Jewish, right? That's why you came to America?"

Before Gustave could answer, September Rose hurried off down the hall, but he caught up with her in homeroom. She was in the back, getting her red coat from her cubby. As Gustave pulled on his coat, she looked over at him, checking to be sure the two of them were alone before walking over to whisper, "The kids all call the music teacher Mrs. Hiney."

"Hiney?"

"Shhh! Yes, Hiney!" She giggled and tapped the back of her gray skirt. "Hiney! Behind! You know?"

Gustave laughed.

"So you're really from Paris? Have you seen the Eiffel Tower?" September Rose made the shape of the tower with her hands.

"Yes. Of course."

"Did you ever go up it?"

"Yes."

"Lucky!" She turned to go.

"Wait," Gustave said. "What means 'French kiss'?"

"Oh, from yesterday in the cafeteria?" September Rose grinned. "It's a way some people kiss. Touching tongues." She stuck hers out, wiggling it, and touched it with her fingertip, and then Gustave understood. "Martha's such a flirt," she added. "Especially with the new boys."

71

"Flirt?"

"Like this," September Rose said. She batted her eyes, flipped her braid over her shoulder, and made a kissy mouth like Martha. She laughed as he nodded. "You get it, huh? Bye!"

She threw on her coat and darted across the room to the door, slipping through a patch of sunshine from a high window. The back of her neck was a smooth, rich brown. It reminded Gustave of something. For a moment he couldn't think what, and then he remembered. The chestnuts that fell from the trees on the Champs-Élysées in Paris. He used to collect them with his friends, rub them with a handkerchief until they were smooth and gleaming, and carry them in his pockets, throw them at things, drop them into the Seine from the bridges. Maybe it was because of the questions she had asked him, but that was what the warm brown of her neck reminded him of. Paris and chestnuts.

# ★ 12 ★

Fridays quickly became Gustave's favorite day of the week. School got out an hour early, so there was never any music class on Fridays. Fridays also always began with algebra, which was now Gustave's favorite subject. As soon as he realized that Americans wrote their numbers a bit differently, it was very easy to follow. He didn't even have to listen to the words. He simply looked at the equations the teacher was writing on the board and figured out what to do by himself. One day, Mrs. Rider was explaining how to solve two equations containing two unknowns, $x$ and $y$. Gustave suddenly saw how to do it, and she called him up to the blackboard. He solved the problem without talking, smiling to himself, while the others were still calling out bewildered questions.

Geography was the next period after algebra. That day, they were starting a new unit on Africa, and Mr. Coolidge had those maps pulled down. As Mr. Coolidge rapped his pointer on the maps and began to speak, Gustave glanced at the book of the boy next to him to see what page he was supposed to be on, then flipped open his textbook. He stopped at a photograph of French soldiers riding on *méharis*, camels. Once, in Paris, he had read a book about those French soldiers who rode camels in Africa. It had seemed like a glamorous and exciting life, a life dedicated to the glory of France. For a while he had wanted to be one of them, a *méhariste*, galloping through the desert under an enormous black sky full of stars.

Gustave absentmindedly twisted the eraser end of his pencil against the page, tearing it. He glanced up and covered the rip with his hand, worried that he would get into trouble. It was a long time ago that he had wanted to be one of those soldiers. He had been younger and stupider in those days. Back then he hadn't known anything about what war was really like.

Mr. Coolidge tapped his pointer on Morocco. "So," he said loudly to the class, and Gustave focused on him again, "what is a 'casbah'?"

Martha waved her hand wildly in the air.

"Yes, Martha?"

Martha ran her fingers through her silky hair, taking her time, making sure the whole class was watching her. "A casbah is a walled-in city like that one in Algiers," she said slowly and clearly, circling her arms like walls around a city. Then she started talking more quickly. Gustave heard the movie star names "Charles Boyer" and "Hedy Lamarr." Suddenly Martha looked directly at Gustave and winked. She drawled in a fake French accent, "Come vid me to ze casbah!"

Gustave's face went hot as the class exploded into laughter. "In the casbah they Frrrrench keeees!" Martha added, giggling. Someone nudged Gustave from behind.

"Oh, I see, you know about the casbah from the movies!" Mr. Coolidge chuckled. Gustave stared at the floor and waited for the class to be over.


At lunch, Gustave sat with Frank again. Leo was there too, and Miles, a curly-haired boy with a cheerful, ruddy face.

"You know Martha likes you, Gus!" Miles laughed.

Gustave shook his head, but the other boys at the table all started talking about Martha and girls and kissing. Leo looked annoyed. After a moment he thwacked Gustave's leg and said, "Hey, Gus, I've been meaning to ask you. Why do you wear those dumb pants?"

His voice was mocking, and after he spoke, the boys all looked at Gustave's legs. He pulled his feet under him. "French," he said curtly.

"Sharp!" Leo sneered. "Or should I say *chic*?"

"I am surprise you know a French word," Gustave said.

Miles jabbed Leo with his elbow and laughed good-naturedly. Leo ignored him and stood up, pulling his own pants up as far as they would go. He waddled around the table like Charlie Chaplin. "Look at me!" he said. "I'm wearing those dopey French pants. Aren't I the cat's meow?"

"Ooh la-la! The cat's meow!" another boy jeered, looking at Gustave. A lot of the other boys made cat noises. Gustave reddened angrily and looked away.

Miles put down his sandwich. "Want to play Battleship?" he asked Frank with his mouth full, getting out graph paper. "Gus, it's a two-person game. Watch, and next time you can play." Gustave turned his back on Leo, observing the game. He had played something very similar in France.

Miles and Frank each had two pieces of graph paper. On each page, they numbered one axis and put letters on the other. Then each boy drew the outlines of ships on one piece of graph paper, keeping that piece hidden behind a propped-up book so that the other boy couldn't see.

"B six," Frank called out.

Miles ran his finger up to B and across to 6. It intersected with a ship he had drawn on the graph paper. "Hit!" he said sadly.

"Take that, you swine!" Frank shouted, marking an X at B6 on his blank piece of graph paper, which he had labeled *Miles's ships*.

"Hey! I'm not the enemy, you are!" Miles said indignantly.

A few minutes later Frank glanced at his watch and got up, stumbling over his schoolbag. "I forgot. I'm supposed to go pick up an extra assignment from the math teacher. See you, fellas. Want to take over for me?" He pointed at his empty seat.

Gustave concentrated on the game. After he had sunk

three of Miles's ships, Miles jumped up. "You win! I'm getting some of that prune pudding before they close." He hurried to the cafeteria line. A minute or two later, Leo said something to Gustave loudly, as if he had said it before. Gustave looked up, startled.

"I *said*, do you want to learn some American, Frenchie? Want to learn what to say to an American girl?"

Gustave shrugged.

"They like you to tease them, see? So if the girls come over today, I'll help you. I'll say the name of some film star. Who do you think is hot stuff? Hedy Lamarr?"

That was the film star that Martha had named in geography class. "No!"

"Okay, so she's not your type. How about Rita Hayworth? So I say, 'Hey, Gus, how about Rita Hayworth?' And you go like this."

Leo let out a long, slow wolf whistle, his hands curving in and out in the shape of a woman's body.

"You got it? Do it!"

Embarrassed, Gustave imitated what Leo had done.

"Swell!" Leo's eyes gleamed. Then I'll say, 'So, Gus, how about *Martha*?' And you say, '*Flat!*' That means she's pretty, like Rita Hayworth. Got it?"

Stifled laughter came from some of the boys.

"She'll love that, Gus!" Leo insisted. "Try saying it. Come on!"

Gustave muttered it quickly, and there was more laughter. Gustave didn't understand everything Leo was saying, and he didn't know the word Leo was telling him to repeat, but something was definitely off.

"Great, Frenchie!" Leo reached over and slapped him on the shoulder. "The American girls are gonna love you!"

The boy next to Leo jabbed him with his elbow and muttered something that sounded like an objection, but Leo just grinned.

The table suddenly quieted. "Hey, here they come!" Leo said, smoothing his hair across his forehead. Gustave looked over his shoulder. Martha and a group of girls crowded behind him, giggling.

"Is there room here for me?" Martha asked loudly, wiggling into the spot next to Gustave and bumping her hip up against him. "So, whatcha eating, Gus?"

She reached over, picked up his apple, and took a bite. Her big hazel eyes locked on Gustave's. Where she had bitten, he saw a smear of red. A girl his age was wearing lipstick? He felt hot, and his skin prickled, but he couldn't seem to look away.

Leo cleared his throat. "Gus has something to tell you, Martha," he said.

Martha stopped chewing and smiled at Gustave. "What do you want to tell me, Gus?" she crooned, as if the two of them were alone.

"Hey, Gus," Leo demanded loudly, "how about that Rita Hayworth?"

Gustave whistled feebly, trying to sound suave like Leo, and curved his hands in and out. Martha's cheeks went pink.

"Yeah, Gus!" one of the boys snickered. The others were silent, grinning and waiting.

Leo leaned forward. "And Gus, how about Martha?"

Martha was gazing at Gustave intently now, her eyes sparkling.

"Come on, Frenchie!" Leo coaxed. "Did you forget your English lesson already? How about Martha?"

There was something wrong with what Leo had told him to say. Gustave was quite sure of that. But no other English words were coming into his head. "Martha?" Gustave said slowly, playing for time. And then he knew what to say.

*"Chic!"* he said loudly, smiling at her. "Cat's meow!"

Just as he said it, Leo whistled a short, sharp note, dropping his hands through the air in two parallel lines. He looked confused when he realized Martha was smiling.

"Hey, wait—you didn't say what we practiced!"

"He said I was the cat's meow!" Martha said haughtily, tossing her head. "And *chic*! That's French for 'stylish'! And the French know style!"

Gustave grinned. Miles had appeared a minute ago and was standing at the end of the table holding a bowl of pudding. He slapped Gustave on the shoulder as he went by. "Good one, Gus!"

# ★ 13 ★

After that, school got a little bit better. In the second week, Gustave had started going to a special language class, once a day, while the others had art or physical education. Three other students who didn't speak good English were also in the class. The two girls were identical twin sisters from Spain, and the other boy, who was older, was from Austria. They had all been in school in America longer than Gustave had. None of them spoke French, not even the teacher, but the class helped.

After a couple of weeks, Gustave discovered that if he didn't fight so hard to understand every word, if he relaxed and kind of let himself float on the surface of the language, like a cork on a bobbing ocean, after a moment his brain often made sense of what he was hearing. And he was starting to feel more confident about speaking in front of several people at once. He never said anything in class, though, except a very few words when he absolutely had to.

Leo started eating lunch with another crowd most days. Gustave usually ate with Frank and Miles. The two of them often played chess at lunch with a pocket-sized chess set, and sometimes they played a pencil game with dots and squares that three people could play. Most of the time Gustave couldn't understand the conversation in the noisy cafeteria unless someone spoke to him directly, but at least nobody bothered him. Even Martha, to Gustave's relief, seemed to have lost interest in him. Lately she had started going with her group of friends to flirt with Leo at lunch. Once she perched on Leo's lap and ate a bite of his sandwich.

Gustave noticed that a lot of kids brought ripe bananas to eat for lunch. But the two green bananas on his apartment windowsill had never turned yellow. When the peel was still greenish gray but had started going dark in spots, Gustave had decided it was time to try them. He'd peeled the bananas and shared them out for dessert. His parents had looked dubiously at the unfamiliar fruit, but remembering the delicious smell of the bananas in the shop, Gustave picked up his piece and took a big bite. His teeth furred over instantly, and a bitter taste filled his mouth. "Eeuh!" he said, spitting it out. "Don't even bother!"

"Manners, Gustave," his mother chided, scooping up the plate with the spit-out lump. She and Papa had dumped their pieces, untasted, into the trash.

September Rose sometimes glanced at Gustave across the cafeteria, but she didn't talk to him again. When he was near her in class or in the hallways, he tried to think of something to say, but it took too long to think of the

81

words. One day during music class, he planned out a sentence in English. As soon as the bell rang, he turned to her and said it. "I like you singing."

"Oh, thanks," she said. "So long." And she was out the door.

Mostly, the first few weeks of school went by in a blur of confusion. Gustave drifted along, trying to be in the right classroom at the right time, trying to decipher the English swirling around him.

Papa had found a job, finally, working as a janitor at a department store. Then Maman got hired to do piecework at home, sewing artificial flowers and feathers and spangles onto hats. Soon the small apartment was overflowing with hat-making materials. But Gustave's parents still had a lot of tense conversations about money. The two of them had started studying English in night school. While Gustave was home in the evenings, struggling through whatever he could do of his homework with the French–English dictionary, Maman and Papa walked to Joan of Arc Junior High three nights a week for night-school classes. There were a few other French men and women, but mostly the students were from different countries. They could hardly understand each other at all, but they laughed a lot, Maman reported. Once, Mrs. Szabo, the teacher, had brought a coffee cake to share. It sounded like a lot more fun than regular junior high school. Gustave's parents were learning about American citizenship in night school too. Some of the other students, who had been in the country longer, were preparing to take the exam to become citizens. One night Papa and Maman came home with a book called *The New American*. At the back were sixty-one questions to study for the citizenship exam. Gustave flipped through it as he ate his breakfast the next morning.

"Are we going to become American citizens?" he asked, alarmed.

"It takes five years before you can apply," Papa said. "So we'll see. Maybe. Or maybe we'll go back to France. It depends what happens with the war."

On the evenings when his parents didn't have night school, they often listened to a secondhand radio·Papa had brought home. When the news came on, his parents fell silent, and Gustave stopped doing homework. They all listened intently to the rapid English, trying to find out how the war was progressing. After the broadcasts were over, Gustave's parents bombarded him with questions about what it had meant, and he answered as well as he could. The broadcasts were mostly about Japan and the Philippines. Sometimes there were alarming stories of German U-boats surfacing within sight of the East Coast of the US and of nighttime explosions at sea. People walking along the beaches found empty, charred lifeboats and smashed pieces of American ships. But there was very little information about what was going on in Europe.

Every afternoon when Gustave came home, he checked the bank of mailboxes in the lobby of the apartment building. So far, there had been no answer from Nicole. Once or twice a piece of mail got put in his family's mailbox by mistake or an advertisement came, and each time his fingers touched an envelope, Gustave felt a rush of excitement and hope. But it was never a letter from France.

One afternoon Mr. Coolidge kept Gustave after school to go over the reading from the night before. Gustave managed to answer some of Mr. Coolidge's questions about African art. "Good!" Mr. Coolidge said. "You understand a lot! Why won't you ever answer when I ask a question in class?"

Gustave shrugged and looked away.

By the time he got back to his apartment building, it was late and the lobby was dim, lit by just one lamp near the door. Gustave went as he always did to the bank of mailboxes, dialed the combination, and reached in. When his fingers felt an onionskin envelope, his heart skipped a beat. He pulled it out. It was pale blue, definitely airmail, though it was too dark to see more. He tore up the stairs, fumbled through his bag with cold fingers to find his key, and unlocked the door. No one else was home. He flipped on the light.

"N.M., La Chaise, Saint-Georges-sur-Cher," it said on the back triangle of the envelope. It was from Nicole! But the envelope looked strange. Both ends had been ripped open and resealed with official tape. It had been opened on one end in France by a censor working for the Nazis. Then it had been opened again on the other end as it came into the US.

It was a disgusting feeling. A Nazi soldier had read his personal letter. Gustave felt as if he had been handed a chocolate bar, and then, just as he was taking a bite, he saw that there was a gigantic cockroach squatting on top of it.

Fighting down nausea, Gustave tugged the letter out of the envelope. As soon as he started reading, he could tell from Nicole's wording that she had known unfriendly eyes were going to slide over her letter before he got it.

*30 January, 1942*

*Cher Gustave,*

    *I'm so glad you got there safely! We hear reports all the time about ships sinking while crossing the Atlantic Ocean, so I was worried. I'm afraid I don't have an answer to your question. Everyone in Saint-Georges is fine, but we heard there was an arrest yesterday in* ▓▓▓▓▓▓▓▓▓▓▓▓▓

    *We have a new teacher at school, Monsieur Faible, who tells us all the important things the Germans want us to know. Studying with Monsieur Faible is very educational. War, he says, is good for the character. It promotes discipline. It helps us learn new skills. He's definitely right. I, for example, am learning to cook. I try to invent new things to do with rutabagas. The Germans don't like them, so that's what we French people eat. I'm so sick of rutabaga soup and mashed rutabagas. So yesterday I made rutabaga pancakes. They still have that same insipid taste, but at least they <u>looked</u> kind of like real pancakes. Papa ate them with enthusiasm. He said I hadn't burned them too badly.*

    *Papa was hungry because he works very hard. All farmers do. I didn't think the pancakes tasted very good myself. But I'm sure you'll be glad to know Papa has been working so much*

*that even my rutabaga pancakes taste good to him. Because he*
*is such a diligent worker, someday I might be able to tell you*
*what you want to know.*
   *Spring is on its way.*

                              *Je t'embrasse,*
                              *Nicole*


Gustave read the letter over and over, hearing Nicole's voice in the words. He could just imagine the mocking glance Nicole would give him as she told him about the "very educational" things she was learning from her new teacher, Monsieur Faible, who sounded like a mouthpiece for the Nazis. Gustave laughed out loud at the thought of Nicole's poor father wolfing down burnt rutabaga pancakes. And Nicole was writing in a kind of code about her father working hard. He was a farmer, sure, and that was hard work, but Nicole meant his other work, for the French Resistance, fighting the Nazis, helping people escape from Occupied France. That was why his "hard work" might bring information about Marcel.

But there was no news about Marcel. And there had been an arrest Nicole was trying to tell Gustave about, but the words had been blacked out by the censor. Had Jews been arrested? Or someone in the Resistance?

"Spring is on its way," she wrote. Even that was a kind of code. Saint-Georges was a lot warmer than New York, but she had written the letter in January, in the depths of winter. Nicole was always an optimist, and she was saying that better days were coming.

# ★ 14 ★

The next day, it sure didn't feel as if spring was coming anytime soon. It started to snow as Gustave was walking to school, and it snowed on and off all day, feathery flakes drifting down outside the classroom windows. When he left the building at the end of the day, the snow had stopped and the sun had come out. Glaring down on the whiteness of the snow everywhere, on the cars, on the trees, on the sidewalks, the sun was almost *too* bright. It was Friday, so Gustave didn't have to do his homework right away. He dropped off his schoolbag at the apartment and ran right back out again. At the front door of the building, he paused, then turned left and headed toward Central Park. Two men with carts were selling roasted sweet potatoes and chestnuts at the entrance to the park.

"Chestnuts?" one called hopefully to Gustave. They smelled delicious, steaming into the frosty air. Gustave reached into his pockets as if that could make money appear there, shook his head, and went past.

A few of the paths had been shoveled, and he wandered along one that wound between tall, snow-covered trees. A few other people were out, but not many. He passed an elderly couple sitting on a bench in the sunshine and a mother with a baby carriage, and then he turned down a narrower path that ran along the edge of the lake. It looked as if it would be a nice place to swim in the summer. Right now, the edge of the lake was frozen, although far off, toward the middle, a patch of water was clear and dotted with the dark shapes of ducks. Gustave searched idly along the edge of the lake for sticks and tossed one out onto the ice. It skittered a long way after it landed, but even that far from shore, it didn't crash through.

Gustave started to compose a letter to Nicole in his head. He wanted to tell her about having a German music teacher, Mrs. Heine, who obviously hated either French people or Jews, or probably both. Suddenly he had an unpleasant thought. Could he even write that? Were the censors reading letters when they went *into* France? Probably. And he didn't want to write anything that might get Nicole into trouble or make the Nazis pay particular attention to her and her father.

He felt a sickening powerlessness, and a rush of memory washed over him. He was watching the Nazi army march, all over again, down the dirt road in front of the house where his family had lived in Saint-Georges, the ground vibrating with the weight of the tanks. The soldiers had looked straight ahead, their faces blank, rifles on their shoulders, their shiny boots rising and falling, as the people from the village stood watching in stunned disbelief. And then the Germans had torn down all the French flags and put up their own flags in their place and installed barriers across the bridges, dividing the country. In his mind, Gustave could still hear the arrogant commands of the German soldiers who had guarded the bridge at the river near Saint-Georges. And that had been in the so-called "free" part of France, the part the Germans *hadn't* occupied. Rage and misery surged up in Gustave, and he bit down fiercely, chewing his own lip, tasting his own blood.

Suddenly a military plane boomed through the New York sky. Gustave felt a jolt of terror. On the left side of the path, an enormous rock jutted out of the earth, offering no cover, but on the right side were thick, snow-covered bushes. Instinctively, Gustave dove for the ground on the right and rolled under a nearby bush. He clung desperately to a stem, pulling himself under as far as he could, oblivious to the snow in his face and the sticks jabbing him. His blood roared in his ears as he waited, head down, for the machine guns to begin.

Then his heart gave a great, almost sickening throb, and he remembered. He wasn't in France anymore. It wasn't a Nazi plane overhead. He was safe in America.

Heat washed over him and then dissipated, leaving him shivering in the cold air. He got on his hands and knees and crawled out from under the bush.

A voice spoke from far above, a girl's voice, high and curious. "Gustave? Is that you? What are you doing down there?"

# ★ 15 ★

Gustave stood, brushing snow off himself, and looked up. Two faces peered at him from the top of the massive rock. One of them was September Rose, wearing her red coat and a blue hat with a pom-pom. The other was a dog—a curious-looking, small, spotted dog with lopsided ears. The faces disappeared, and Gustave heard the girl and the dog scrambling down the other side. After a moment, September Rose came around the rock through the bushes, shoving branches out of her way, with the little dog eagerly pulling ahead of her at the end of a leash.

"Were you playing a game?" she asked.

"Sort of." Gustave squatted down. "What's your dog's name?"

"This is Chiquita." At the sound of her name, the little dog's ears shot straight up, and Gustave laughed.

September Rose beamed. "Watch! She does tricks. Cheeky, sit." The little dog sprang up onto her hind legs, barking.

September Rose tousled her dog's ears. "Well, we're working on that one. So, what were you playing?"

"Nothing. If I throw the stick, will she bring it back?"

"Fetch, you mean? Hey, your English is getting lots better. Not bad after only a month!"

"Five weeks."

"Five weeks—still pretty good! How come you never talk in class? Yeah, sometimes she'll fetch. But I don't want to let her off the leash right now, with all the trees around. She's kind of an escape artist. You can walk her with me if you want to, though."

"Sure."

As they started down the path, Gustave looked at September Rose more carefully. There was something different about her today. She had a long string of beads looped twice around her neck, and against each cheek she had coaxed a lock of hair into a dramatic curl.

"Are you going to a party?" he asked.

September Rose ran a finger through the beads and twisted them. "Oh, these, you mean? No, I just like them. My granma won't let me wear them to school. She won't let me do my hair like this for school either. This is my Josephine Baker look." She touched the curl on her cheek with her right forefinger, put her left hand on her hip, and tossed her head back in a glamorous pose. "Hey, did you ever hear Josephine Baker sing in Paris?"

The name was vaguely familiar—Gustave knew Josephine Baker was a famous Negro jazz singer who had moved from America to France. But in Paris he had never

91

gone to the theater, except sometimes to the movies. "No. Never."

"When I grow up, I'm going to be a singer like her. And I'm going to go to Paris. So you should tell me all about the city, so I can learn about it first, okay? Did you ever see Josephine Baker walking her pet leopard in Paris?"

"Leopard?"

"An enormous, spotted cat!" September Rose put her hands up by her face like claws and snarled, baring her teeth. Chiquita stopped abruptly and growled. She laughed. "It's okay, Cheeky, I'm just pretending! Josephine Baker's pet leopard is named Chiquita. That's where I got Chiquita's name from. Her Chiquita has a diamond collar! When I'm a rich and famous singer like her, I'll buy one for you, Cheeky!" She squatted down and patted the little dog, then stood back up. "Josephine Baker walks the leopard through the streets of Paris. You never saw her doing that?" She sounded disappointed.

"No. Paris is big. She must live in a different *quartier* from me."

"Neighborhood?"

"Yes, a different neighborhood. I never saw anyone with a leopard where I live!"

"But did you ever walk on the Champs-Élysées?" she asked eagerly. "I read that she likes to walk there."

"Sure."

"What's it like?"

"Oh." It was like a hand squeezing his heart, remembering Paris before the war. "Beautiful. Fancy shops. Fancy people. Tall trees with white flowers. But it's not the same now, with the Nazis come."

"Yeah, I guess. I wonder if Josephine Baker is still giving concerts. So tell me more about Paris. Do the ladies wear very elegant clothes? The girls too?"

"Before the war, yes, some of the ladies, the rich ones. Not so much girls. My father sold cloth when we lived in Paris, nice cloth."

"Really? Like silk? I always wanted a silk dress!"

"Of course silk. Also cotton, wool. But now there is not so much new cloth in France. Most people wear old clothes. If they have lots of new, maybe they are friends with the Germans and that is why they have new clothes."

"I never thought about that. I wonder what Josephine Baker uses for costumes for her performances."

"Maybe old costumes."

"Yeah, maybe."

The path curved left, past a bench where an elderly woman, her legs covered by a red plaid blanket, was eating crackers and tossing crumbs to the pigeons. Up ahead, in a spot where the path was well cleared, someone had drawn a grid in yellow chalk with numbers in the squares.

"Someone's been playing hopscotch!" September Rose said.

Gustave stopped to look at it. The spaces were large, and there were rocks on the five, six, seven, and eight, so to jump the board successfully, you would have to make a mighty leap on one foot from four to nine.

"That looks hard," September Rose said. "I bet no one

could do it, with the stones blocking those spaces, so they never finished the game."

"I can do it," Gustave said. "I won this game a lot at school in France!" He jumped onto the one and two squares with both feet, hopped forward onto his left foot on the three triangle, and then hopped sideways to four. He stood there on one foot, wobbling slightly, getting ready, and then he hurled himself through the air to nine. He landed, miraculously, inside the square and fought for balance, then he hopped quickly onto the ten and turned around, getting ready for the way back.

"On your way back, pick up one of the stones," September Rose challenged him. "Then I'll try."

The hop from ten to nine was easy. Gustave balanced there, thinking about which stone to scoop up. Eight and seven were closest, but if he picked up one of them, that would make the board much easier for September Rose. So he put his right leg out straight behind himself for balance, leaned down carefully, and scooped up the rock on five without falling or touching the pavement. He hopped back over the board and waved the rock triumphantly at September Rose. "Did it!"

"I never saw a boy play hopscotch before."

"In France everybody plays. Why not?"

"Yeah, no reason. Okay, let me try." She handed him Chiquita's leash. "I'll even throw this rock back onto the five, so the board is just as hard for me as it was for you."

She tossed the rock into the five triangle. Then she started off, hopping quickly and neatly from two feet on the one and two squares to one foot on the three triangle and then the four triangle. She barely paused for an instant before she made the long hop from four to the exact center of nine and then on to ten as if it had not been difficult at all. She did the turn on one foot, hopped quickly onto the nine and stood there, smiling, her hands on her hips. "See? Easy!" she bragged.

"You pick up a rock too."

"Of course. I'll get the one on six." She leaned over to scoop it up, but as she did, she wobbled and put a hand down.

"Oops! Butterfingers!" she called.

"You touched. You're out! I win!" Gustave shouted.

"No, I said 'butterfingers.'"

"So? You touched. What does 'butterfingers' mean?"

"That's the rules here. Don't you play it that way in France? If you touch and remember to say 'butterfingers,' you aren't out."

"Not in France."

"Well, this is America! When I go to France to sing for my first international audience, I'll remember, and when I play hopscotch, I won't call 'butterfingers'!" She hopped rapidly onto the six and then to the four and the three, leaped triumphantly onto both feet on one and two, and then jumped off the board, whooping and wildly circling her arms.

"Did it!" she called, flushed and triumphant. "Tie!"

"It's harder the way we play in France, with no 'butterfingers.' What does 'butterfingers' mean?" Gustave handed September Rose Chiquita's leash.

"You say it when you drop something. I guess it's like

if you had butter on your fingers, they would be slippery. But also it's a candy bar. You haven't had one yet?"

"No."

"Oh, you've gotta try it. Chocolate with peanuts. They're one of my favorites. But they're really hard to find these days. A lot of the chocolate's going off to feed the soldiers. If I ever find one in a candy store, I'll give you a bite. *If* you tell me more about Paris!"

Chiquita was straining on the leash. September Rose took a few running steps, catching up with her. "Come on!" she said over her shoulder. "Chiquita won't stay still any longer."

They passed a group of girls playing jump rope, and then they were next to a wide-open field.

"Can Chiquita fetch now?" Gustave asked.

"Sure." She unsnapped the leash.

Gustave waved a stick at the little dog, then tossed it out over the snowy grass. She ran after it and trotted back proudly with it in her mouth. "Good dog, Chiquita," he crooned. He tried to take the stick from her, but she gripped it tightly with her teeth, so he played tug-of-war with her for a while. Then Gustave wrenched the stick loose and threw it out over the field as far as he could. She raced after it, leaping over lumps of snow, but before she got to the stick, she swerved, darted off to the right, and disappeared.

"Oh no!" September Rose shrieked, giggling madly and taking off over the snowy field. Gustave tore after her. "See what I told you?" she called over her shoulder. "Escape artist! Chiquita!" she shouted. "Come back!"

Gustave whistled as loudly as he could while running. "Chiquita!"

But there was no sign of her. She had vanished behind a clump of trees. September Rose ran around one way while he ran around the other. They almost collided on the other side.

"No luck?" she asked, panting. She seemed more exasperated than worried.

Just then Gustave saw a stubby tail sticking up from a snowbank about twenty feet away. "There!" he called.

September Rose streaked past him. As she reached the snowbank, she grabbed her dog's collar. Chiquita was gobbling down something bright orange. September Rose snapped the leash back on. "Don't *do* that, Chiquita!" she scolded, breathing heavily and laughing. "Naughty girl!"

"What's she eating?" Gustave asked, reaching for it. "Is it all right for her?"

"Yeah. Don't worry. Someone must have bought a roasted sweet potato and thrown some of it away. Those are her favorite thing, those and apple cores. She's amazing. She can smell them from hundreds of feet away and right through snow. At least we caught her this time." She sighed and rubbed Chiquita's ears, starting to walk again.

"I love her. But she's trouble with a capital *T*! She scares me when she runs off. Last summer, we were visiting my cousins down in Maryland on the Fourth of July, and there was this big picnic, with fried chicken and corn on the cob and peach pie and everything. I brought Chiquita, of course. That's when I found out that she can't stand loud noises. There were fireworks—"

"Fireworks?"

"Yeah, you know." September Rose acted out a firework going off, squatting down and jumping up exuberantly, throwing a spray of snow into the air and waving her arms. "*Boom! Boom! Hiss!* Lots of bright colors? Red, blue, gold, green? Pfshhh!"

"Yes. Fireworks." He tried the word.

September Rose talked more slowly and clearly. "Yeah. I was holding Chiquita on my lap." She held her arms close to her chest to show him. "But when the noise started—*BAM!*—she began quivering. . . ." September Rose acted it out, and he nodded. "And then suddenly, *zoom!* She tore out of there and disappeared. We looked for her for hours. I cried. I thought she was gone for good. But then when we got back to my cousins' house, there was this gigantic hole in the screen door. She had run home and jumped right through the screen! We found her hiding in the closet, shaking. Little Cheeky! She was so scared, poor girl! But I was too, until we found her."

Gustave nodded. He had understood most of the story. "I never had a dog."

"Alan gave her to me when she was a puppy. That's my big brother. He's bossy, but he's pretty great. Do you have any brothers or sisters?"

"No. I have a cousin, though. Jean-Paul. And he has a baby sister."

"Are they still in France?"

"No. They came with us. But he lives not close—in the Bronx."

"Yeah, that takes a while to get to." She glanced at her

watch. "I have to get home soon. But you wanna see something funny first?" She leaned down and made a snowball, and the small dog yipped in excitement. September Rose dropped the leash. "Ready, Cheeky?" She held the snowball back as Chiquita panted. "Fetch!" She threw it into a snow-covered field, and Chiquita hurtled after it, yipping, then burrowed down into the snow where it had landed. After a while, she popped her head up and looked back at September Rose, mystified.

September Rose squealed with laughter. "She doesn't understand why it disappears! It's so funny—she never learns."

Gustave whistled, and the little dog came tearing joyfully back as he made another snowball. "Catch!" he shouted, and he tossed it high in the air. Chiquita leaped up, and as she snapped her jaws around it, the snowball burst into a shower of powder. September Rose burst into giggles again, and Gustave laughed until his stomach hurt at the little dog's baffled, enthusiastic face as snow sprayed over all three of them.


That evening after dinner, Gustave got out a piece of air-mail stationery and started a letter to Nicole.


*20 February, 1942*

*Chère Nicole,*

*I wish I could send you some food from America. There's so much here. In the park and on the street corners, they sell sweet potatoes and roast chestnuts. They smell just like the roast chestnuts at home. A couple of weeks ago, Maman asked me to take the trash to the garbage bin behind the apartment building. When I lifted up the lid, I saw someone had thrown a huge roast turkey into the garbage! The whole thing! It was still warm and steaming. Only a little bit of the white meat had been cut off. I almost took it out of the garbage, because even though we had just had dinner, it had mostly been potatoes, so I was still hungry. In fact, don't tell my parents, but I did tear off and eat just a tiny bit. I mean, it was still clean. The part I ate wasn't touching anything dirty or anything. And it was so good. Then I ran back upstairs and told Maman and Papa what I'd found, and they couldn't believe me, so they both came down to see it. Maman wouldn't let us eat any of it, though. In New York, there's lots of meat in the markets, not like in France, but we don't usually have enough money to buy it.*

*Papa has a job now. He cleans in a department store, and Maman makes hats at home. There are always feathers and spangles all over the apartment.*

*Also, about food. I was just walking in the park with this girl from school that I ran into. Her dog found a nearly whole sweet potato someone had thrown away. Just tossed it into a snowbank!*

*So what new recipes are you trying? Are there still concerts in Paris, do you know? School is all right. I'm getting better at English, but it's hard. Some of the guys are friendly. Some aren't.*

Gustave wanted to tell her about Mrs. Heine, the German music teacher, but he didn't want to say anything that might make the German censor angry or suspicious of Nicole. He thought about it and then wrote:

*I have a music teacher named Mrs. Heine. As you can imagine, I am her favorite student, because I have such a beautiful singing voice.*

He could just see the way Nicole would laugh when she read that. She would certainly know he meant the opposite of what he was writing.

*Either that or it is something else about me that makes her so tremendously fond of me. On my second day of school, she made me sing in front of the whole class. You can imagine how much I enjoyed that. This one kid told me that her name is the same as the American word for rear end. How unfortunate for her.*

*I know you'll keep me up to date on what is going on at school in Saint-Georges, on your new recipes, and on everything else important, right?*

*Gustave*

He signed his name and looked up. Papa and Maman were sitting on the sofa together, drinking tea and listening to music on the radio.

"Can I take one of the airmail stamps you bought?" Gustave asked.

Papa lifted his head from the back of the sofa where he was resting it. He had dark circles under his eyes. "Go ahead. But bear in mind that these letters to France are expensive."

"I won't write too often, Papa. And Nicole knows where we live now. So she can send news."

Gustave's parents exchanged a glance.

"Yes," Papa said gently. "That's true."

# ★ 16 ★

Gustave had understood, since his first day, that September Rose didn't want him to sit with her at lunch, and by now he was pretty sure it was because boys and girls weren't friends at this school, not if they didn't want to be teased. Martha and Leo were different. They were always hanging around together. People certainly teased them about being boyfriend and girlfriend, but they both seemed to like the attention. They weren't trying to hide anything—lately they went around holding hands, and once Leo had put his arm around Martha's waist right in front of everybody.

Still, Gustave wished he could talk to September Rose at school. Every afternoon the week after his encounter with her in Central Park, Gustave walked over to the big rock where they'd run into one another, hoping she and Chiquita would be there, but they never were. Central Park was so big that he might easily never run into her there again. After school on Friday, Gustave meandered around the park for hours, sticking to the places where people seemed to walk their dogs, but he still didn't see her. When he finally got home, his fingers and toes were numb from the cold.

On Sunday night Gustave and his parents went to Aunt Geraldine's for dinner. It was a long, slow trip on the subway up to the Grand Concourse in the Bronx. The apartment building was on a beautiful, wide street and it was large and elegant. Gustave ran up the curving stairs to the second floor and pushed the doorbell. Jean-Paul answered at the first ring, smiling broadly. Aunt Geraldine was right behind him. Jean-Paul was wearing new pants that went all the way down to his ankles, Gustave noticed with a twinge of envy. He also had a new brown sweater and he would almost have looked like an American if Gustave hadn't known that he was French.

"Come in, come in!" Aunt Geraldine cried, kissing Maman and then Papa and Gustave and bustling around hanging up coats. "We have the best news. A Red Cross postcard came from David yesterday, forwarded from France."

"How is he?" Maman asked worriedly.

"It seems he's all right! Jean-Paul, show them Papa's postcard. He couldn't say much, of course. The cards are surely read by the Nazis as they leave the camp. It's mostly just check boxes; there isn't a lot of room to write. But he checked, 'I am in good health,' and he sent his love to me and the children, and he also wrote—what was it, Jean-Paul?"

"He said, 'Tell Christophe's family he is here with me and well.'" Jean-Paul recited the words from memory, bringing the postcard down from the mantelpiece and handing it to Maman.

"So it's such good news, you see!" Aunt Geraldine cried. "We'd been so worried."

"Why? I don't remember Christophe and his family," Maman said.

"We couldn't figure it out at first either," Jean-Paul explained excitedly. "But then we remembered he'd mentioned a friend named Christophe when he first went into the army. We don't know him or his family. But you see, the name—it's a Christian name! So if Papa is with Christophe, it means he's still in a camp for French prisoners of war."

"Ah," Papa said slowly. "That *is* good news."

"I don't get it," Gustave said quietly to Papa.

"They haven't figured out he's Jewish, so he's in a camp with the other captured French soldiers," Papa said. "The camps for soldiers are—" Papa hesitated. "Well, it seems those are better places to be than the camps for Jews."

"Tonight we have so much to celebrate! A letter from David! And Berthold has a job now! Congratulations!" Aunt Geraldine smiled at Papa. "And you're working too, Lili! The boys are starting off well in school. We're all so lucky. Jean-Paul, why don't you show Gustave your room?"

"Yeah—come look at my American comic books. The kids at school all trade them."

"Oh, those foolish comic books!" Aunt Geraldine said to Maman and Papa. "I wish he would spend half the time reading for school that he spends poring over them!"

"But they're so good for my English, Maman!" Jean-Paul said. "They're easier to understand because of the pictures."

"Sure! *Zip! Pow! Blam!* Even I understand that much English! Go on!" Aunt Geraldine put her arm around her son affectionately, and Gustave noticed that Jean-Paul was now nearly a head taller than his mother. He had put on some weight in America too. After a month and a half here, he wasn't so scrawny as he'd been on the ship.

Jean-Paul had comics out all over his bed, and he had his own room. The apartment was enormous compared to Gustave's. Madame Raymond, the relative they were living with, had two extra bedrooms, Jean-Paul explained, giving him the tour. His mother shared a big bedroom with Giselle, and Jean-Paul had a narrow maid's room off the kitchen. It had only a tiny slit of a window, but it did have a model airplane hanging over the bed. "It used to be her son's room," Jean-Paul explained. "When we got here, there were some old books and games and also another airplane that he never finished that she said I could work on. I had to buy new paints, though. His were all dried up."

"Did those pants used to belong to her son too?" Gustave asked.

"These?" Jean-Paul looked down at his pants and then at Gustave's French ones. "No. Madame Raymond collected used clothes from her friends for me and Giselle. Your parents didn't get you any American pants yet?"

"No."

Jean-Paul looked embarrassed. "Sorry. That's tough. I only have two pairs—one regular pair and one fancy. If I had more, I'd give you one. But since I only have two, I know my mom would kill me."

The rich, meaty smell of *cassoulet* was coming from the kitchen. "Dinner!" Aunt Geraldine called.

As Aunt Geraldine served, she chattered nonstop to Maman about life in the Bronx, about her favorite bakery and the broken cookies they always saved for little Giselle; about Madame Raymond, who was very particular about food and how the kitchen was kept but kind about everything else; about the cold New York weather; and about the park nearby where she took Giselle to play. Aunt Geraldine was especially excited because she had met a French rabbi while doing Madame Raymond's fruit shopping, which had to be done at a specific market that was several miles away by bus.

"But it was worth the long bus trip with Giselle after all!" she exclaimed. "The fruit there is delicious, and Rabbi Blum is so nice. His family is from Alsace. He wants us all to join his synagogue, your family too."

Aunt Geraldine paused to hand around helpings of dessert, ladyfingers drizzled with kirsch.

"Oh, my favorite! How nice of you to make it!" Maman spooned up the spongy cookies flavored with cherry brandy. "But about Berthold's job."

"Oh yes, of course. I'm sorry, Berthold. Congratulations! Tell me all about it."

"He's working at a fine department store," Maman

explained. "For now he's a janitor, but that way, you see, he can be the first to spot an opening when there's one in sales, as soon as he can speak English better."

"Don't expect to be hired in a good position while you have an accent," Aunt Geraldine said bluntly. "That's what I hear. But at least you have a job and some money coming in." She poured coffee from Madame Raymond's silver pot into a fragile, flowered teacup and handed it to Maman. "Anyway, now that we're all getting settled, you must come to Rabbi Blum's synagogue with me. It's a lovely old building on the Upper East Side. To be with other French Jews, I think it's all right to take a bus on the Sabbath, don't you?"

"Real coffee!" Maman held the cup below her nose, savoring the aroma. "What luxury! What do you think, Berthold? We've seen several synagogues much closer to our apartment."

"Oh sure! But this synagogue is French," Aunt Geraldine insisted. "The children and I have already gone twice. Nearly everyone there speaks French. You'll see. It feels just like home."

"Really? There are enough French Jews in New York for a whole synagogue?"

"Yes! Most of the people at this synagogue have been here quite a few years, but almost everyone is originally from France. The boys need to prepare for their bar mitzvahs. They are so behind. I feel terrible that we've had to put that off."

"I know." Maman nodded.

"Time for us to get out of here before they make us

start chanting prayers!" Jean-Paul jumped up, pushing his chair back with a screech, and the grown-ups laughed. He licked his finger and picked up the last few crumbs from his dessert plate as he took it into the kitchen. "The best part is that there's a French Boy Scout troop connected with the synagogue, the Franco-American Boy Scouts, and I'm in it! You've got to join too. Want to help me work on the model airplane?"

"Sure."

As Jean-Paul got out the paints, he told Gustave about the Boy Scouts. He had already gone to one planning meeting and a hike. "The rabbi is the troop leader, but there aren't enough boys our age for a whole troop, so we join together with some French Catholic boys. One of their priests is a leader too."

"They don't mind being with Jews?" Gustave took the airplane piece Jean-Paul handed him and began dabbing it with silver paint.

"They don't seem to. We're all French. It's great to be somewhere where everybody speaks French, not like school."

Gustave watched Jean-Paul carefully attach a propeller. "How *is* your school?"

"It's all right. They started me in second grade, because I couldn't speak English at all, not like you, so I was with all these stupid little kids. I felt like a giant in there. But two weeks ago, they moved me up into third. I'm still a giant, but they'll move me up again as soon as I learn more English."

"Do you have any friends?"

"Well, there are some boys I play tag with at recess. They think I'm great because I'm so much faster than them! It's all right. What about you?"

"There are some guys I eat lunch with. And sometimes they choose me for their team at recess. There's a girl from school I talked to in the park one time. But she doesn't talk to me at school. I know she doesn't want people to say we're girlfriend and boyfriend, but still, she could at least talk to me a little."

"Women!" Jean-Paul said. He pushed another airplane piece toward Gustave. "You want to paint this silver?"

"Sure." Gustave took the tailpiece. "My mother told your mother we heard from Nicole, right? I got a letter with part of it blacked out. It was something about someone being arrested. But she didn't have any news about Marcel."

"Yeah." Jean-Paul had his head down and was concentrating on the propeller. "I don't think we're likely to get any news about him, you know," he muttered after a while.

"We might. Nicole's father is in the Resistance, and he's still trying to get information."

Jean-Paul just kept painting his airplane piece silently, without looking up.

"Time to go, Gustave," Papa said, opening the door. "Ah, that's a nice airplane you're making there, Jean-Paul."

"Thanks," Jean-Paul said. "Bye." He stayed in the room, painting, as Gustave went out to the kitchen and started putting on his still-damp shoes.

"So, I hope things keep going well with the job, Berthold," Aunt Geraldine said as his parents put on their coats. "It's hard to imagine you as a janitor, I must say. I guess you can't do much else with your foreign accent. It's a bit of a comedown for you! No fine clothes at work when you're a janitor, hmm?"

"It'll do for now," Papa said stiffly, winding a scarf around his neck.

"It's such good news about David. Don't be annoyed with Geraldine, Berthold," Maman said as they waited on the cold subway platform for the train home. "She just says whatever she's thinking. She doesn't mean any harm. She's always been that way."

"Yes," Papa said shortly. "Always rude!"

"Oh, you know you don't mean that! She's your sister-in-law, and you love her."

"True. I do love my rude sister-in-law!" Papa said. Gustave listened, grinning to himself as he watched a pigeon calmly strutting around the empty subway track and pecking at the ground between the rails.

"That was some meal, wasn't it?" Maman commented. "They certainly are living well. Madame Raymond must give her a good salary."

"Hmm."

"But our jobs pay enough to manage on. We're here, and we're safe. We need to take it one day at a time." Maman kissed Papa. Gustave looked away, scuffing his left shoe along the cement. He knew Papa *did* find it hard working as a janitor. He came home exhausted and limping every evening, ate dinner quickly, changed out of his blue janitor's coveralls, and then three evenings a week, he left with Maman for two hours of night school. It was odd seeing him going off to work in that faded blue jumpsuit. Before the war, Papa had always gone to work sharply dressed in a suit with polished shoes. There had sometimes even been a brightly colored silk handkerchief peeking jauntily out of his pocket. Where are those silk handkerchiefs now? Gustave wondered suddenly. They must have been left behind, somewhere in France.

The train pulled into the station with a whoosh of heated air and the shrieking of brakes. The pigeon fluttered calmly up to the platform just in time and began strolling about again. The doors of the train hissed open, and Gustave and his parents got on. The doors shut and the subway train started up with a jolt. Colored lights flashed as the train rattled through the dark tunnel.

Jean-Paul had a pretty nice setup there in the Bronx, Gustave thought as his parents talked to each other. Good food, his own room, even the model airplanes. But why was Jean-Paul sure that they weren't going to hear about Marcel? An unpleasant thought floated into Gustave's head. What if one day he got a letter from Nicole with information about Marcel and his mother, and it was bad news? Until this moment, he had always imagined that when he finally heard some news, it would be good. But it might not be.

# ★ 17 ★

By the end of the school day on Monday, most of the snow on the streets had melted. There was a strong wind, and the sun kept coming out and then disappearing behind large banks of cloud. It was March, but it still felt like winter. Gustave pulled his coat tightly around him, remembering what they said in France about changeable March weather: *"Quand il fait beau, prends ton manteau."* *When it is warm, bring your coat.* That was even more true here, in this cold American city.

As Gustave approached Quong's Hand Laundry at the corner of Amsterdam and 91st Street, he saw that the sidewalk in front of the store was partially blocked by a large, strange-looking yellow bike. It was a giant tricycle, really, with a wide basket between the two front wheels. It looked clunky and slow, but Gustave felt a sudden pang, missing the bicycle he had given to Nicole before he left France. She was no doubt riding it recklessly, the way she had ridden her old bike. Maybe even right now, an ocean away, she was swooping up and down the hills around Saint-Georges.

This old tricycle on the sidewalk wouldn't win any races, but Gustave stopped to look at it. As he did, he noticed a sign in the window of the laundry: HELP WANTED. DELIVERY BOY.

If he had a job, he could buy those pants. And he could have some pocket money again. Through the window, Gustave saw the rack of secondhand clothes, and, with his heart pounding violently, he pushed open the door.

Mr. Quong looked up from his work at the counter. "Can I help you?"

Gustave stood up as tall as he could, trying to look and sound confident. "I would like ze job." As he spoke, he heard his French accent on the word "the," and he flushed.

"Ah." Mr. Quong looked him over closely. "Can you ride a bike?"

"Yes."

"How old are you?"

"Thirteen." Gustave was glad that his birthday had been last month.

"My last delivery boy just quit with no warning. He turned eighteen, and he went right down to the army recruiting station and enlisted. The job is riding the bike and delivering laundry packages to customers three afternoons a week. A quarter per day, and you keep the tips. I'll give you a try. What do you say?"

"Yes!"

"Good. Come around the counter."

Gustave did, and the cat followed, meowing insistently. "I'll feed you in a minute, Molly," Mr. Quong said absentmindedly. He showed Gustave a pile of packages wrapped in brown paper and tied with string, each one neatly labeled with a name and an address. Molly rubbed against Mr. Quong's ankles and then Gustave's, meowing again.

Looking at the addresses, Gustave had a sinking feeling. "I need to tell you—I am immigrated, two months ago, from France. I don't know all the streets yet."

"Ah." Mr. Quong nodded. "I was an immigrant too, from China. You'll learn." He rummaged around behind the counter and pulled out a folded-up piece of paper. "I'll give you this map. I'll number the deliveries so you know the best order to do them in. My customers don't live too far away, all within a mile or so. Once you learn, it'll be easy. They pay me when they drop the clothes off, so you don't have to collect any money when you deliver, except your tips, of course. Afterward, you lock the delivery bike in the alley. I'll show you where. Can you start right now?"

Gustave nodded. He carried the packages out to the delivery bike, stepping around the cat, who seemed to be getting in his way on purpose. Even without tips, in just three weeks he would have more than enough to buy the navy blue pants! A gust of wind roared down the street, and he adjusted his scarf around his neck. Straddling the bike, he waved goodbye to Molly, who had jumped back onto her blanket in the window, shoved down on the rusty pedals and started off.

It was harder to get around than it had looked. Some of the streets were one-way, and that wasn't marked on the map. Cars honked at him, taxis swerved, and people shouted. Busses roared by, leaving foul-smelling exhaust in their wake. And Gustave hadn't noticed before, but now he realized how many other delivery men and boys there were riding bicycles on the street, some of them zipping in and out of the dangerous traffic like maniacs. One cut in front of Gustave just as he was going over a manhole cover, shouting something incomprehensible over his shoulder, and Gustave nearly toppled over. There were also more hills than you noticed when you were walking, Gustave thought, and the delivery bike was clunky and heavy, difficult to pedal up hills. Still, it was great to be back on something with wheels.

Mr. Quong had numbered the packages so that Gustave delivered first to the addresses on lower numbered streets and then worked his way uptown. The first package, for an address on 71st Street, was especially bulky. Gustave found a place to lock the bike the way Mr. Quong had shown him and trudged up six flights of stairs. On the apartment door was a rectangular white banner bordered in red with a blue star in the middle. As Gustave was examining it, the door opened and a tired-looking woman stood in the entryway with a baby on her hip and other children shrieking behind her.

"Oh, the clean diapers! And you brought them all the way up the stairs instead of leaving them at the bottom like the other delivery boy. Thank Heavens! I really need those. Can you put them on that table?" She gestured to a table near the door, and then, to Gustave's surprise, she reached into her apron pocket and handed him a nickel. "This is for you."

"Thank you!" Gustave bounded down the stairs and out the door to the street. His first American tip! He squeezed the coin happily and felt it getting warm in his hand; then he tucked it deep into his pants pocket.

The next delivery was to a run-down-looking apartment building on West 83rd Street. Gustave found the address and locked the delivery bike, but then he couldn't find his way in. At the first delivery, he had walked right into a hallway and gone up the stairs, but this building was different. It had a faded green door with a cracked pane of glass in the window, but it was locked. Next to it was a small grocery store. Gustave walked in. Dusty cans lined the shelves, and in the front were newspapers and magazines. A thin man with faded, coppery hair was alone at the cash register.

"Excuse me. I need deliver to this address," Gustave said, showing the man the package.

The man was chewing on something. "Yeah, next door. We own it. Wait."

He disappeared into the back of the shop. Gustave went out and stood in the cold by the locked door. Across the street, two older boys were throwing rocks against a garbage-can lid propped against a window. They shouted whenever one of them knocked it down onto the sidewalk with a clatter. Gustave watched until the man came back and unlocked the door. He looked hard at Gustave. "Third floor," he said curtly.

Gustave ran up the stairs and knocked.

"What do you want?" shouted a voice behind the door.

"Delivery!" he called. The door opened a crack and a hand reached out, grabbed the package, and slammed the door. He could hear the bolt sliding back into place.

When he came out onto the street, the man was still standing at the door, but the boys had disappeared. Gustave unlocked the bike, straddled it, and pushed off. He was nearly at the corner when he heard a shout. "Stay offa our street, Jew-boy!" A rock clanged on the back tire rim and someone laughed just as another rock struck his hand.

Shaky with anger and fear, Gustave pedaled as fast as he could, uptown and away.

When he got to a busy intersection, he stopped, his leg muscles trembling, and sat down on the curb next to a grimy pile of snow. He pushed the top layer off, grabbed a clean handful from underneath, and held it against his sore hand. At first it stung badly, but after a minute the cool felt good. He left it until it melted into slush and fell off. He looked at the list of addresses and started off again, his legs shaky, his knees aching with the effort.

*Jew-boy.* He heard the jeer in his head each time he pushed down on the pedal. *Jew-boy. Jew-boy.* After a while it shifted, turning into a taunt he had heard in France: *"Youpin. Youpin."*

By the time he got to the last delivery address, on 99th Street, it was nearly dark. His head was aching, and his fingers, clutching the cold handlebars, were numb. Gustave found a railing and locked Mr. Quong's bike to it. He took the last package out of the rusty metal basket, climbed three flights of stairs, and rang the doorbell. This door had a blue-star banner on it too.

Nothing. He rang the bell again, impatiently, stamping water off his feet. He could hear a small dog barking excitedly inside. What if no one was there? He hadn't thought to ask Mr. Quong what to do if that happened. But after a moment he heard quick, light steps coming to the door. He saw the peephole darken as someone peered out, and then the door swung open. There in the entryway stood September Rose.

"Hey, it's you! Why are you here?" she blurted out.

Gustave felt awkward and very aware of his nose, red and drippy from the cold outside.

"This is for you," he mumbled, holding out the laundry package.

September Rose took it. "Oh. From the laundry. You deliver for Mr. Quong now?"

"I started today."

"Do you have a lot more to do?"

"No—yours is the last."

September Rose hesitated in the doorway, looking at him as if she wanted to say something more. Her hair was curled closely against her cheeks, and she was wearing her long chain of beads looped around her neck again. Over her shoulder, Gustave glimpsed a small, glittery room, crowded with a plush pink sofa and other pieces of furniture. Warmth and a rich, sweet, spicy smell drifted toward him, making his stomach growl.

"Have you done the geography reading yet?" September Rose asked.

"No." Remembering all the schoolwork he still had to struggle through, Gustave felt bone-achingly cold and tired.

"It must be hard, doing homework in English."

"I just do the part I can."

"They don't make you do it all? Lucky!" She grinned.

All at once a yapping ball of fur came rushing to the door, and Chiquita jumped up on Gustave, her light front paws scrabbling at his legs. "Hello, girl!" he said, rubbing her head. "So that was you, barking! Find any sweet potatoes lately?"

Down the hall, the door to another apartment opened, and an elderly woman peeked her head out. She had short, tightly curled gray hair and skin a bit darker than September Rose's. She looked at Gustave suspiciously. "Seppie?" she demanded. "Everything all right? What's that boy doing here? Where your granma at?"

September Rose came out into the hallway. "Everything's hunky-dory, Miss Noelle," she said, holding up the brown paper package. "Granma went down to get the evening paper. This is Gustave. He delivers for Quong's Hand Laundry. He's in my class at school."

"Chiquita looks mighty friendly with him."

"Of course. She's a mighty friendly dog."

Miss Noelle looked hard at Gustave. "Well, you finished delivering the laundry. You be going, hear?"

September Rose grinned at Gustave, rolling her eyes slightly. "See you at school, Gustave," she said. "Or maybe in the park?"

Maybe she had been looking for him there too.

"Sure," he said. "See you."

# ★ 18 ★

ustave chained the bike in the alley by the laundry. Mr. Quong was just locking up.

"Any problems with the deliveries?" Mr. Quong asked, pulling down metal shutters over the shop windows.

Gustave hesitated. "Some boys threw rocks at me on Eighty-Third Street."

Mr. Quong looked at him intently. "Hmm. That was a new customer. I'll tell him he has to pick the laundry up himself if he comes back. I don't want you to have to deal with that again. Did you have any trouble finding the addresses?"

"No, sir. I found them all."

"It'll get easier and faster," Mr. Quong promised.

It was dark, and much later than the time Gustave usually got home. When he arrived at the apartment, Papa was there too.

"Where have you been?" Maman cried. "We've been worried!"

"Working," Gustave said. He couldn't keep himself from smiling. "I found a job! I'm a delivery boy for Mr. Quong's laundry."

"You found work!" She sounded astonished. "In America!"

"I'll give you half the money," Gustave said hesitantly, quickly recalculating how long it would take to earn the pants.

Maman and Papa smiled at each other. "You keep the money. Just be sure that the job doesn't interfere with your schoolwork," Maman said.

"It should actually be good for his English," Papa said, settling into his chair with a sigh and rubbing his bad leg. "Yes, you keep the money, *mon vieux*. A boy needs some candy now and then. And eventually you can pay for little things—like stamps for your letters to France."

"Sit down," said Maman. "Dinner's ready."

"So, what's this Mr. Quong like?" Papa asked.

"He's nice. He's an immigrant too, he told me."

"From China, it sounds like."

"Yeah. He has a cat—hey, we have meat today!" Gustave watched as Maman served him a thin sliver of pot roast and a mound of carrots, turnips, and potatoes, ladling sauce on top.

"Yes. There was a bargain on cheap cuts at the butcher's," Maman said. "Was the work hard? Gustave! Wait until everyone is served!" Maman tapped his hand, and he put his fork down.

He certainly wasn't going to tell her about the

stone-throwing boys. "It was hard finding some of the addresses, but—wow, this smells so good. It's like before the war!"

Gustave delivered for Mr. Quong again on Wednesday. There was another address in the west eighties, but everything went smoothly. On his third delivery day, Friday, dark clouds loomed, and shortly after he started off, freezing rain began to patter down on the streets around him. Mr. Quong had given him a tarp to wrap the laundry packages in to keep them dry, but between the rain and the cars splashing him from head to foot, before long Gustave was soaked through to the skin with icy water. The deliveries took a long time, but, to his relief, again nothing bad happened. It was nearly pitch-black outside by the time Gustave got back to Mr. Quong's shop and chained the delivery bike in the alley.

Mr. Quong smiled at him sympathetically as he came in. "Ah, you look cold. No problems with your deliveries today, right?"

Gustave shook his head.

"Would you like some tea?"

Gustave shivered. "No, thank you—I have to go home."

"All right. Good work this week." Mr. Quong made a mark in his notebook, then handed Gustave three quarters.

The coins were warm and solid in his hand as he ran back to the apartment, thinking excitedly about everything he could buy. He couldn't save it all, because he was going on a hike with Jean-Paul and his French Boy Scout troop over the weekend, and he would need two nickels for each way of the long ride on two different subway lines, the IND and the IRT. But counting the nickel tip from Mrs. Markham, the lady with all the diapers, he would have sixty cents left over. The first money he had earned in America!

The following Sunday, Gustave and Jean-Paul raced across a field at Van Cortlandt Park in the Bronx. The French Boy Scouts, visible from a distance because of their kerchiefs, were gathering near the entrance to a trail. The sun was shining, and what had been ice on the field was turning to mud. A young priest in a dark shirt with a white neckband held out his hand to Gustave and smiled. *"Bonjour. Bienvenue,* Gustave! I am Father René. Welcome to the Franco-American Boy Scouts. Let me introduce you to these five rascals, Bernard, André, Guy, Maurice, and Xavier."

"This is my cousin," Jean-Paul said to the five boys. They shook Gustave's hand enthusiastically, all of them except Maurice, who was tall, with an aloof, narrow face and dark, intense eyes. He just nodded coolly.

"Maurice is kind of the unofficial leader," Jean-Paul whispered eagerly. "He won't talk to you, except to order you around, until you earn your totem name."

Gustave's hands prickled with excitement. "How do I do that?"

"You'll see!"

"Hi!" said Xavier, grinning. He was chubby and looked a little younger than the others.

"I'm glad you're here," said Bernard, who had dark, wavy hair. "We need more scouts."

"You and Jean-Paul just came to the US, right?" said Guy. Guy was tall and lanky, with an inquisitive face.

"In January," Gustave said. "What about you?"

"I've been here since I was eight. Before that, we lived in Corsica."

"Hey, wait!" said André. "You go to Joan of Arc Junior High! I've noticed your French pants in the halls."

"Yes! What grade are you in?"

"I'm in ninth."

"Oh. I'm in seventh."

*"Allons-y, les gars,"* said Father René. *"Let's go!* We have a long hike today. Who's up for some tree identification?"

"In winter?" asked Gustave.

"Sure! A good scout can identify trees from the bark!" Father René said, starting off down the trail. "All right, Xavier, what's that one?"

"Oak?"

"Beech!" Father René laughed. "You boys need to brush up! André, what's this?"

Father René hiked energetically up the wooded path, talking about trees. Gustave breathed in deeply, enjoying the smell of the woods and the French voices all around him. The sun sparkled on the needles of the pine trees and lit up their craggy bark. Bernard was up ahead, wearing a pair of French *pantalon de golf,* just as Gustave was, with warm socks and sturdy shoes. After a while Father René stopped quizzing them about nature and started singing. It was a familiar French song about the emperor and his family coming to visit every day for a week, starting with *lundi matin,* Monday morning:

*"Lundi matin, l'empereur, sa femme, et le petit prince . . . ,"* he belted out. *On Monday morning, the emperor and his wife and son . . .*

*"Came to my house, to shake my hand for fu-un!"* the boys roared back, even Gustave, because here, singing this silly song from back home, it didn't matter if his voice sounded like a dying frog.

*"But since I was away, the little son did say/'Since that's the way it is, we will come back TUESDAY!'"* the song went on, and then repeated through all the days of the week. The scouts belted the words out goofily at the top of their lungs, the French sounds soaring into the sweet-smelling woodsy air.

When the song ended, they hiked in contented silence for a while, listening to the birds and the wind and the distant roar of cars from somewhere far away in the city.

"Are you thinking about going to the Lycée Français?" Xavier asked Gustave, pausing to let him catch up so that they could hike side by side.

"There's a French school in New York?"

"Yeah, I go, and so do Xavier and Bernard," said Guy, joining in. "It's a private school."

"I'm pretty sure we can't afford that."

"Not now anyway, Gustave." Jean-Paul joined the conversation. "Maybe when your father gets a better job.

My mother said that later maybe I would go. Madame Raymond said she might be able to help with my tuition."

"My father says you can't do anything in France without *le bac*," added Bernard. "So he wants me to get the French high school diploma in case we go back after the war."

"I never thought about that." Anxiety twisted in Gustave's stomach, interrupting his happy mood. "But he means if the Allies win the war, right?"

"Of course!"

"If we don't win, France will be a slave country to Germany," Guy said. "And Belgium, Poland, Norway, Denmark, Czechoslovakia, Austria, and all the others too—it would be horrible. The Allies have to win."

"It would be even worse for us Jews," Bernard said quietly, looking at Gustave.

The thought of Germany winning the war was too unbearable to contemplate. His mind held the thought for only an instant before shifting away—to how it would be now that he knew another French boy at Joan of Arc Junior High, to being hungry, to the blister forming on his right heel.

"I hear there's so much homework in high school," Xavier said. "Chemistry and physics and all those exams—yuck! Anyway, it's far away. Who wants to think about that now?"

"It's next year for me, and Maurice is already in high school," André said, joining the conversation. "You can always try to get into Stuyvesant High School if you want to, Gustave. Joan of Arc is all right for junior high, though. Especially now that there are two of us there."

"Sure."

"Boys!" Father René called a halt to the hike as they came to a low summit. The path split here, one branch diverging to the left and the other winding ahead through the trees. "I know you have some *private* scout business to attend to." He grinned. "I'll just hike this side trail by myself for the next hour or so. I'll meet you all back here at one p.m. sharp. Maurice, you have a watch? I'm counting on you to get the troop back here, yes?"

*"Oui, mon père."*

"All right then. Use good common sense, boys! Don't do anything *too* foolish." He grinned again and headed up the trail. As he disappeared, the boys gathered around Maurice.

"Gustave Becker," Maurice said, speaking to him for the first time. "You want to be a full member of our troop, the Franco-American Boy Scouts of New York, Troop 582?"

"Yes!"

"Joining our troop is a great honor, and you must earn it. We have two very difficult challenges for you today. Tests of your physical and mental strength."

Xavier giggled excitedly, and Maurice turned on him sternly. *"Éponge Tenace!"* Tenacious Sponge! "Please treat this occasion with the seriousness it deserves."

*"Oui, Lion Exigeant!"* Yes, Demanding Lion!

"Your first challenge, neophyte"—Maurice turned

back to Gustave—"is to crawl under these bushes, all the way to the stream. You have three minutes by my watch to get there and back, or you fail." Gustave looked anxiously in the direction Maurice indicated. It was a long way to the stream through very dense shrubbery.

"Reach into the stream and get a rock from the bottom," Maurice continued. "Then crawl back to the path and show us your sleeve to prove you made it all the way to the stream. You have to stay down. You can crawl or wiggle on your stomach, but you can't stand up. Pretend there's enemy fire overhead. I'm timing you—now go!"

Gustave dropped to his belly and slithered forward through the bushes as fast as he could, shoving his way along through the wet underbrush. Branches poked into him. Mud seeped up through his jacket and pants. Maman wasn't going to be happy.

"One minute down!" he heard the boys shouting behind him. "Two to go!"

He bore to the right, where the bushes seemed slightly less thick, and got up to his knees to crawl furiously ahead. That was much faster, but a sharp stone poked into his right knee. "Ah!" he gasped, but he kept going. The stream was right ahead of him now. He lay on his belly on the muddy bank, plunging his left hand down into the stream. Bitterly cold water soaked the sleeve of his jacket. He scrabbled around on the bottom and grabbed a smooth rock. Done!

He turned around to crawl back with his fist clenched around the stone. A branch slapped him sharply in the face.

"Two minutes down!" came a shout from farther away.

Mustering all his energy, ignoring the branches in his face, he crawled and slithered back at a furious speed, realizing that the way to the stream had been downhill, and that now he was going uphill.

"Two and a half minutes down!" came the call. "Thirty seconds left!"

He plunged ahead through the sticky mud, slipping once so that half his face got caked in it, and then, scratched and panting, he pulled himself onto the path out of the last of the bushes just as the call came. "THREE MINUTES!"

"You did it, Gustave!" Jean-Paul pulled him to his feet. "Boy, are you filthy!"

Gustave straightened up, panting.

"You barely made it, neophyte," Maurice said, his sternness wobbling for a moment into a smile as Gustave combed his fingers through his hair, pulling out globs of mud and leaves. "Did you get the rock?"

Gustave held it up triumphantly.

"You're plenty wet!" Bernard said. Gustave glanced down at his jacket and twisted the cloth of his sleeve, squeezing water out onto the path.

"So. We march on in silence now, men," Maurice commanded. "The neophyte has completed the first of the two challenges."

They hiked forward. Gustave's damp skin tingled, half frozen, and his muddy shoes sloshed along the path. *Half done,* he thought triumphantly. How hard could the other challenge be? He could do another one like that, no problem.

Maurice raised his hand. "Halt!"

Beside the path was a narrow clearing with rows of logs set like benches. The other boys looked at each other, grinning, and arranged themselves on the logs. Gustave started to sit with them.

*"Non!"* barked Maurice. "You stand here with me and face them. They must see your face clearly. Here." He pulled a handkerchief from his pocket. "Wipe some of the mud off so they can see you," he said in a more normal tone of voice. Gustave did.

"And now for the second of the two great challenges," Maurice intoned, sternly again. "This is the truth challenge. You have to answer some questions. To show your purity of spirit, you must reveal your soul to your comrades."

Gustave looked nervously from Maurice to the others.

"There are three questions," Maurice said. "Face the men when you answer. Question one. Who is your best friend?"

Gustave released a breath he hadn't realized he was holding. That wasn't so private or personal. The answer was easy. "I have two. Jean-Paul—" he pointed at his cousin "—and also, back in France, Marcel."

Jean-Paul's face shifted, unreadable.

"Good. Now for question two," Maurice commanded. "Remember, you must answer honestly. Who is the most interesting girl you have seen in America?"

A snort came from Xavier. The others looked at Gustave, grinning, anticipatory. Jean-Paul was smiling again, smirking almost. Gustave's face went hot. Martha at school *was* exceedingly pretty—he knew that a lot of boys would name her. But . . . "September Rose," he said, blushing. "This girl from my school."

"Oooh—ooh!" several of the boys howled at once.

"SEPTEMBER ROSE?" Maurice bellowed the name so loudly two crows started up, cawing, from a nearby tree. "That's an unusual name."

Gustave's blush deepened. "I guess."

"Is she blonde?" Guy demanded.

"A tall, curvy American blonde?" Bernard grinned.

"Answer!" barked Maurice.

"No. Black hair."

"Ooh, sexy!" said Xavier.

"As if you would know anything about sexy, Tenacious Sponge!" André elbowed him.

"And now, for the third and final question. Remember, you must tell the absolute truth."

Gustave nodded.

"This is the Franco-American Boy Scouts. Face the men as you answer. When you have been here a year, which will you be more, Gustave? French or American?"

Strangely, that was the most personal question yet. Memories of France flooded through Gustave. Crusty baguettes. Cuckoos calling in the woods in spring. Fields full of sunflowers. But then other memories hit him like a slap. Graffiti on the street: *Jews out of France.* And what he had felt, to his shame, when the border police let his family cross into Spain, leaving France behind: relief.

Deep, exhausted relief. But he still knew what the answer was. "I am French," he said firmly. "France is *ma patrie*." *My fatherland.*

Maurice nodded. "That's what we all say when we first get here," he said.

"No, I said Corsica was," Guy said.

"Yeah, sure, but that's part of France," Maurice answered. "Gustave, you have two countries now. France and America. We all do. So because that was your answer, there is one more thing we have to do, to complete your initiation. Bernard, the knife?"

Bernard pulled a pocketknife out of his side pocket, flipped open the blade, and handed it to Maurice. Gustave eyed the sharp blade.

"Kneel," said Maurice. "You are both French *and* American now. There are a lot of people in America who are two things, especially in New York. But you've got to be both. So we have to make America part of you, and we have to make you part of America." He straightened up and spoke in a booming voice. "Neophyte! Your blood will mingle with the soil, joining you forever to your new country. Hold out your hand."

Gustave held out a shaky palm, and Maurice drew the blade of the knife across Gustave's forefinger. A dark drop of blood welled up and fell to the ground, and then another and another. Maurice pushed the blade back into the pocketknife, flipped out a metal hook, and, squatting, used it to dig around the spot where the drops had fallen. Gustave watched him churn up the dirt.

"Let me," he said suddenly. Maurice shrugged and

handed him the knife. Gustave dug and churned with the metal hook of the pocketknife, mixing the blood into the dirt until neither was distinguishable from the other.

"Now you're part of America," Maurice said, gesturing ceremoniously. "Rise!"

Gustave got to his feet, watching curiously as Maurice took a canteen out of his rucksack and poured water into a tin camping mug. Bernard and Xavier and Jean-Paul scooped up soil from another spot and plopped it into the water, stirring. "Mmmm—yummy!" said Bernard mockingly, and they all laughed.

Maurice handed the murky cup of water to Gustave. "When you've drunk this down, you will have successfully completed your initiation," he said, grinning. "This is the soil of your new homeland. Drink it down and make America part of you."

Gustave looked at the muddy water. It was disgusting. Would it really change him to drink it? He brought it to his lips.

"Chug it! Chug it! Chug it!" the boys chanted. Gustave lifted the cup and gulped mouthful after mouthful of the bitter drink. He held the empty cup out to the boys triumphantly and flipped it upside down. "Did it!"

The boys cheered jubilantly. Maurice clapped him on the shoulder and then waited until the others settled down. "Well done, Gustave!" he said. "You are one of us now. I will give you your totem name. It is . . ." He paused, and the younger boys waited. *Méhari Pondéré.*

"Oh yeah! That's good!" said Guy. "He has such a serious face."

"And he's reliable," said Jean-Paul. "You can count on him. Like a *méhari* in the desert."

*Serious Camel.* Not a bad name, thought Gustave. Those *méharis* were an important part of the French army in northern Africa, galumphing along, carrying people and supplies. He could live with that name.

"And now can we meet Father René and go to Nedick's?" asked Xavier. "I'm starving!"

"Me too!" said Jean-Paul.

Gustave shifted nervously, sticking his hands into his pockets and fingering the two nickels there. He was suddenly very hungry too, but the only money he had was for the subway ride home. The rest of his money was in a jam jar on a shelf in the apartment.

André must have read the worry on his face. "Father René'll treat," he said, slinging his arm around Gustave's shoulder. "Let's get Méhari here his first Nedick's orange soda to wash away the taste of that delicious drink we made him guzzle. And maybe you deserve a hot dog too!"

They started back down the trail to meet Father René. Jean-Paul began singing *"Il était un petit navire,"* "There Was a Little Ship," and the others joined in, Gustave too. He was scratched and bruised and cold, and his finger stung where it had been cut. He was covered with mud, his mouth tasted like dirt, and he was exhausted. And, for the first time since arriving in America, he felt supremely happy.

# ★ 19 ★

As he got ready for bed that night, Gustave realized that he was looking forward to the next week. Maybe he would have another laundry delivery for September Rose. And he'd probably see André at school. It was funny to think that there had been another French kid at the school and that Gustave hadn't even known it. He might have crossed paths with André every day without even looking at him.

During homeroom, the principal made announcements over the loudspeaker. Because of the crackling and static, Gustave always had a hard time following them. Today all he understood was "lots of schools," "victory," "rally," and "war effort." Joan of Arc Junior High School had been invited to do something. Gustave didn't know what, but the class started talking excitedly, so it seemed like it was going to be a big deal.

"Quiet!" Mrs. McAdams shouted. "Raise your hands!"

As Gustave listened, he started to figure it out. He heard the word "audition" over and over, which meant the same thing in French. After a few minutes he noticed words he'd heard before in music class—"soprano" and "alto." Then he heard "chorus," and he realized that they must be talking about a group from Joan of Arc Junior High going to sing at a rally, and he lost interest. He certainly wasn't going to audition for that!

Suddenly Mrs. McAdams turned to him. "YOU UNDERSTAND, GUS?" she boomed. "RALLY FOR VICTORY IN THE WAR! CHILDREN WILL SING! TEACHERS PICK THE BEST! *LA-LA-LA!*" She sang in a fake voice, making the class snort with laughter. Gustave nodded, cringing in embarrassment.

Gustave walked from homeroom to science with Frank, joining up with Miles and Leo in the hallway. As they arrived at the science classroom, Gustave caught sight of André in a group of older students going in the opposite direction. André waved. Miles, Frank, and Leo stared at Gustave as he waved back.

"Was he waving at you?" Miles asked excitedly.

"How do *you* know a ninth grader?" Leo demanded.

"Boy Scouts," Gustave said.

"I'm in Boy Scouts too," Leo said, sounding as if he were accusing Gustave of something. "But all the kids in my troop are in seventh grade, like us."

"It's the Franco-American Boy Scouts. We're different ages, but we're all from France."

"Andy's French?" Leo sounded incredulous. "But he doesn't wear those dopey French pants. No offense, Gus."

After lunch they had recess in the small play area outside the school. The blacktop was packed with kids, some shouting and running around, some basking in the sun against the wall, talking. A group of ninth grade boys had dibs on the basketball hoop, as usual. Gustave had never played the game—he went to his English class for foreign students when the others had physical education.

"Race you to the other side!" called Miles. "Ready, go!" He, Gustave, and Frank darted across the blacktop. Miles made it to the wall first, with Gustave and Frank half a pace behind. Just then, a stray orange ball bounded toward them.

"*Attention*, Gustave!" André shouted in French, then switched into English. "A little help?"

Without thinking, Gustave jumped up, brought the ball down with his knee, and kicked it back to André. The ninth grade boys waiting under the basket laughed.

"This is basketball, kid, not soccer!" André shouted. "Use your hands. Come learn how to play!"

Gustave ran over. At first he was terrible at maneuvering the ball with his hands, and none of his shots went in. But then André showed him how to bend his knees and push evenly with both hands during a set shot, and another ninth grader, Lou, showed him how to use the backboard. By the time the bell rang, Gustave had actually gotten the ball through the basket three times.

"We'll make an American of you yet, Serious Camel!" André said to him in French as they went in. "Come and join us anytime."

"Why did the ninth graders want you to play basketball with them?" Leo asked as Gustave slid into his seat for history. "You're terrible!"

"He was getting better at the end," Miles said loyally. "I wish the ninth graders would let us all play."

"They shouldn't always hog the baskets," Frank said.

"We could draw a circle on the wall and shoot at it even if we can't use a basket," Leo said. "Me and Gus against you and Miles, tomorrow at recess. What do you fellas say?"

Gustave looked at Leo, surprised but pleased. "Sure!"

Gustave's good mood faded when Mr. Coolidge announced the homework. In addition to a reading assignment, Mr. Coolidge gave them a handout about a long-term project on a historical figure. "It should be about someone you admire," Mr. Coolidge said. "I expect you to do research at the public library and use at least three sources. You'll have to write an essay and give an oral report. A speech to the class," he said, speaking more slowly and clearly and looking at Gustave. "Everyone will do it. No exceptions." Gustave nodded reluctantly. His stomach tightened at the thought of trying to speak in front of everyone. At least the due date was in April, almost a month away. He didn't have to worry about it for a while.

*   *   *

140

After school Gustave looked through the pile of packages waiting for him on Mr. Quong's counter. He was happy to discover one at the bottom addressed to "Mrs. Leonora Walker" at September Rose's address. A light rain was coming down as he started out, and his bike splashed through puddles. But he was getting much quicker at delivering now, as Mr. Quong had predicted. He worked his way uptown, saving September Rose's address for last.

Gustave hurried up the stairs and then paused outside her door, catching his breath. He ran his fingers through his hair and knocked.

The door opened immediately, and September Rose peeked out. She was wearing a pink sweater. Her long string of beads was looped around her neck, and she had the curls again, one against each cheek. "Hi!" she whispered, stepping into the hallway. Chiquita slipped out the door from behind her, whining excitedly and jumping up on Gustave. "Chiquita, quiet!" September Rose hissed. "I gotta warn you. My granma is about to give you the third degree. Miss Noelle told her about you and me talking in the hall that other time."

"The third degree? What's that?"

Just then the apartment door at the end of the corridor opened a crack, and Miss Noelle peeked out. Chiquita bounded down the hall toward her, yipping, and Miss Noelle pulled her door closed again. At the same moment, a voice from inside September Rose's apartment called, "Is that the delivery boy? Invite him in, Seppie. I'll be right there."

"She's gonna ask you a lot of questions," September Rose whispered. "And I mean a *lot*! Come on in."

Gustave rubbed his feet extra carefully on the mat outside before going in so that he wouldn't leave any marks on the carpet.

"He's here, Granma," September Rose called, and then looked back at Gustave. "Sorry," she mouthed, raising her eyebrows.

An elderly woman in a blue flowered dress came out through a swinging door that led into a kitchen. She was round and small, but she moved with majesty as she came toward him. "This the boy?" she asked. "Chiquita, down." The little dog dropped immediately onto the floor, wagging her tail and looking up hopefully. "I want to talk to you, young man," she said, ignoring the little dog. "I am Mrs. Walker, September Rose's grandmother."

This was obviously a formal situation, so Gustave did what his mother had trained him to do back in France. "Hello, madame—um, I mean, hello, Mrs." That didn't sound quite right, but he held out his hand. Mrs. Walker looked surprised, but she shook his hand, her manner thawing slightly.

"You're Gustave?" she asked.

"Yes, Mrs."

"Ma'am," September Rose murmured.

"I mean, yes, ma'am."

"What's your last name?" she demanded.

"My name is Gustave Becker."

"You're a foreigner?"

"Yes, I'm from France."

"He's from Paris, Granma!" September Rose interrupted. "Where I want to live when I grow up."

Mrs. Walker hushed her. "You live nearby?"

"On West Ninety-First Street."

"I see. And what does your father do?"

"Granma!" September Rose protested.

"I'm just trying to get to know the boy, Seppie."

"In France he had a store. He sold cloth and shoes.
Right now, he is a janitor."

"A janitor—really?" Mrs. Walker looked surprised.
"And your mother? Does she work too?"

"She's a seamstress. She sews things on hats. Flowers
and . . ." He couldn't think of the English word. "Shiny
small things."

"I think you mean spangles. That's keen!" said September Rose. "I like sewing too. Maybe she could teach
me."

Mrs. Walker was still looking at Gustave curiously.
"So," she said, a bit more mildly. "You know my Seppie
from school. You have classes together?"

"Yes."

"And lunch!" September Rose said, grinning. "We
have lunch together—along with *Mar-tha*!" She chanted
the name mockingly.

"Who is Martha?" Mrs. Walker sounded a bit bewildered.

"Oh, she's just this girl in our grade who's a big flirt.
She was flirting with Gustave for a while, but now she's
back to flirting with Leo. Martha thinks she's the cat's
meow, right, Gustave? She just *loves* being the center of

attention." September Rose giggled, batting her eyes. "This is what she's like: 'Kiss my hand, Leo! I mean, don't kiss it! I mean, do! Ooh, look everybody, he's kissing my hand!'" She grabbed Gustave's hand and mimicked the way Martha had pulled her hand back and forth with Leo, giggling wildly. Chiquita jumped up and ran between the two of them, whining.

Mrs. Walker laughed. "You children—Lord have mercy! I'm glad you have a new friend, Seppie. Pleased to meet you, young man. Miss Noelle saw you the other day and she got me all worried," she added, a bit apologetically. "She always keeps an eye on things in our building."

September Rose snorted. "'Keeps an eye on things'! That's one way to put it. It's like living in the same building as the FBI!"

Mrs. Walker shook her head at her granddaughter. "She's just looking out for you. Gustave, you and Seppie can talk right here in the living room. No need to lurk in the hallway and alarm Miss Noelle again!" At the door to the kitchen, she looked back. "You know, I think you're the first white person I ever had in my home. Thought I'd never live to see the day."

"Sorry—she's so old-fashioned," September Rose whispered, blushing. "So, this is our apartment. Make yourself at home."

Chiquita seemed to think the last comment was addressed to her. She jumped up onto the sofa, turned in a tight circle, and settled down with a sigh. Gustave looked around. The room had high ceilings. Light streamed through the tall windows onto bright, stuffed furniture;

a big radio in a wooden cabinet; a thick, soft rug; and photos on the mantelpiece above the fireplace. Overhead, something moved and glittered. When Gustave looked up, he realized that the shiny figures of birds dangled from the ceiling as well as from the mantelpiece and from hooks around the room. In the center of the mantelpiece, in an ornate frame, with more glittery birds around him, was a photo of a middle-aged man in a military uniform. He had a high forehead, deep-set dark eyes, and close-cropped hair. His posture was stiff and proud, and he gazed steadily out of the frame. Something about the man's eyes was familiar.

September Rose came over to look at the photograph too. Her mouth looked sad and vulnerable in a way Gustave hadn't seen before, and he suddenly realized who the man must be. "Is that your father? He's a soldier?"

September Rose nodded silently, running her finger gently around the frame. She seemed to be far, far away, and Gustave wanted to pull her back into the sunny room. "What are these?" he asked, indicating the metallic birds.

September Rose touched one with the tip of her finger. "My Granma makes those. She's a tin-can artist. She makes a bird for every day my father's away. It's kind of like a prayer. Pretty, aren't they? Especially when the sun shines. This one's my favorite." She cupped a pale blue one with a long neck, then tapped it gently, making it sway and tinkle against the other birds dangling around it. "There are even some outside on the fire escape. I'll show you."

September Rose led Gustave into the kitchen and

pushed up the window. A brisk wind whipped in. Outside, a wind chime made of dangling tropical birds swayed and jingled above the fire escape. "See? Granma made that too."

"Mmm-hmm." Mrs. Walker was at the stove with her back to them. "September Rose Walker, shut that window now! It's windy out there!"

September Rose slammed it shut, and a last bit of breeze rushed through the kitchen, making the birds dangling from the ceiling collide noisily. Chiquita had trotted into the kitchen behind them, and now she sat next to the kitchen table, sniffing the air.

"Those are all made out of tin cans?" Gustave asked.

"Yes. Granma paints some of the birds and some she leaves shiny. She makes them for her friends too. Each one's different."

"They're amazing," Gustave said.

"I know! I tell Granma they could be in a museum."

"Not my birds." Mrs. Walker pulled a pie out of the oven. She glanced up at the ornaments, still jingling against one another in the stirred-up air. "No one's taking away my birds. They for Martin, your daddy, my baby boy. To bring him home."

Her voice was hushed, and nobody spoke for a moment. Then Mrs. Walker opened a cupboard and pulled out glasses and blue-patterned dishes. "Who's hungry?"

Chiquita gave a little squeak and jumped up, balancing on her hind legs.

Mrs. Walker snorted. "I don't make pie for dogs! Seppie, you never had your after-school snack. What's your daddy call you? String Bean? And looks like Gustave could use some banana cream pie too." She took a bottle of milk out of the refrigerator and poured them each a tall foamy glass.

"Banana pie?" Gustave whispered as he and September Rose sat down. "Pie made with bananas?"

"Sure! Don't you have it in France? Banana cream pie with sliced bananas on top. It makes it super sweet."

"It smells delicious," he told Mrs. Walker. "When we got bananas one day, they stayed green and then turned sort of gray. How do you make them ripe? We don't have them in France."

"Oh, sugar!" Mrs. Walker put a slice of pie on his plate. "I'm so old, I don't buy green bananas!"

"Don't say that, Granma! You're not so old," September Rose protested, handing a small chunk of pie down to Chiquita.

"None of that, Seppie!" Mrs. Walker tapped her arm as Chiquita gobbled the bite of pie. "When I buy bananas, I buy them yellow. But they aren't in the market too often nowadays. Most days I eat a can of fruit salad," Mrs. Walker said. "That's what I mostly make the birds out of. I love those red cherries. They go down easy. Martin loves that fruit salad too." She sighed.

"You and Daddy love fruit salad! I get tired of it." September Rose put down her fork, pushed back her chair, and stood up. "Gustave, how are you trying to ripen your bananas? You gotta keep them warm. Like at the equator.

We think that's where my dad is. He's not allowed to say in his letters where he is, but we know it's someplace warm."

She held out her skirt and started to sway back and forth like the Hawaiian girls in a movie Gustave had seen once in Paris with Marcel and Jean-Paul. "You know the jingle from the radio, right?" September Rose said. "Watch—I'll be Chiquita Banana."

September Rose started to sing, rocking her hips and swaying her arms to the syncopated beat. It was a song about bananas and how you could tell when they were ripe. Her voice was warm and rich, and it filled the small, bright kitchen. How could she sing like that with people listening—so easily, so lightly?

> *"Bananas like the climate of the tropical equator,*
> *So never put bananas . . . in the refrigerator!"*

September Rose twirled around with her hand on her hip as she ended the song. Chiquita jumped up on her, yipping.

Gustave clapped. "Are you going to try out for that chorus for the Victory Rally?"

"I guess."

"You'll be picked for the solo, I'm sure."

"Maybe." September Rose sat down and took a big bite of pie.

"Don't you get embarrassed, singing in front of people?" Gustave asked.

Mrs. Walker laughed. "Not my girl Seppie!"

"Why would I get embarrassed?" September Rose

asked. "I'm going to be a famous singer when I grow up, just like Josephine Baker. I'm going to sing to audiences of hundreds in Paris!"

"Josephine Baker indeed!" snorted Mrs. Walker. "You go right ahead and sing, Seppie, but you keep your clothes on your back while you do it."

"I *know*, Granma! I just love the way she sings and dances! And her curls, of course." She turned her cheek toward Gustave. Now that he was up close, Gustave was surprised to see that her curls were drawn on, not real.

"I thought that was hair!" he said.

"I *want* to get my hair done like Josephine Baker's for real, but Granma *won't let me*," September Rose complained. "So I have to draw the curls on with an eyebrow pencil."

"Your hair's a gift," Mrs. Walker said tiredly, as if they'd had this same conversation many times before. "Your daddy's going to want to see his little girl in braids when he comes back from the war. We're going to leave it be."

"For now," September Rose said meaningfully.

"Did you ever hear Josephine Baker sing here in New York?" Gustave asked.

"No. Just on the radio. She used to perform in Harlem sometimes, but I read an article in an old magazine that said she doesn't like to sing in America, because even with a Negro singer performing, they won't let Negroes be in the audience. It makes her mad. It makes me mad too. It's not like that in Paris. She said so in the article."

Just then they heard the apartment door open.

September Rose stiffened. "I thought Alan was working this afternoon," she whispered nervously to her grandmother.

A moment later a young man stood in the doorway. "Who's *that*?" he demanded, staring at Gustave. "And what's he doing in our kitchen?"

# ★ 20 ★

"Sit down, Alan," said Mrs. Walker calmly, cutting another slice of pie. "Gustave, this is September Rose's brother. Please excuse his rudeness. He must be tired. Alan, this is Gustave. He goes to school with September Rose."

Alan dropped his pile of papers onto the table. "What's he doing hanging around Seppie?" he demanded, folding his arms across his chest.

"Geez, Alan! He's my friend!"

Alan glared at September Rose. "We talked about this!"

"Not in front of our guest, Alan," Mrs. Walker said sternly. "You can stay and have pie with us all, or you can go to your room."

Alan sat down with a thud. Feeling uncomfortable, Gustave excused himself and headed toward the bathroom. He took a long time in the little room, splashing water on his face and drying it on a pink embroidered towel. He walked back hesitantly.

"He goes to my school," he heard September Rose hiss as he approached the kitchen. "You said that was all right."

"I said it was okay to be friendly to the white kids *at* school. Out of school is different. You could get yourself into trouble, especially with a boy. Granma, tell her!"

"I'm the one who invited him in," Mrs. Walker murmured. "He talked to Seppie at the door one day when he was delivering for Quong's. Miss Noelle got me all worried over it."

"He's from France, anyway. He's not American," September Rose jumped in. "It's different."

"People won't know that just seeing you and him together."

"He seems like a very nice boy, Alan, very polite," Mrs. Walker said. "Anyway, hush! He's our guest right now. We'll discuss it later."

Gustave hesitated in the kitchen doorway. Mrs. Walker turned and saw him. "Would you like another piece of pie, Gustave? Seppie is having one."

"Go ahead, Gustave. You don't have to go just yet, do you?" September Rose asked. "Granma's trying to fatten us up a little."

Alan scraped his chair back loudly and crossed his arms, scowling. "You all know I have a Negro Youth Group meeting here at five-thirty," he said. "It's going to be crowded enough in the apartment with just us."

"Oh, that's today?" September Rose reached for the

papers. "Are those the flyers? Let's see! 'Democracy—At Home and Abroad,'" September Rose proclaimed, holding one up for Gustave to see. "Ooh—they're swell!"

"Here are the other two," Alan said, pulling flyers from the stack.

"'Don't Buy Where You Can't Work!'" she read, holding one up and then the other. "'Victory Abroad, Victory at Home!'"

Gustave leaned closer and looked at the two "V"s on the third flyer. "What is 'Victory at Home'?" he asked September Rose quietly.

Alan snorted.

"Victory against race discrimination," September Rose said. "Like the theaters Josephine Baker won't sing in because they don't let Negroes be in the audience. Places we can't live. Jobs they won't hire us for. Stores that won't let us try on clothes."

Gustave nodded, feeling a bit sick. It sounded all too familiar.

September Rose turned to Alan. "Where are you going to post the flyers?"

"Around Baumhauer's Department Store, on One Hundred and Twenty-Fifth Street," Alan said. "I dressed up and applied for a job there last week. So did Willie and Roberta. 'We don't hire coloreds,' they said. They wouldn't even let Roberta use the customers' restroom as we were on our way out. But they're happy to sell us stuff and take our money."

"Alan, honey." Mrs. Walker looked at her grandson worriedly. "I don't know if that second flyer is such a good idea. 'Don't buy where you can't work?' They aren't going to like that, if people stop shopping at their store."

"That's the whole *point*, Granma. We're going to picket too. If they lose enough money, maybe they'll finally hire some of us."

"Your daddy went and got himself a good job without doing any of that. Paid well too. Thirty-eight dollars a week before he went off to war. That's real good wages."

"Sure, Granma. But I don't want to drive a garbage truck."

"Sanitation truck," said September Rose.

"That's just a fancy name for garbage, Seppie," said Alan. "I know it's good money. But even Dad says, 'It's good money, but it smells!' And who knows if he'll be able to get his job back when he comes home."

"I *wish* you'd let me join your group," September Rose said. "I'm old enough."

"You're just a kid. It could get dangerous. You don't understand anything!" Alan threw a glance at Gustave. "I changed my mind about the pie. I'll wait for supper." He left the room.

"I didn't know he applied for that job, did you, Granma?"

"No, I sure didn't. But it was asking for trouble. Everyone knows they don't hire our kind. I wish that boy had more sense." Mrs. Walker began clearing up. "Say goodbye to your classmate. His mother'll be expecting him."

"Thank you for the pie, Mrs. Walker," Gustave said. "It was delicious."

"You come again now, hear?" She smiled at him. "Anytime."

Mrs. Walker started to hum the Chiquita banana song as she ran the water.

September Rose watched until her grandmother had turned her back, then ran her finger over her plate and licked it, grinning conspiratorially at Gustave. "Anyhow, that's probably what you're doing wrong."

"What is?"

"The bananas. That's probably why they didn't ripen. Like the song says, 'You never put bananas in the refrigerator.'"

"We don't have the refrigerator. I put the bananas on the windowsill."

"You don't have a refrigerator? Why not?"

"Seppie—hush!" Mrs. Walker swatted her with a dish towel.

"What? Anyway, probably too much cold air is coming through the window glass. Try someplace warmer."

She walked him to the front door.

"Could my father get that kind of job, the garbage job?" Gustave asked her.

"If they're hiring. And if he's strong enough. The workers have to jump up and down from the back of the truck all day."

"Oh. No, he has a bad leg. He can't jump," Gustave said.

The two of them were standing alone in the living room. September Rose dropped her voice to a whisper. "I'm sorry Alan said all that. He's just being bossy and overprotective. When I started junior high, he told me I could be friendly to white kids in school, but not outside of school, especially boys. He said when a girl was in junior high or older, it was asking for trouble."

"Why? What kind of trouble?"

"Oh, you know, sometimes people might yell dumb stuff at you on the street or whatnot. I just tell Alan, 'Uh-huh, uh-huh,' and then I do what I want where he can't see. I mean, nearly all the kids at our school are white. What am I gonna do, not be friends with anybody except Lisa and the people from our church?"

Gustave nodded.

She smiled a little shyly. "Anyway, I've been meaning to say, you can call me 'Seppie' if you want to. That's what my family calls me, and my friends. Hey, maybe one day soon after school we can go to the library to work on our reports for history. You've probably never been there, right? I could help you get signed up for a library card."

"I did go, once, but I didn't get a card. That would be swell!"

September Rose laughed. "You're learning to talk just like an American!"

Gustave felt himself smiling as he pedaled away from September Rose's building. "That's what my friends call me," she had said. He hadn't misunderstood. She had said it twice. When Alan had walked into the kitchen, she had told him, "He's my *friend*!"

# ★ 21 ★

"I just don't know who to do this stupid history report on," Gustave said as he carried the soup to the table.

"Does it have to be someone American?" Maman asked, ladling the soup into three bowls.

"No. Anyone in the world. Any historical figure you admire. A lot of kids are doing athletes and stuff."

"That's a funny kind of historical figure! You should do someone more significant. How about Napoleon?" Papa took his bowl of lentil and potato soup from Maman. "You used to have a book about him, I remember."

"Yeah, when we lived in Paris. Maybe I could do it on him. I'd have to find some new books."

"Or what about Joan of Arc?" Maman asked. "You could teach those American kids about the important Frenchwoman their school is named after."

"I don't know. They might think I was showing off about France or something." Gustave blew on his soup too hard to cool it, and some spilled out the other side of the bowl.

"Careful!" Maman said, mopping it up. "Well, I think you should do it on someone from France so you already know something about the topic, don't you? That will make reading the books in English easier."

Papa broke off a piece of bread and handed the loaf to Maman. "What about the man who designed the Statue of Liberty? Do these American kids know she was a gift from France? What was his name, Lili?"

"Bartholdi. Or what about Gustave Eiffel, who designed the Eiffel Tower?"

"I just don't want to give a speech in English, with everybody listening and looking at me." And wearing weird French pants, Gustave thought. So far he had been able to save sixty cents from his earnings and tips, but that was a long way from the two dollars the pants cost at Mr. Quong's. He stirred his soup vigorously.

"I know you can do a good job, Gustave," Papa said. "Just memorize the speech ahead of time and then deliver it."

"We're amazed when we hear you speaking English now," Maman said. "And you understand the radio broadcasts so well. I was telling our night-school teacher, Mrs. Szabo, about it, and she says to be patient, because grown-ups learn so much more slowly."

"Ah, to be young!" Papa said, ruffling his hair.

"Huh. That's what *you* think," Gustave said. "If you were young, *you'd* have to do an oral report."

Maman giggled as she cleared away the soup bowls.

"Ai-yai-yai, what a disaster that would be! Who's ready for some dessert?"

Gustave peered at the bowl of fruit salad Maman handed to him. These days Maman had a new trick: she'd buy cheap pieces of old fruit that they were going to throw out in the markets, and she'd use the good bits to make fruit salad. Too often he had spooned up mealy apple or orange pieces going sour. Today it looked all right. He took a bite.

"I need to talk to you about something else," he said.

"That sounds serious!" said Papa.

"It is. One day when I came home, I saw that your *New American* book was open to the citizenship questions. Were you studying them? Are we going to stay in America forever?"

"We don't know, *chéri*," Maman said slowly, setting her teacup down. "So much depends on what happens with the war. Lately we've been thinking that even if the Allies win, we might stay."

"We've been talking with people at night school," Papa said, taking a sip of tea. "There may be a better future for you here."

"In any case, it takes five years to become a citizen," Maman said. "Nothing is happening right now. But what do you think? Can you see us becoming Americans, all of us, together?"

"Maybe." Gustave bit into a sour piece of fruit, grimaced, and pushed his bowl away. France was home. But France was also the place where he had seen that vicious graffiti: "Jews out of France." It was where Philippe, a cruel boy at school, had left a note on his desk saying "Hitler was right. Death to the Jews." And where the police had raided their house, destroyed their things, and threatened his parents. Only some French people were like that, of course. Other people, like Nicole and her father, risked their lives to help Jews. And being French was who Gustave was.

Right now, he couldn't imagine living in France. But he also couldn't imagine never living there again.

"Of course, when you're grown up you can make up your own mind. You may want to go back one day," Papa said.

He might. If the Allies won the war. If there was still a France.


The next Boy Scouts meeting was closer, at Father René's church on West 23rd Street, so Gustave only needed a nickel each way for fare. As he pulled open the heavy door of the Church of St. Vincent de Paul and walked into the velvety hush inside, he realized that he had never been inside a church before. He had to walk past a crucifix hanging on the wall to get to the stairs that went down to the basement, where the Boy Scouts met. The eerie, tormented figure on the cross made Gustave shudder. He was glad when he'd found his way to the big, plain room in the basement. He was a few minutes late, and all the other scouts were there, sitting at a long table, talking in French. Some of them were eating sandwiches and some were practicing knots. There were several boys he didn't know, ones who hadn't been on the earlier scout hike. "Come join us, Serious Camel!" André called. "How's your figure-eight knot?"

Father René smiled a welcome. "It's just me again today. The rabbi's mother has been ill," Father René explained to Gustave. "He's usually more involved."

Father René was a whiz at knot tying. By the end of the meeting, Gustave could do a good half hitch, a half-knot, a square knot, and a figure-eight knot. The figure eight, with its intricate symmetry, was his favorite.

"Two weekends from now, your schools have Thursday and Friday off," Father René said at the end of the scout meeting, "so we'll be going on our annual March camping trip. We'll assemble early Thursday morning and drive up to Osprey Lake." The boys whooped in excitement. Father René turned to Gustave and Jean-Paul. "We go every year. There's a grand estate up there with an abandoned mansion on it. The man who owns it was a Boy Scout himself when he was young, and for years he has been letting scouts go and camp there—on the grounds in summer and inside the old building when it's cold."

"It's fantastic!" Bernard said. "We make a fire in this huge old fireplace in this gigantic empty room. We cook over it and sleep next to the embers, because it's really cold up there in the mountains. Sometimes it snows and we get to play in it in the morning. I can't wait!"

"I have some spare sleeping bags for anyone who needs one," said Father René. "But bring your warmest clothes, and everyone bring a warm blanket too. Do you each have an old blanket to bring?" he asked Jean-Paul and Gustave.

"Sure," said Jean-Paul. Gustave nodded. The one he slept under was definitely old.

"Good. So we'll see each other then."

"I'll bring the potatoes again, Father René," André said. "They are so good roasted when it's cold out."

"Sure. Anyone who wants to can bring something for our feasts. Rabbi Blum and I will make sure there's enough food for us all."

"Can you bring marshmallows again?" Maurice asked Guy.

"Definitely!"

"Ooh, yeah! Bring lots!" said Xavier.

"Just don't eat the whole bag yourself this year, Tenacious Sponge!" said André.

"Then you better try a little harder to keep up with me, Talkative Chipmunk!"

When Gustave got home after Scouts, Papa was alone in the apartment, sitting on the sofa drinking a cup of tea and reading a French newspaper. Classical music was playing on the radio. "Ah, Gustave," he said. "Good to see you. There's a letter here for you, from France. With no return address."

"From Nicole?" Gustave threw his coat toward the hook on the wall, not bothering to pick it up when it missed and fell to the floor. He ran to the table. It was

Nicole's handwriting! Trying to ignore the tape on the ends showing that the censors had already read it, Gustave slit open the light blue envelope. As he did so, he looked in distaste at the stamp. It was a new one, but it wasn't one he wanted to save for his stamp collection. It had a picture of Maréchal Pétain, the new leader of France, the one installed by the Nazis. Pétain was French, but he did everything the Nazis wanted him to do. Awful things like passing laws making life hard for the Jews. Gustave looked more closely at the stamp and grinned. Ever so lightly, someone had drawn a line across Pétain's face, crossing him out. Yes, this letter was definitely from Nicole. He drew the fragile paper out carefully.

*10 February, 1942*

*Cher Gustave,*

*I haven't heard from you since my last letter. Write to me! Tell me about your glamorous life in America! I'm sure pretty soon you'll see a movie star in a fur coat. Do people ride around everywhere in shiny cars? Do you have steak and chocolate cake at every meal? There's no important news for you, but I will try to make this a colorful letter anyway. We're short of food and fuel in our village, but everyone is getting by, just barely. My fingers are blue as I write this, because we have had no charcoal for the last week. We are burning wood to keep warm, but we don't have much left, so Papa is rationing it. We only use a tiny amount each day, which means I'll be lucky if my ink doesn't freeze. And I need the ink to stay thawed* because after I finish this letter, I have to do my homework for our oh-so-wonderful new teacher, Monsieur Faible.

Speaking of Monsieur Faible, he talked to our class indignantly last week about something that happened in the cinema in ▓▓▓▓There had been rumors about a ▓▓▓▓▓▓▓▓▓
▓▓▓▓▓▓▓▓▓▓▓▓▓▓▓▓▓▓▓▓▓▓▓▓▓▓▓▓▓▓▓▓▓▓▓▓▓▓▓▓▓▓
▓▓▓▓▓▓▓▓▓▓▓▓▓▓▓▓▓▓▓▓▓▓▓▓▓▓▓▓▓▓▓▓▓▓▓▓▓▓▓▓▓▓
▓▓▓▓▓▓▓▓▓▓▓▓▓▓▓▓▓▓▓▓▓▓▓▓▓▓▓▓ No one knows where they were taken.

Later, there was an unfortunate occurrence at the cinema in the city of ▓▓▓ The German-made newsreels that play before films now, as you can imagine, are very informational in telling us about the fine contributions the Germans are making to France these days. This newsreel showed Hitler giving a speech. The audience was very eager to hear Hitler's inspirational words translated into French for their benefit. Unfortunately, however, it seemed many people in the theater had bad colds or maybe even bronchitis or pneumonia, because there was so much sneezing and coughing throughout the newsreel that it completely drowned out the words and it was impossible to understand what was being said. What a shame!

Monsieur Faible went **white** and then bright **red** as he was telling us about it.

In other news, I have been riding my bicycle often, sometimes with Claude. You remember him, I'm sure. He's nice.

Stay strong. We do. Soon the crocuses will be sprouting.

Je t'embrasse,
N

Gustave read the letter several times, trying to be sure he completely understood it. She had written it before his letter had arrived, telling her about eating the turkey out of the garbage—that was pretty obvious! It had taken her letter a month to get here. The bit at the end was quite clear. She was riding her bike often. He knew what that meant. She was helping the Resistance, helping send signals to people escaping out of the occupied part of France. But she was biking with Claude? She was letting him help, the way Gustave had helped? Gustave felt a twinge of jealousy.

"So what's the news?" Papa asked. "How are things in Saint-Georges?"

Gustave plunked down next to Papa on the sofa, and a musty smell rose up. "It's cold there," he said. "Or it was a month ago. Nicole says there's almost no charcoal. She says she's still working for the Resistance."

"She says that?" Papa put down his tea, alarmed, and reached for the letter. "Even with no return address, they could trace it back to her, and she and her father could get into terrible trouble."

"No, of course not, Papa! She's smart. She says it in code, the way she did last time. She just says she's riding her bike. But I understand what that means. But then there's this whole long, confusing thing in the middle about a teacher I know she doesn't like and a story he told them. Part of it is blacked out."

"May I see?" Papa took the letter. Then he grinned. "*Monsieur Faible. Mr. Feeble.* I bet that's not his real name." He studied it some more and chuckled. "I'd like to have been in that cinema when all that coughing was going on! Don't you see? They were trying to drown out the newsreel because it was celebrating Hitler."

"Oh, that makes sense. But it's the part that's blacked out that I'm especially trying to figure out. Look, here you can see the tops of some of the letters. The censor didn't quite cover up the whole word." He showed Papa. "I think this word is 'kids' and that one is 'teachers.' You can see the tops of the letters, see? Do you think she was saying kids and teachers from a school disappeared?"

"Oh, who can say?" Papa murmured, studying the paper.

"But why would they arrest people from a school, Papa? It wouldn't be our school in Saint-Georges, because she says 'the cinema in the city of' whatever it is. First of all, there's no cinema in the village, and also nobody would call Saint-Georges a city. But do you think she was writing about a school?"

Papa looked at Gustave with a peculiar expression. "I don't think there's a lot of point trying to figure out what those words might have said. It could have been anything. Probably she mentioned the name of a city, and the Nazi censor blacked it out so that their enemies wouldn't find out what's going on in their territories."

"I guess you're right." Gustave sat next to Papa on the sofa, half listening to the music from the radio and reading the letter over again. The word "colorful" seemed to be written a bit more darkly than the other words. Why?

And then he saw it. She was drawing his attention to the colors she mentioned in the letter. She had named three colors, and all three colors were written just a bit more darkly than the other words: her **blue** fingers and then Monsieur Faible's face turning **white** and then **red**. *Bleu, blanc, rouge.* The forbidden colors of the French flag. Nicole had sneaked them into the letter in a secret act of patriotism, a secret act of rebellion against the occupying Germans. Gustave laughed out loud in delight. "Papa, look!" he said. "There's something else here we didn't see before!"

# ★ 22 ★

ustave wrote back to Nicole the following evening. He printed instead of writing in cursive, because there was something special he wanted to do.

13 March, 1942

Chère Nicole,

I am writing letters—you just hadn't gotten my last one yet when you wrote yours. I couldn't read your whole letter because part was badly blotted with black ink. I think you were saying something important about students. Was it students our age? Otherwise, I understood everything in your letter well. I felt as if I could see everything in bright colors when I was reading it.

Something funny happened in school today. You remember my favorite teacher ever, Mrs. H., the one who loves my singing so much? (Surely by now you've gotten my last letter.) Well, some kids played a trick on her the other day. She's always talking about how much she hates swing music—it's really popular right now. So she was playing the piano while we sang Beethoven's "Ode to Joy." It's a Christian hymn. For some strange reason I didn't know the hymn. Do you have any idea why? Anyway, Mrs. H. played one page, and then the boy who turns the pages for her flipped it over, and the next bars she played sounded funny. She looked confused.

Then I heard giggling and I recognized the tune she was playing. It wasn't Beethoven. It was "It Don't Mean a Thing (If It Ain't Got That Swing)"—a Duke Ellington song that everybody's been humming and whistling lately! In the back of the room, I heard someone singing quietly "boo-wop-a-bop, boo-wop-a-bop, a-bop"!

Some kids had pasted the music on top of the Beethoven sheets in her songbook! Mrs. H. crashed her hands down on the keys. "Who did this?" she shouted, but nobody would admit it. So she yelled at us the rest of the period, giving us a long lecture about not messing with her things and about how bad and decadent swing music is.

I found out who had played the trick because after the bell rang, I heard some guys laughing, and when they got into the hall, one of them said to another, "Gimme some skin!" It's a kind of handshake some kids do here. Everyone thought it was really funny.

But poor Mrs. H. You can imagine how very sorry I felt for her. It made me think of your teacher, Monsieur F., the one you like so much.

I hope you'll send me important news soon.

By the way, I don't think I ever told you the name of my

169

*school. I go to Joan of Arc Junior High. It's a skyscraper school!*
*And I live near a Joan of Arc statue. A bit of France here in*
*New York. My favorite part of France too.*

*Stay strong.*
*Gustave*

Gustave looked over his letter, wondering if he dared to add the symbol he wanted to add, wondering if it was dangerous to do it. He was pretty sure Nicole knew that Joan of Arc was connected with the French Resistance. But just to be absolutely sure, he added the faintest line crossing each "J" a second time. The censors wouldn't see that, and even if they did, they couldn't be sure it wasn't a random mark. But Nicole would know what the double-crossed "J"s were, Gustave thought triumphantly. The symbol of the French Resistance—the Cross of Lorraine!

To pay for an airmail stamp, Gustave took a quarter and two dimes out of the jar where he was keeping his earnings from Mr. Quong. Now he only had a nickel left. At this rate, it was going to take a long time to save enough to buy those secondhand pants. But it was worth it to send the Cross of Lorraine to Nicole. A secret symbol of defiance. A secret symbol of hope.

Cousin Henri and Jean-Paul were waiting outside Grand Central Terminal when Gustave got there on Thursday afternoon. Cousin Henri had invited the two of them to see *The Jungle Book*, a new movie about a boy raised by wolves.

"This sounds like a great movie!" Jean-Paul said, jumping over a puddle as they headed down 42nd Street.

"I know! It could really happen—a boy could be raised by wolves. There was a case in France once, right, Cousin Henri? That boy from Aveyron?"

"Sure," said Cousin Henri, stopping in front of a plate-glass storefront. "Victor was his name. People talked about him a lot when I was growing up. My mother used to scold us, 'Don't eat like the wolf boy!' Surprise! Who's hungry?"

"I am!" said Jean-Paul excitedly.

"But I thought we were going to the movie!" Gustave said.

"We're stopping in here first," said Cousin Henri. "I thought you two should try out an Automat. These were one of my favorite things when I first came to New York. It's a special kind of American restaurant where you buy your food out of machines."

The restaurant was huge. It had a marble floor and vividly colored stained glass. Banks of small compartments with glass windows lined the walls under signs reading CAKES, PIES, DINNERS, and SANDWICHES. It was like a palace celebrating food. People filled the room, talking, laughing, peering through the small windows, and eating at the tables. Gustave could smell beef and chicken and mashed potatoes, and through it all the strong, bitter aroma of coffee.

"I can't believe how much food there is in this country!" Gustave said.

Cousin Henri laughed and handed Gustave a dollar.

"My treat! Pick anything you'd like. But first you need to take this to the 'nickel thrower.'" He said the last word in English.

"What's a 'nickel thrower'?"

"It's the woman in that booth over there. She takes your dollar and gives you a pile of nickels to use in the machines."

At the glass booth a bored-looking woman was chewing gum. She took the dollar and, using her rubber-capped forefinger, flipped them twenty nickels with impressive speed.

"Come on," Jean-Paul called, grabbing some of the nickels and pushing the rest toward Gustave. "I'm getting a sandwich!" Jean-Paul ran off. "Or maybe cherry pie!" he called over his shoulder. "What are you getting?"

"I don't know yet."

There was so much delicious-looking food, it seemed impossible to decide. But when Gustave came to the bank of windows marked CAKES, he stopped. Behind the panes of glass were individual slices of cakes with cream, cakes with fruit, chocolate cake, lemon cake, cakes with dripping pink icing. Now he knew exactly what he wanted. A cake shaped like a pie with a crumbly-looking crust and a rich, creamy filling. Ahead of him, a man worked the machine and took out a plate with mocha-frosted cake on it. Gustave did the same thing, sliding two nickels into the slot and turning the knob. The glass door clicked, and Gustave lifted it up and slid out the plate.

"Ah! Cheesecake!" Cousin Henri smiled when he sat

down. Jean-Paul was already there, biting into a thick sandwich. "That's one of my favorites too."

"Are you going to get a slice?" Gustave asked, pouring the extra nickels onto the table.

"I'll just have coffee. Watch—this is my favorite machine!"

It was directly opposite their table. Cousin Henri fed it a nickel and lifted the handle, and from the golden head of a dragon, a stream of coffee poured into his cup.

"Cool!" said Jean-Paul.


Gustave could still taste the delicious creaminess of the cheesecake when they got to the movie theater. The movie had already started, so they went in quietly. Gustave stopped at a row with a lot of empty seats. The first seats of the row in front were filled with tall young men in soldiers' uniforms, so Gustave kept walking down the row until he came to three spots where no one would block the view. He settled into a plush seat.

On the huge movie screen, in brilliant Technicolor, a small boy toddled into a wolf's den. The soldiers laughed loudly as the baby patted the wolf cubs and plopped down among them. A few minutes later the baby on screen had grown into a twelve-year-old boy. The boy, Mowgli, dove into a river to get away from a tiger, and then Gustave and Jean-Paul gasped in unison as the camera moved back to show a crocodile swimming behind him.

It was an exciting movie, especially when Mowgli

encountered humans for the first time and when the tiger came on screen. At one point Jean-Paul leaned over to ask Gustave to translate what a girl had said to Mowgli, and Gustave suddenly realized that he was watching a movie in English without even noticing that it wasn't in French.

When the movie ended, the lights came back on, and some people filed out while others stayed in their seats to watch it again. "We missed the very beginning," Jean-Paul said. "It'll show again in a few minutes, right? Can we stay and watch it, please, Cousin Henri? Other people are staying."

"Sure," Cousin Henri said.

After a short time the lights lowered again, and the black-and-white images of a newsreel started to flicker on the screen.

"In news from Europe," boomed a deep voice, "escaped prisoners tell frightening stories about the camps in Poland." A photo of bare feet behind barbed wire filled the screen, then the boots of German soldiers and a snarling, slavering dog lunging forward at the end of a leash. Gustave felt himself go cold. "Political prisoners . . . unwanted people . . . civilians from occupied countries," he heard. "France." Yes, he had just heard "France," pronounced the funny American way. The images on the screen rushed on: a line of prisoners seen from the back, mostly men, but also what looked like the black hair of a boy. "Cold . . . starvation," the announcer said. "Death."

Gustave's stomach lurched. The screen seemed to waver in front of him. He pushed himself to his feet. Jean-

Paul sat still, blank faced. Gustave shoved his way blindly to the end of the aisle and ran to the men's room. The lights glared on the white tile, and a searing pain flashed behind his eyes. The stall door stuck and then gave way, and he almost fell toward the toilet as he threw up.

When Gustave came out of the men's room, Cousin Henri was waiting in the lobby. "Are you all right?" He put his arm gently around Gustave's shoulders. "Maybe that cheesecake was too rich for you, eh?"

Gustave felt as if he might throw up again if he opened his mouth to speak. The pattern in the carpet swam in front of his eyes.

"Let me get you something. Come." Gustave let himself be led to the refreshment counter, where more American food gleamed, colorful, plentiful, tantalizing.

"One Coke," said Cousin Henri. Gustave started to shake his head, feeling ashamed about all the food he was eating and all the money Cousin Henri was spending on him. But the young woman behind the counter was already handing Cousin Henri a green glass bottle.

"Here." Cousin Henri smiled slightly. "Coca-Cola— the taste of America! Go ahead, try it—it will settle your stomach."

The bottle was cold and smooth in Gustave's hand. The coolness felt good. He tipped it toward his mouth.

Coca-Cola fizzed on his tongue, startling him. The taste was intensely, cloyingly sweet and utterly disgusting. It was like medicine, like cod liver oil. He swallowed what was in his mouth to be polite, but he shuddered as it went down, intense pain shooting through his head again.

"There now, that's better, isn't it?" Cousin Henri asked worriedly.

Gustave nodded, but he couldn't take another sip. Instead he turned and walked back into the theater toward their seats. Jean-Paul was still watching the screen. The newsreels had finished, and the movie was starting up again. Maybe Jean-Paul hadn't understood enough English to know what the newsreel was about. But there had definitely been a boy on the screen in that prison camp. A boy Marcel's age.

Elephants moved across the screen and then gibbering monkeys swung. The soldiers in the row in front laughed, and one of them tossed a piece of popcorn up in the air. Couldn't the American army do something about those prison camps where people were starving? Why wouldn't America at least let more Jews in? The movie blurred in front of Gustave's eyes, and he blinked hard to clear his vision. Now it was past the point in the story when they had first come in, but Cousin Henri and Jean-Paul were still happily watching. On the screen Mowgli was coming to the human village again. Buldeo, the angry man from the village, was saying they shouldn't let Mowgli enter, that he wasn't a person like the villagers. "He is a wolf," Buldeo said, his face huge and scowling on the giant screen. "Let one in, and all will follow."

"He's a boy!" Gustave wanted to shout at the movie. "Let him in! He's not a wolf. He's a human being!"

## ★ 23 ★

The next Saturday Gustave went with Maman and Papa to the French synagogue on the Upper East Side. His parents wanted to meet the rabbi and arrange for him to begin tutoring Gustave for his bar mitzvah. The rabbi was already working with Jean-Paul. The plan was for both of them to get bar mitzvahed together in the fall, a few months late. It was going to mean a lot of studying between now and then.

They walked across Central Park to get to the East Side. The snow was completely gone now, and the ground was thawing, leaving unsightly stretches of mud where there would soon be grass. A faint reddening on some of the trees showed where leaves would be sprouting in a week or two. But there were no flowers yet, not even snowdrops or crocuses, Gustave noticed.

Papa was walking slowly and heavily, and Gustave had gotten ahead of his parents. He paused, and as they approached, he heard a snatch of their conversation. "I don't know how we are going to be able to afford to pay the rabbi for tutoring Gustave," Maman murmured. "And a suit for him to wear on the big day? His clothes are looking so disreputable. How are we going to afford that?"

"We'll work something out. I might have a lead on a better job." Papa paused and rubbed his leg.

"Why didn't you bring your walking stick?" Maman scolded. "Sabbath or no, we'll take the bus home."

The synagogue was small and old and friendly-looking. They went in, and Papa collapsed into one of the back rows. Maman went upstairs to the women's balcony. Jean-Paul turned around from a pew in the front and hurried back to sit with them. He was wearing an American suit with long pants that went all the way down to his ankles.

Services at the synagogue were very similar to the way they had been in Paris, partly in Hebrew and partly in French. The rabbi had a kind, weary-looking face. After services most of the congregation went down to the basement for *kiddush*, the meal after prayer. The room filled up quickly. Gustave was surrounded by so many voices speaking French that he could have been back in Paris. There was something familiar even about the strangers' faces around him, something that tugged at him, reminded him of home.

"Want to see what I brought?" Jean-Paul pulled Gustave into a corner behind some drapes. "My mother said not to, so don't tell." He pulled a rolled-up Superman comic from the inside pocket of his suit jacket. On the front, Superman was punching a cowering villain. *"Pow!"* it said above him in large, electric-looking letters. Gustave flipped the pages as Jean-Paul animatedly explained the stories.

"Too bad he isn't in the American army," Gustave said, handing it back. "The war would be over tomorrow."

"Yeah." Jean-Paul turned to a large picture. "Look—here he stops bad guys who are about to blow up a dam."

Aunt Geraldine came toward them out of the crowd of people, and Jean-Paul quickly stuffed the comic back into his suit pocket, trying to look innocent. "Gustave, *viens ici!*" Aunt Geraldine said. "I want to introduce you to Rabbi Blum. His family came from Paris too, some years ago. He's tutoring Jean-Paul, and he'll be tutoring you too. He also leads the Boy Scouts. Come, Jean-Paul, let's let them talk."

The rabbi was drinking a cup of coffee. He had kind, bright eyes in a thin face and curly, graying hair. "I've heard a lot about you from your aunt and cousin. So you'll be studying Torah with me. Are you looking forward to your bar mitzvah?"

"Well, I'm a terrible singer. I don't want to sing in front of everybody," Gustave said.

Rabbi Blum chuckled sympathetically. "Chanting Torah isn't the same as singing. Don't worry. Just be loud and clear, and you'll do fine. We'll practice until you can do it in your sleep."

Another man tapped the rabbi on the shoulder, and he started to move away.

"Wait, can I ask you something?" Gustave blurted out.

*"Bien sûr." Of course.* The rabbi paused, looking patiently at Gustave.

"Do you know any way to find people—Jews—in France? Ones who have disappeared?"

The rabbi suddenly looked exhausted and much older. "That's a lot harder than the singing problem. Have you asked the people at the Hebrew Immigrant Aid Society?"

"My father did. He filled out some forms. But we haven't heard anything."

"That's probably the best thing you can do. But, Gustave . . ." The rabbi hesitated, looking at him sympathetically. "I know so many people here who are trying to communicate with friends and relatives in Europe without any luck. It's just chaos over there. We may have to wait until after the war."

Something in the room was making Gustave dizzy. The man behind Rabbi Blum tapped him on the shoulder again, insistently, and the rabbi clasped Gustave's hand and moved away.

"Hey! Come on!" Jean-Paul was in a line across the room, waving at him. Gustave made his way between the groups of people. The room was too crowded and too bright, and the rapid French conversation felt too loud.

"What took you so long?" Jean-Paul asked cheerfully. "Look, there's challah and pastries! I saved you a spot in line."

A stout woman with two small children was just ahead of them. The older boy yanked her arm, swinging on her, and banged against Gustave's shin. Gustave stepped back and rubbed it. "I asked Rabbi Blum if he could help us find Marcel."

"What? You asked him about . . . Marcel?" Jean-Paul's voice dropped to a whisper at the last word, as if there were something shameful about talking about him.

Rage surged up in Gustave. "Yeah. *Marcel!* Our best friend, remember? Who's stuck back in Europe? Or don't you care? Doesn't *anybody* care?"

Jean-Paul's face flamed, and his voice got louder. "Of course I care! But you act like you don't know anything about what's going on. It's dumb to talk about it. There's just *no point.* Talking about it just gets everyone upset."

"Shut *up!*" Gustave shouted. "Of course there's a point!"

Heads turned in their direction. The boy in front of them stopped swinging on his mother's arm and looked at them with wide eyes.

"Don't you get it?" Jean-Paul yelled back. "They kill Jews for no reason at all! After you left Paris and the Nazis came, I saw them beat up an old man, right in front of me. He could hardly walk. He didn't get off the sidewalk and into the gutter fast enough for them. They kicked his cane out from under him and they beat him *to death!* Right there on the street!"

The man behind them put his hand on Jean-Paul's shoulder. "Hey! Shhh!" he said. Jean-Paul shrugged away from the man's hand, but his voice got quieter.

"It was horrible," he said. "Blood was everywhere. Marcel is probably dead, Gustave. You're not stupid. You know it's true. Why won't you just admit it? You know his family's from Poland, and the first people the Nazis took were the Polish Jews living in France. If the Nazis got him, Marcel is probably dead."

The room was suddenly impossibly bright and clear. It shattered into fragments, and then the shards pulled back together dizzyingly, slightly askew.

"It isn't true! The Nazis might not have gotten Marcel. He isn't dead! How can you say that? He isn't!" Gustave backed away, knocking over a folding chair. "I'm going!" he shouted. "Tell them I'm going home!" Slipping in between groups of people, he ran toward the stairs, up, and out onto the street.

It couldn't be true. Marcel couldn't be dead.

# ★ 24 ★

Gustave's legs were walking. He didn't know where they were heading, but it wasn't home. He had started out at a run, then gradually slowed. By now, he might have been walking for hours. He wasn't sure. The soles of his feet burned, but his legs, sore and heavy, just kept going and going, mechanically pushing against the pavement, heading down one block after another. Traffic roared by, and buildings loomed up around him. After a while he realized he was no longer in an area of clean, elegant buildings, neighborhoods full of men in hats, women pushing baby carriages, laughing girls playing jump rope. Here, the streets were almost entirely empty.

He kept walking between buildings that looked like factories, breathing in exhaust, hearing the clang of machinery. The city seemed at once to stretch on forever ahead of his feet and to imprison him, with its tall walls, garbage-strewn streets, impersonal buildings, and relentless noise. After a long time he had to stop, because he was at a river. It had to be the East River. For a long time he watched it tumble by, dirty gray water under a somber gray sky. A bridge loomed up beside him, and he wanted to be on it, to be suspended above everything. He searched until he found the ramp to the bridge and then made his way along the pedestrian walkway, hearing the traffic honk and rumble as it crossed. When he was somewhere near the middle of the bridge, he stopped, peering through the metal barrier at the water beneath him. Far in the distance, against the pale sky, a greenish silhouette rose up. It was the Statue of Liberty. He was seeing it for the first time. Her arm was raised high, holding up her torch.

*He's probably dead. You're not stupid. You know it's true. Marcel is probably dead.*

Jean-Paul's voice in Gustave's head was relentless. None of the noise around him could make it go away. Under his feet the girders thrummed with the weight of the traffic, which went on and on, heartlessly, as if it didn't matter, as if the lives of Jews didn't matter, across the ocean in Europe, out of sight and far away. Gustave took a deep breath of the polluted, foul-smelling air.

Yes, he did know. Of course he knew. Marcel could be dead. However much he drowned it out with other thoughts, with the activities of his daily life here in America, he knew it. It was knowledge that Gustave pushed away into the darkness, but it kept coming back, lurching up, making his stomach sick. It was knowing Marcel might be dead that gave him nightmares, that woke him, gasping and sweating, in the night. That was why

Jean-Paul's eyes went flat and lifeless whenever Gustave said Marcel's name. Gustave had known it, of course, although he hadn't let himself say it in his head. But he did now. *Marcel Landau could be dead.*

Far below Gustave's feet the water churned, gray and turbulent. Over him the sky opened, the pale gray now streaked with white clouds, far away, inaccessible, offering no help, no hope. His best friend might be dead. He might have died as a boy, died without ever having had the chance to grow up. "Died" was too polite a word. If he was dead, he had been murdered.

But Gustave's own heart still throbbed and beat inside him, powerful, pulsing. He was just a small speck in all that space, a small speck in the heartless, roaring, ignorant, insensible world. Yet inside him, energy rushed. It almost seemed wrong, how alive he felt. Why couldn't he share it with Marcel, give him half of his own boundless life?

But he couldn't. And how did you go on living, how did you keep on passing through the days in a world in which such hideous things were true?

Gustave stood on the bridge, clutching the cold metal railing with his worn gloves, staring down at the river, watching the water flow on and on, for what might have been hours. Gradually, he realized that he could no longer see the water clearly. He looked around. The sky was darkening. Traffic continued to pass, rumbling, over the bridge. In the buildings on either side of the river, lights were starting to come on. The lights along the next bridge lit up suddenly, swirling up and down like a

185

strand of pearls wrapped around a woman's fingers. The bright edge of the moon was rising on the Brooklyn side of the river, slowly gliding up into the sky. It hung there, huge and luminous and yellow, reflected across the dark ripples of the water. Gustave watched it moving above the horizon, getting smaller and smaller. He wished that he could understand what the moon was trying to tell him. He couldn't. But somehow, slowly, his grief quieted. The night air was cold and clear. He walked down off the bridge and started toward home.

# ★ 25 ★

"**Y**ou can't just disappear like that! What were you thinking, wandering all over the city?" Papa looked angrier than he had in a long time.

"I told Jean-Paul to tell you I was leaving," Gustave said.

"Your mother was so worried she cried! You've been gone for hours. That's not acceptable. You need to be punished. No Boy Scouts this week. No fun activities. You just go to school, to Hebrew lessons with the rabbi, and to your job. The rest of the time you come straight home, you hear me?"

"Fine," Gustave said dully. Papa didn't understand anything. Gustave didn't want to go to Boy Scouts anyway. If he did, he'd have to see Jean-Paul.

"Are you all right? Why did you run out of the synagogue?" Maman asked, twisting her hands. Her eyes were red, and Gustave felt a pang of guilt.

But talking about Marcel out loud would make it more real. "I just wanted to get out of there," he muttered.

All week Gustave felt slow and heavy, clumsy, and strangely numb. On Sunday he had his first lesson with Rabbi Blum, who gave him prayers to practice afterward, so he had more homework than usual to do in the afternoons. Understanding English felt harder, as if he had sunk under murky water and couldn't push himself back up to the top. Even riding around doing laundry deliveries for Mr. Quong made his knees ache and his calves feel heavy. And after he got home, eating dinner felt like work, all that chewing, and nothing tasted good enough to be worth the effort. In his last class on Friday afternoon, Gustave ignored Mrs. McAdams droning on about sonnet structure and focused on running the tip of his pencil around and around the long, oval-shaped pencil groove at the top of the desk. He watched as the groove got darker and darker. It was strangely satisfying.

"Gustave . . . Gustave!" a voice whispered insistently. "I said, do you want to walk Chiquita with me today?"

His head jerked up. September Rose was standing in front of him in her red coat, fidgeting impatiently. Everyone else was gone, even the teacher.

"The bell rang! Class is over! What's going on with you? It's like you've been sleepwalking all week. Are you worried about that oral report or something?"

Gustave shook his head. He had forgotten all about it.

"Is something wrong in your family? Is somebody sick?"

"No."

"Is it about France? You're worried about the war? Or about someone in France?"

He blinked, and for the first time that afternoon, his eyes focused, and he really looked at her, startled that she had guessed. "Yes. A friend."

"Oh," she said, suddenly looking awkward. "I didn't want to be right. Did you get some bad news or something?"

"No. No news. Nobody knows where my friend Marcel is. It's like he disappeared from the earth." Gustave was surprised to hear himself telling her about it.

"That's really rough. I worry about my dad too. But at least I get letters." She zipped and unzipped her bag several times, looking at him nervously, as if she didn't know what to say.

Then a smile came over her face. "In my dad's last letter he talked about hot dogs. Do you know how they cook hot dogs in the army? They deep-fry them! Isn't that revolting? My dad said they were dripping with grease, and the ketchup slid right off!" She laughed. "He writes a lot about the disgusting food. But do you want to meet me in Central Park later? I'll go home and get Chiquita, and we can walk her together."

"I can't. I'm being punished. I can do my laundry deliveries, but then I have to go right home." He felt a jab of frustration.

"Ooh—what did you do?" September Rose's eyes gleamed.

Just then the classroom door opened, and Mrs. McAdams walked in. September Rose jumped back to her desk and zipped her bag closed. "What are you two still doing here?" Mrs. McAdams asked suspiciously. "September Rose, you know better. GUS, CHILDREN NOT ALLOWED AFTER SCHOOL. NO! NO! NO!" She wagged her finger at them.

"Sorry, Mrs. McAdams. I just left something under my desk. I had to come back and get it," said September Rose. She left the room immediately. Gustave pulled his schoolbag onto his shoulder and followed her out the door.

That weekend, Gustave had his second lesson with Rabbi Blum. He sat at the kitchen table in the rabbi's apartment, repeating the Hebrew prayers, chanting them sluggishly. Long ago, back in Paris, in the old synagogue gleaming with polished wood, those prayers had pulled at him like music, rising and falling, mysterious, half understood. Now they felt lifeless.

*"Arrête!" Stop!* Rabbi Blum burst out.

"I told you," Gustave said flatly. "I can't sing or even chant. I know what it's supposed to sound like, but I can't make it come out like that."

Rabbi Blum peered at him through his glasses. "We need to talk. Your heart isn't in what you are doing."

"I practiced." He had gone over the prayers the night before—for a few minutes, anyway.

"I'm going to ask you a big question," the rabbi said.

190

"An important question. Do you believe in the existence of Adonai?" Rabbi Blum's voice was reverent as he pronounced the Hebrew name for God.

Gustave shrugged. The floor of the rabbi's kitchen was made of buckled brown-and-white linoleum.

Rabbi Blum banged the table sharply, spilling some tea out of his cup. "Look at me, Gustave! Pay attention!"

Gustave looked up, startled.

"I mean it. Tell me honestly. Do you believe that Adonai exists?"

"No. I don't." He had said it out loud, and the floor hadn't collapsed under them, the apartment building splintering into fragments, furniture and people falling down through the air. He had said it out loud, and nothing had happened at all.

The rabbi looked at him quizzically. "You're sure?"

"Yes, I'm sure. Of course I'm sure." Gustave looked at him furiously. "How could He? How could Adonai let such awful things happen in Europe? Adonai can't exist."

"Mmmm." Rabbi Blum sat back in his chair. "Yes. It's easy to think that."

"Easy? It isn't easy!"

Rabbi Blum nodded slowly. He rubbed his scalp, making a tuft of his curly, graying hair stick up. "There's something I find useful when I feel doubtful about the existence of Adonai," Rabbi Blum said, looking at him intently.

Gustave stared. The *rabbi* sometimes doubted the existence of God?

"A wise American philosopher once wrote that when

there is no way of knowing which of two possibilities is true, when there isn't enough evidence to know, either way, it is reasonable just to choose one or the other. And he thought we should choose the belief that has better consequences."

Gustave stared at him angrily. "What does that even mean?"

"We should believe the thing that makes better things happen. For example, if I don't believe in Adonai, I might despair. But if I believe in Adonai, even though there is no way to prove or disprove his existence, it has good consequences. I feel stronger, more connected to the world, more connected to other Jews."

"But it's your job to say that, right? And if you believe in Adonai, you get to keep your job," Gustave said bluntly. He didn't mean to be rude, but right now he just didn't have the energy not to say what he thought.

"Well, yes. It does have that good consequence too." The rabbi smiled and reached out, tousling Gustave's hair. "I think you've had enough religious instruction for this afternoon. Go on home and eat your dinner."

Gustave had his coat on and was at the door when Rabbi Blum stopped him. "I know you're worried about your missing friend, and I'm very sorry," he said softly. "Many, many of us are also worried about friends and family members in Europe. But you need to go on. There's no alternative. I don't mean to say that you should forget. But you have one life to live, one infinitely precious life. You must *live* it. You must live it with all your heart, with all your energy."

Right now it didn't feel as if he had any energy at all. But the rabbi meant well. Gustave nodded.

Rabbi Blum put his hand on the door, holding it open as Gustave stood in the hallway. "I notice you missed the Boy Scout meeting this week," he said, lingering in the doorway. "But you're surely going to come on the camping trip, aren't you?"

Gustave didn't really feel like going anymore. But Papa had been so excited back when Gustave had told him about the camping trip that he had gone out specially and bought him a new pair of wool socks and a khaki army blanket at the secondhand store. So Gustave kind of had to go. He nodded.

"Have you ever been camping in cold weather before?" The rabbi was clearly trying to make light conversation.

"Sure."

"Ah. Then you know how things are done. Lots of layers. And wear your warmest clothes. *À bientôt!*" *See you soon.* To Gustave's relief, the rabbi let the door close.

The last time Gustave had been camping in the winter was a few years ago, in the mountains with his Boy Scout troop in France. Jean-Paul and Marcel had been there too. They had roasted potatoes over the fire and eaten them, and then Marcel had had the brilliant idea of putting the leftover baked potatoes at the bottom of their sleeping bags to keep their feet warm. For a moment it had felt absolutely wonderful. But then the troop leader had come running over. "*Non, non, non!*" he had exclaimed. "What if wild animals smell food and come into the tent at night? Do you want them nibbling your feet off?"

So the three of them had quickly taken the potatoes out of their sleeping bags. Then Marcel ate his, even though he had just been rubbing his toes against it.

To his surprise, Gustave found himself grinning as he walked down the street away from the rabbi's apartment. That was Marcel, all right! Totally disgusting—but in a good way.

# ★ 26 ★

After school on Tuesday it was surprisingly warm, but rain was pouring down, and Gustave didn't have an umbrella. He turned up his collar and raced down the street, darting from awning to awning, shaking the water off when he got underneath one. When he reached the awning outside the grocery store on the corner, somebody else was waiting under it too.

"Hey, Gustave! Are you still being punished?" It was September Rose, holding a striped umbrella.

"No. It's over. Finally!"

"Yay! Then do you want to walk Chiquita together today? We can go up to my apartment and get her and then go to the park."

"Seppie, it's raining!"

September Rose shrugged. "You can share my umbrella. Dogs still need to be walked even in the rain. What do you say?"

"Sure, I guess." He was already wet through, so he might as well.

"So I decided I'm going to audition for the victory chorus," September Rose told him as they walked to her apartment, sharing her umbrella. "Listen. Here, hold this so I can sing." She handed him the umbrella. Giggling, she danced out into the rain and sang a song about a flag. She darted back under the umbrella and dried her face with her sleeve. "Did you like that one?" she asked. But without waiting for an answer, she slipped back out into the rain and, dancing down the pavement, she sang another song about waiting for a letter. "Which one do you like better?" she demanded, coming back under the shelter.

"The letter one."

"Me too, I think." She squeezed water out of her hair. "But I'm also thinking about singing this other one. It's a boy telling his girl to wait for him while he's away at war. It's kind of funny and sweet. *Don't sit under the apple tree/With anyone else but me . . . ,*" she sang, dancing a few steps. One of her feet hit a puddle, sending up a spray of water, and she shrieked gleefully. "Well, I have to think about it. Do you want to go to the library this weekend to work on our history projects?"

"I can't. I'm going camping with my Boy Scouts troop."

"In this weather? You French Boy Scouts are tough! How about next Tuesday? It's the auditions, but we can meet somewhere after."

"The Joan of Arc statue?" he asked. "You know that one near school, at the end of Ninety-Third, in Joan of Arc Park?"

"Sure."

The rain was starting to lighten as the two of them turned onto September Rose's block. As they made their way around a large display of dripping suitcases on the sidewalk in front of a store, two older Negro boys zoomed by them on bicycles, splashing through a huge puddle and sending a spray of water in their direction. One of them turned, glared at the two of them walking side by side under the umbrella, and yelled some English words Gustave had never heard before.

September Rose stiffened, and a mottled crimson darkened her face.

"What's the matter? What did he say?"

"Just something stupid. Bad words."

"But what did it mean?"

"I'm not gonna repeat stuff like that, Gustave!" she snapped. "He called me something bad!"

"Creep." Gustave looked after the boys, but they had disappeared.

"Yeah, stupid creep. I'm not gonna let it bother me."

They walked the rest of the way to September Rose's apartment building in silence. Gustave stopped when he came to the railing where he usually locked Mr. Quong's delivery bike. "Do you want me to wait outside while you go get Chiquita? So your brother doesn't get mad at you?"

"No, come on up. He's never home this time of day. Only Granma will be there, and she likes you. Anyway, I have to feed Chiquita first, so it'll take a few minutes."

As soon as September Rose opened the apartment door, Chiquita ran toward them, yipping and jumping up on September Rose. Somewhere else in the apartment, voices were shouting.

"You got to stay away from those hooligans! Look at you!"

"We're doing what needs to be done! Anyway, it's my business. Stay out of it!"

A door slammed, and Mrs. Walker came down the hall and collapsed into a chair in the kitchen, rubbing her eyes.

"What's wrong, Granma?" September Rose cried.

Mrs. Walker pulled her into a hug. "It's that brother of yours. I just don't know what to do with him," she said, her voice trembling slightly. "You should see how he came home. Hello, Gustave." She wiped at her eyes. "I'm sorry—you caught us at a bad time."

"Why's he here this early? Is he hurt? What happened to him?" September Rose looked terrified.

"He got beat up. He won't say how. I'm at my wits' end. I just don't know how to get him to stay out of trouble. He's bruised and he's got a terrible black eye. Will you run to the butcher and get him a piece of liver to put on it?"

September Rose reached into a sugar bowl in the cupboard for some coins. "Sorry, Gustave," she whispered. "I can't go to the park after all. We'll walk Chiquita another time, okay?"

"Okay." Gustave headed toward the door. Chiquita followed him, whining hopefully.

"Wait!" September Rose called out. "I forgot." She darted into the apartment. In a moment she was back, shoving something into his hand. "I got this for you. I wanted you to feel better about your friend and everything. It was *so* hard to find. You would not believe how many markets I looked in before I found it. About a million! See you."

She closed the door, and Gustave looked at the object she had given him. It was wrapped in notebook paper secured with a rubber band. His name was printed on the paper in capital letters. As he unwrapped it, the delicious smell of chocolate wafted up. It was a candy bar, a kind he had never seen before. "Butterfinger," he read out loud. It was the word September Rose had taught him the day they'd played hopscotch. On the back of the lined paper was a note:

Hi, GUSTAVE!
I'M SORRY YOU'RE WORRIED ABOUT YOUR FRIEND. KEEP YOUR CHIN UP. HOPE THIS MAKES YOU FEEL BETTER. FROM SEPPIE AND CHIQUITA.
P.S. DON'T DROP IT—HA-HA!

Gustave smiled. When he got outside, the rain had stopped, and a faint rainbow arced high over the pale buildings through a sky filled with tumultuous clouds.

After dinner that night Gustave poured the money from his savings jar onto the tablecloth. One dollar and fifty-five cents. Mr. Quong was letting him skip his Friday deliveries so that he could go on the Boy Scout camping trip, but because he had worked Monday and would work tomorrow, he would still earn fifty cents this week. So after Mr. Quong paid him, he would finally have enough to buy the pants! Gustave wouldn't take them camping, because he didn't want them to get messed up, but when he went to school on Monday, he'd be dressed like a normal American boy.

Gustave put one nickel back in the jar and zipped the rest carefully into a pocket in his schoolbag.

During school the next day, and while he was riding around doing his deliveries afterward, he kept fingering the outside of the pocket nervously, making sure that he could still feel the coins. After his last delivery, as he was biking back to the laundry, Gustave suddenly got worried that somebody else might have bought the pants since he'd last checked on them. He chained the bike and ran inside to the used-clothing rack. Molly pattered over to him, meowing and rubbing against his legs. For a moment he couldn't see the pants. He rummaged through the clothes on the crowded rack, searching. There was the blouse with the stain, there was the men's jacket, there was the child's dress with the duck on the pocket—and there they were, jammed between two much bigger pairs of pants. Gustave pulled them off the rack and squatted down to rub Molly gently behind the ears.

"There you are, Gustave!" Mr. Quong came out of the back. "I have your pay for you." He opened the cash register and took out two quarters. "Are you interested in those pants?" he asked, looking up. "Do you want to try them on? You can change in the room back here."

Between the lines of drying clothes, Gustave pulled on the new pants. They were perfect in length, and when he put his belt on, he could tighten them slightly so that they fit around the waist too. He pushed his way through some hanging sheets back out to the front.

"Ah, they fit you nicely!" Mr. Quong smiled. "I didn't know you wanted those."

Gustave unzipped the pocket of his bag and counted out the money, added the new fifty cents, and pushed it over to Mr. Quong.

"No, no, that's too much." Mr. Quong handed him back some of the coins. "Employees pay half price. For you, they are just one dollar."

"Half price?"

"Sure! It's a tradition in this country. And you know what?" Mr. Quong jumped up. "I have just the tie to go with those pants. It's an old silk one, from before the shortages. Very fancy." He rummaged around in a cupboard under the counter and pulled out a navy blue tie with diagonal red pinstripes. "Here—no charge."

Gustave accepted the tie hesitantly. Lots of the boys at school wore them every day. "It's nice." But was it taking charity?

Mr. Quong smiled at him. "You work hard for me—you've earned it. You'll look just like the other boys at school now. Just like an American!"

# ★ 27 ★

It was a long drive to the mountains for the Boy Scout camping trip. Gustave watched out the window for a while as they left the city and the landscape gradually opened up into suburbs and then apple orchards and farms. After a while mountains loomed up, blue and misty in the distance, and as they ascended, the scenery got more and more wintry-looking, more like February than late March.

Father René's gleaming black sedan was packed with scouts, talking and laughing. It was a bit more crowded than Rabbi Blum's car, but Gustave had chosen this one because Jean-Paul had been sitting in the backseat of the rabbi's. Gustave listened to the boys around him chattering mostly in French but with a few English words mixed in. After a while he dozed off. He woke when Guy poked him.

"*Réveille-toi*, Gustave!" *Wake up over there!* "Do you

know this American song? It's great for long drives. We're going to sing 'A Hundred Bottles of Beer,' Father René!" he called out tauntingly.

"No, no! Anything but that!" Father René pretended to bang his head against the steering wheel.

Guy laughed. "Yeah! It'll be great for Gustave's English! Remember how hard English numbers were when you first got here? Come on, fellows!" Guy started singing at the top of his lungs in English. *"A hundred bottles of beer on the wall, a hundred bottles of beer . . ."*

All the others sang too, and after a moment even Father René joined in with his deep baritone. The tune was singsongy and repetitive and annoying, and that was the fun of it. After a few verses, Gustave got the hang of it and sang too: *"If one of the bottles should happen to fall, ninety-six bottles of beer on the wall!"*

At about bottle eighty-two, Gustave could tell from the pressure in his ears that they were climbing steeply up into the mountains. They were down to seventeen bottles and still going strong when Father René turned the car into a country lane and stopped when overgrown shrubs blocked the dirt road and he couldn't drive any farther.

"Here we are!" he announced. "And now, please, no more bottles of beer!"

The boys piled out and started getting gear from the back as Rabbi Blum's car pulled up behind them.

"This is it?" Gustave asked André. "It looks like the middle of nowhere. I thought we were going to camp in a deserted mansion near a lake."

"Yeah, this is it. The road is overgrown because no one's lived here for years. We park the cars here and hike to the house. It's a couple of miles."

Rabbi Blum was arranging loads. "Three miles, more or less! Great exercise. Here you go, Gustave. You're a hard worker—you can take a heavy one with food in it, right?"

"Sure."

The rabbi handed Gustave a few packages and helped him stuff them into his backpack. "You did well at your last lesson with me," he said to him in an undertone. "Are you feeling a bit better about the bar mitzvah and everything?"

"Yeah. I mean, boys in my family have been having bar mitzvahs since forever. I guess I want to do what my father did, and his father."

The rabbi smiled. "Sure! And before him, your grandfather's father and his father and his father. I often like to think about that too."

Father René and André came over and handed Gustave a faded sleeping bag. "André can show you how to tie this onto the pack. You can use some of your knots."

"It's so much less gear than if we were carrying tents," André said, showing him how the sleeping bag went over the pack. "Still, those shoes don't look so great for hiking."

Gustave looked at his feet, embarrassed. He was wearing the only pair of shoes he had, the ones he wore every day. The leather on the right shoe was starting to separate from the sole, and the tread was worn down to almost nothing. The other boys all had much sturdier-looking shoes.

"You'll be fine," said Rabbi Blum, shouldering his pack. "This trail is rough, but it's quite flat."

"Come on!" Maurice squeezed past, bumping Gustave's shoulder with his pack and starting down the trail.

"Everybody ready? *On y va!*" *Let's go!* called Rabbi Blum.

They all headed down the path. At first it was narrow, and their way was blocked by snow-laden branches that they had to push aside, walking single file. After they had gone about half a mile, though, the path widened. Gustave saw Jean-Paul up ahead of him on the trail, looking back and waiting. There wasn't any way to avoid him.

"How come you didn't ride with us?" Jean-Paul asked when Gustave got close. Gustave shrugged and kept walking. Jean-Paul started hiking alongside him.

"Look, Gustave . . ." Jean-Paul went red. "I'm sorry about yelling at you in the synagogue."

"Don't worry about it," Gustave said stonily. He looked down, making his way around roots gnarling the path.

"I mean, of course I care about Marcel! He was my best friend too, except for you! I just got mad because I know how bad it is there. And you kept acting as if it wasn't. As if we might get a letter from him anytime," Jean-Paul ended limply.

Gustave winced. He had said "was." Marcel "was" his best friend. And he didn't even seem to have noticed what he had said.

Gustave hiked along the partly frozen mud of the trail.

It was getting late, and over the tree line he saw a crescent moon already up in the pale sky. The image of the yellow moon rising into the sky over the East River that night he had stood on the bridge came back to Gustave, full, luminous, calming. When you didn't know what to believe, the rabbi had said, when there was no evidence either way, you had a choice. Nobody knew for sure what had happened to Marcel. Jean-Paul thought he knew, but he didn't, not really. Gustave knew what choice he was going to make, what he was going to believe. Until he knew something else for sure, he was going to believe that Marcel was alive. No matter what anyone else thought. No matter what anyone else said.

Gustave and Jean-Paul hiked on side by side, silently, along the trail lumpy with roots, across an ice-glazed stream, up a slight rise, and over a tree that had long ago fallen across the path and had now begun to decay.

"So," said Jean-Paul, shoving Gustave playfully. "Friends again?"

Gustave didn't have to think the same things Jean-Paul thought to be friends with him. He shoved his cousin back, and they both slipped slightly on the muddy path. "Friends."

"Are we almost there?" Xavier asked Father René after another mile or two. A wind had picked up, and the air was getting distinctly colder.

"Almost. Let's take a short break, boys."

Gustave shrugged off his pack, letting it fall onto the

side of the path, and stretched his arms and shoulders. His back, sweaty where the pack had pressed against it, quickly felt cold in the evening air. The others were doing the same thing.

"We're nearly there," Maurice said confidently. "I remember. The trees get farther apart here, and then we climb up a hill. From there we can see the mansion and the lake."

"That's right. Good memory, Maurice," said Rabbi Blum. "So—let's make our last push. We want to gather some wood to make a fire in the fireplace and warm that gigantic room a little before nightfall."

They hiked up the last long hill. No one was talking anymore. The only sound was feet crunching through the snow. At the top of the rise, Bernard ran ahead through the pine trees. *"Et voilà!"* he said with a grand gesture. *There it is!* And then he looked back at them all, his face bewildered. "It isn't there!" he said, sounding stunned. "The mansion's gone!"

# ★ 28 ★

"What? *Ne raconte pas de bêtise!*" *Nonsense!* "Of course it's there!" Rabbi Blum shouldered his way ahead through the tree branches. The boys crowded behind him. A hillside, bare except for a bit of strewn rubble, looked out over an icy lake. Pale pinks and blues streaked the sky and the surface of the ice.

Father René had been retying his hiking boot. He crunched up behind the scouts, and they all stood there gazing at the empty expanse, their breath making clouds of steam in the frosty air. "It appears it isn't," he said. "It must have been torn down."

"What are we going to do?"

"We don't have tents!"

"It's freezing!"

"I know how to build a lean-to, Rabbi!"

Everyone was talking at once.

The two men looked at each other. "It's awfully late

to go back," Rabbi Blum said. "Maybe looking for wood to build a shelter *is* our best bet. It's going to be a chilly night, though."

Father René nodded. "Let's go have a look around before we decide what to do."

The scouts ran down the hill, dropping their packs at the bottom and scattering, looking for large, fallen branches. Gustave found one caught in the crook of a standing tree and tugged at it, knocking a shower of powdery snow down onto his head. Jean-Paul ran over to help him, but the branch was thoroughly stuck. They were working at it, struggling sweatily, when they heard Xavier shriek from across the field. "Come see what I found!"

The boys ran toward him, the snow spraying out around their feet, and the men came trudging behind more slowly and heavily. "What's that?" Xavier called, pointing at a small roof just visible over the trees. "I think it's a shed or something."

The boys raced across the snowy field, then pushed through trees and underbrush. In another clearing stood a stone silo with a partially collapsed roof. Maurice was trying the door when the adults came panting through the trees, swatting at low-hanging branches.

They all crowded round, peering through the doorway. Inside was an empty, dusty room with some disintegrating hay in a corner and a few broken boards leaning against a wall.

"This is perfect!" said Maurice. "Can't we camp here?"

"Well, it isn't the Ritz! But I think this is our best bet," said Father René briskly. "Maurice, can you get the boys organized?"

The sky was dusky, and wind rattled the branches of the trees. Under Maurice's direction, Gustave and Jean-Paul and the others gathered firewood, Maurice cleared a fire circle, and he and André started a campfire, while the two men unpacked the food and then began to cook. Xavier, Bernard, and Guy spread out the hay so that it covered part of the floor of the silo and laid out the old blankets on top of it to make a warm surface for the sleeping bags.

"Is that nearly ready, Father?" Jean-Paul asked, dumping a load of wood next to the campfire. "I'm starving."

"Me too!" Xavier said, sticking his head out of the silo.

"Soon!" said Father René cheerfully. He was frying potatoes and onions in a skillet over the fire. "Time to toast the frankfurters."

"Finally!" Maurice grabbed a stick and shoved a frankfurter on it, holding it out over the fire. Gustave took one and put it on a stick too, and so did the others. The frying onions smelled delicious. The stars were coming out now, over the lake, and sparks from the campfire swirled upward into the freezing air.

"This is so much better than camping in the mansion!" Maurice exulted as he took a plate of fried potatoes from Rabbi Blum. "A lot more exciting!"

"Exciting—yes, that's one word for it," Rabbi Blum said wryly. "I think we're in for an awfully cold night."

* * *

It *was* very cold. Even though they wore their jackets and their hats inside their sleeping bags, even though they had extra blankets, and even though they all huddled close together in the corner of the silo on top of the hay, it was almost too cold to sleep. Gustave's icy feet woke him up several times in the night, no matter how tightly he curled into a ball. Then, as soon as the sky got light, he woke up for good. The others were still sleeping. Gustave's breath made clouds of steam in front of his face. It smelled like pine in the silo, and the air was sharply cold in his nose, almost cold enough to freeze. He pulled his scarf up, and after a few breaths he was warmer and the scarf was slightly damp. He was too cold to get out of his sleeping bag, so he lay there, looking at the pale blue glimmer of the lake through the broken part of the silo door.

"Rise and shine! Rise and shine!" bellowed Maurice suddenly, and the morning stillness was over as they all started getting up, groaning and stretching.

Xavier got out of his sleeping bag, ran off to the woods to relieve himself, and then came racing back again immediately. "It's too cold!" he called out, his teeth chattering, getting back into his sleeping bag.

"None of that, none of that! You're right, it *is* too cold to sit around," ordered Father René. "François, I'm not going to bother starting a fire," he said to Rabbi Blum, who was adjusting his yarmulke on his head with fumbling fingers. "Let's all just get packed up on the double, march back to the cars, and drive into the village for a hot breakfast somewhere. I saw an inn when we drove through yesterday. We need to get these boys warmed up."

"Good idea. Let's go."

The thought of eating inside a heated building got them all moving quickly, and soon, with everything stuffed back into their packs, they were heading to the trail. It was too cold to sing or even talk, so they hiked silently and speedily through the woods. Gustave's nose and fingers were very cold, and he could hardly feel his toes, even though he had on wool socks. The path felt a lot longer hiking in this direction. But finally they were at the clearing, and then in the cars, and then starting off, and gradually the car warmed from the heat of their bodies.

"Ah! The snowy countryside is so lovely, don't you think?" Guy warbled in a falsetto, and everyone laughed.

"Right now I'd just like to look at its beauty from inside a nice warm inn," said Father René. "Preferably next to a fire. While drinking hot coffee!"

"Or hot chocolate!" said Xavier. "Do you think they'll have it?"

"I'm sure! And ... there it is!" announced Father René, turning in at the inn's driveway. The car crunched over snowy gravel and came to a stop. Behind them Rabbi Blum turned in too. The boys piled out of the cars and hurried into the warmth.

The lobby of the inn was huge, with heavy beams overhead and the antlered head of a deer hanging on the wall over a roaring fire in a stone fireplace. Xavier laughed when he saw the deer. "When I was little, back in France," he said, "the first time I saw one of those, in a castle, I ran around to the other side of the wall to see where the rest of the deer was!"

Rabbi Blum took charge. "First, everyone into the restroom to tidy up a little. I'll supervise and make sure you all come out looking respectable. René, do you want to go talk to the people at the restaurant?"

"Sure. I'll take these two with me." He and Xavier and Gustave washed and slicked their hair quickly in the restroom first and then went down the corridor that led to the inn's restaurant. The corridor was wood paneled, with a plush, crimson carpet. The restaurant smelled deliciously of coffee and pancakes and sweet syrup. Gustave's stomach growled. A friendly-looking man about the age of Gustave's father, impeccably dressed and wearing horn-rimmed eyeglasses, came forward to greet them. "May I help you?" he asked Father René.

Father René spoke effortlessly in English. "We haven't been staying at the inn, but I wonder if you could serve us breakfast anyway," he said to the host, smiling his usual, charming smile. "My Boy Scouts are very cold and hungry. They camped out last night in an old silo. We were supposed to spend the night in the old Woodress place out on Osprey Lake, but last night we were shocked to find that it wasn't there!"

"Oh, yes." The host looked intrigued. "It was finally torn down last summer. I'd heard that Boy Scouts used to camp there. Well, you must certainly need a hot breakfast!" he said sympathetically. "I'll even give you all hot chocolate on the house! How's that, boys?" He peered at Xavier and Gustave through his glasses, smiling.

"Swell!" Xavier grinned.

"I have a big table over there." The host pointed at a long wooden table by the window. Sunlight streamed in over the dark wood, and near one end a fire burned in another large stone fireplace. "Let me just have a waiter set it up for you. How many?"

Rabbi Blum, followed by the rest of the boys, came into the restaurant at that moment. A tall, supercilious-looking man who had joined the host glanced at Rabbi Blum's yarmulke with a peculiar expression and then tapped the host on the shoulder. The two of them walked a few feet off and spoke briefly.

"I'm going to have waffles *and* pancakes," Xavier said excitedly. "You said we could have whatever we wanted, right, Father René?"

"Excuse me." The host was back. His face had lost its earlier friendliness, and his eyes too slid to Rabbi Blum's yarmulke and then to Father René's face. "I apologize. Mr. Blanchard, our manager, tells me that table has been reserved. I'm afraid I can't seat you."

"Another table would be just fine. Or two tables, close to one another," Father René said. "We're not fussy."

"I'm sorry. All of our tables are full for breakfast this morning."

Rabbi Blum came forward. "What do you mean?" he asked, sounding angry. "I see quite a few empty tables. There. And there and there." He gestured at the nearly empty room.

"I'm sorry, sir," the host said coolly. "These tables are reserved."

The manager stepped forward. "They are reserved for guests of the hotel," he said impassively. "We cannot help you at this time."

He looked at Rabbi Blum's yarmulke again, and Gustave suddenly realized what was going on. He felt shaky with rage.

"Very well." Father René spoke abruptly. "Let's go, boys."

"No waffles with melted butter and maple syrup," Xavier said mournfully when they got to the lobby.

The two troop leaders were conferring in undertones, speaking English. Gustave edged closer to listen.

"It must be a restricted hotel," Rabbi Blum said angrily. "They won't serve Jews. Look around. Do you see anyone else who seems Jewish here?"

"But Gustave was with me when we came in," Father René said, sounding confused. "And the host was very friendly at first."

"I guess he didn't realize Gustave was Jewish, but he saw my yarmulke when I came in. In any case," Rabbi Blum said, "they don't want us, and I wouldn't spend any money here anyway. We'll find somewhere else."

"These boys are ravenous. And there's nowhere around for miles." Father René turned to the scouts. "Who cares if this restaurant is all booked up? We scouts don't need to eat in a restaurant, do we? We're not softies! Now that we've warmed up, let's all go have a campfire breakfast, the way we planned to at the old mansion. We'll find a picnic spot close to the village, overlooking another spot on the lake. Are the same boys riding with me?"

Outside, the sun was higher and brighter, and the air seemed warmer, maybe because they had been standing in a heated space for a while. When they came to an open spot on the road overlooking Osprey Lake, the men parked and the boys ran around gathering firewood for a campfire. Rabbi Blum got food out of the back of his car, and André used the powdered milk to make hot chocolate in a saucepan. Xavier took Guy's bag of marshmallows and dropped one in each cup. Rabbi Blum started frying eggs as Father René sautéed potatoes.

Gustave took a mug of hot chocolate in his gloved hands. Osprey Lake stretched away, pale blue and glittering, to the horizon. Gustave took a hungry sip of hot chocolate, sweetened by the sticky melted marshmallow on top. Its richness ran through him, warming him and making him feel calmer. Even his toes felt warmer in his beaten-up shoes, although he was standing in the snow.

It was breathtaking here. America was a beautiful country. Maybe even almost as beautiful as France. But he still felt confused and angry. This was America! It was supposed to be a country where all people were equal, but that inn wouldn't serve Jews.

Some of the other scouts were sitting on a log by the fire, eating the first plates of eggs while Rabbi Blum made another skilletful. They were talking about which of them had tasted coffee and whether it was better than hot chocolate. None of the other scouts seemed to have noticed or cared very much about what had happened in the restaurant.

"Here." Jean-Paul was making toast by holding chunks of bread on a stick over the fire, and he handed a piece to Gustave. "To tide you over until you get your eggs. Doesn't food cooked over a campfire taste better than anything else in the whole world?"

"I know. Especially when it's so cold."

"Hey, whatever happened with that girl you said was interesting? The one who was named after a month?"

"September Rose. Seppie. We're friends." Thinking about her, Gustave wondered what was going on with her family, whether her grandmother and her brother were still fighting, and whether his black eye was getting better.

"Ooh, is she your girlfriend?" Jean-Paul teased him.

Gustave flushed. "No, just my friend." He took a bite of the bread, which was crispy on the outside and soft and warm inside, tasting somehow like the fire and the smoke and the fresh, pure air all at the same time.

Jean-Paul glanced at Gustave, his face reddened from the heat of the fire. "I guarantee my toast is better than what we would have gotten in that stupid inn anyway," he said. "I wouldn't eat their food if you paid me."

A look of recognition flashed between them.

# ★ 29 ★

The city felt crowded and dirty compared to the frosty landscape around Osprey Lake. But it was also warmer. On Monday morning Gustave left his gloves at home for the first time, and as he walked to school, he noticed buds on some of the trees, and green shoots poking up from fenced-in areas of soil along the sidewalk. He was wearing his new blue pants and tie. He passed strangers on the street, and none of them stared at him or seemed to notice him at all. Nobody would know now just by looking at him that he hadn't been born in America. As he ran up the school steps, Gustave noticed that he was whistling "La Marseillaise," the French national anthem, quietly to himself.

Posters about the rally in Battery Park were up all over the school. VICTORY! they announced in large letters. YOUTH RALLY. BATTERY PARK. MUSIC! ENTERTAINMENT! SUPPORT THE WAR EFFORT! Gustave walked self-consciously to homeroom, expecting someone to comment on his new clothes at any minute, but nobody did. In fact, nobody said anything about them until lunch.

"Hey—new pants!" Miles said. "They look good."

Leo looked over. "Yeah, you look normal now, Gus. So, did you fellows hear about the rally? There's going to be dancing!"

"Not dancing, roller-skating!" Stephen said.

"That's not what I heard," Leo insisted.

And that was it. Gustave looked like one of the crowd now. He fit in. It felt great and not quite real at the same time, as if he were wearing a costume.

In third period there was an all-school assembly. It began with the usual sorts of announcements about the sewing club and basketball, and then Mrs. Hale, the principal, walked onto the stage. "I know we are all excited about the Victory Rally and the auditions for the chorus," she said, smiling. There was a surge of cheering in the auditorium. "But I do have a few things to say about it," she went on. "I want you all to remember that whether or not you are in the chorus, every one of you who attends the rally will be representing Joan of Arc Junior High. It'll be a big crowd, full of students from schools all over the city, and I expect you all to be on your best behavior. There will be police there, of course, keeping order—if you get separated from your group or need help, check in with one of them.

"And now, an important announcement. The rally organizers have also decided to hold a scrap drive, so they are asking everyone who attends to bring some tin cans. Ask your mothers and your other relatives and friends to save them. The metal will be used to make military equipment—airplanes, tanks, ships, and smaller equipment too. Any questions?"

Stephen's hand was up. "Is it true there's going to be roller-skating at the rally?" he asked.

"Yes. There's a wooden platform up in the park because of some construction work, and the fire department is going to put a railing around it and turn it into a temporary roller-skating rink. There's also going to be music and a bonfire. You can bring your own roller skates or rent a pair there."

Miles's hand shot up. "But, Mrs. Hale," he asked worriedly when she called on him, "Battery Park is right on the water. Won't the light from the bonfire be dangerous? In the newspapers it says ships are getting torpedoed by U-boats, and that lights along the coast let the Nazis see where our ships are."

"Yeah!" Frank called out. "That's why they dimmed the lights at the Statue of Liberty."

"Let's remember to raise our hands before speaking. Yes, that's right, Miles, Frank. I'm pleased that you are all paying such good attention to the war news. But don't worry. The firemen are building the bonfire behind a barrier so that the light won't shine out to sea. The ships along our coast will stay safe."

When the students returned to homeroom, Mrs. McAdams hushed them and turned to Gustave. "DO YOU UNDERSTAND, GUS?" she boomed at him. "MRS. HALE SAYS TO SAVE CANS AND WASH THEM. WASH, WASH?" She did it in pantomime.

"I understand," he said, trying not to sound impatient. She didn't need to baby-talk at him anymore! "The cans will be used to make airplanes."

"YES, GUS!" She sounded astonished. "GOOD BOY!"

"Gus gets everything now, Mrs. McAdams!" Frank said without raising his hand. "You don't have to shout."

"VERY WELL!" She sounded amazed.

Yes, Gustave understood perfectly well. However, his mother almost never used commercially canned food unless she absolutely had to. She said canned food wasn't French. Gustave could ask his aunt, but somehow he was pretty sure that elderly Madame Raymond, who was so fussy about fruit, also didn't tolerate canned food. He didn't want to be the only one at the rally empty-handed. He thought about the problem on and off all morning.

At lunch, when Gustave was waiting in line to buy milk, someone tapped him on the shoulder. September Rose was standing behind him. "Are you going to have a lot of cans to bring?" she asked abruptly.

Gustave shook his head.

"I'm not going to have *any*!" she burst out indignantly. "My granma uses all of ours to make her birds! I can't ask her to let me have them. Those birds are so important to her—it would be mean! But what am I gonna do? There's Miss Noelle next door, but she saves all her cans for Granma. I mean, I could go door to door and ask, but Granma would never be okay with me talking to strangers like that."

Door to door? Suddenly Gustave had an idea. "I know

Mr. Quong's customers. They aren't strangers. When I deliver for Mr. Quong, I could ask them for cans. Hey . . ." He glanced at her awkwardly. "You could come. I mean, if you want to. We could share the cans."

"Sure!" She beamed at him as she picked up a bottle of chocolate milk. "That'd be swell!"

After school, when Gustave and September Rose got to Mr. Quong's, Gustave realized he hadn't thought about how Seppie was going to keep up with him when he was biking. "Do you mind riding in the basket?" he asked. "You can hold the packages."

"*Whee!* This is the life! My own chauffeur!" September Rose shrieked, kicking her feet in the air as he started off.

With Seppie in the basket, he couldn't bike nearly as fast as usual. But it was fun to have company, and September Rose helped explain about collecting cans.

"It's for the war effort," Gustave said to Mr. Davis, the first customer.

"Lots of junior highs are gathering for a Victory Rally," September Rose jumped in. "We're all collecting cans so factories have metal to build tanks for the army and binoculars and things, and ships for the navy, and planes for the air force. I mean, isn't it amazing to think that your empty can of peas could be bobbing in the ocean in a few months, on its way to defeat the Japanese?"

Mr. Davis laughed. "It *is* amazing! I have some empty cans in the garbage. I'll get them."

A few of Gustave's customers shook their heads, but most of them found one or two empty cans.

One building had a doorman who wouldn't let September Rose in. "I'm sorry," Gustave said, feeling his face get hot as the doorman stood there with his arms crossed over his massive chest. "I have to deliver this."

"Go ahead," September Rose said stiffly. "I'll wait outside."

Gustave had started with the uptown customers today, and as he got down to the last packages, he noticed a thick bundle for Mrs. Markham, the woman with all the small children who had given him his very first nickel tip. He and September Rose climbed up the six flights of stairs with the bulky package.

"I bet she'll help," said September Rose, as Gustave was about to knock.

"How do you know? You never even met her!"

September Rose pointed at the blue-star banner on Mrs. Markham's door. "She has a banner just like ours. Haven't you noticed? It means her husband's in the war."

"Oh! I thought it was just to be patriotic." Gustave knocked and stood back, studying the banner.

"Hello, madame!" he said when she opened the door, holding her baby on her hip. "More diapers?"

"What else?" She smiled at him, looking tired, and pushed a wisp of sandy-colored hair behind her ear. Then she noticed September Rose behind him. "Who's that? Is that colored girl with you?" she murmured nervously.

"This is my friend September Rose. We're collecting cans for the war effort," he said. "Do you have any?"

"For the Victory Rally," September Rose added. "Our school is participating."

"Oh, you're doing a scrap drive?" Mrs. Markham seemed to have recovered from her surprise. "Yes, I read somewhere that we should start collecting them. I have a few in the garbage, I think." She opened the door wider and they stepped into the entryway. "Here, can you hold baby Robbie for a minute?" Mrs. Markham passed the baby to September Rose. Then she rolled up her sleeves and started going through her kitchen trash can. "Yes, there's one!" she said triumphantly, holding it up. "And another from yesterday." She rinsed the cans and dried them on a towel. Then she opened the cupboard and pulled out a can of wax beans and removed the top with a can opener. "I'll make these for dinner tonight, so you can have this one too," she said, dumping them into a saucepan and washing out the can. "Do you need a bag?" She pulled a shopping bag out of a drawer and put the cans in it. "Here, this will make them easier to carry. Just bring it back next time you come."

"Great, thanks!" said September Rose, handing her back the baby. "Bye, Robbie! He's sweet!"

Mrs. Markham cradled her son, rubbing her chin on the baby's fuzzy head. "Anything to bring the men home. I see your parents got you some new pants," she said to Gustave.

"No. I bought them. From tips and delivery money."

"Good for you!"

"Oh, yeah, I didn't notice before," September Rose said. "They look nice."

Gustave's legs were exhausted by the time he'd pedaled the two of them back to Mr. Quong's laundry, but
the bag Mrs. Markham had given them was stuffed with
cans, and several others were rolling loose around Seppie
in the basket of the bicycle. When they got back to the
laundry, Mr. Quong saw what they were doing. He asked
Gustave to watch the desk for a minute and went upstairs
to get them another bag and a few more empty cans to
add to their collection. Gustave and September Rose had
to stamp on a few to be able to cram the last ones in.

"Do you want to come to my apartment?" Gustave
asked. "We could wash and flatten the rest there, so
they'll be easier to carry."

"Are you sure?" September Rose asked.

"Why not? It's closer than yours."

With their overloaded schoolbags and the extra bags
of cans, it was tough going. Halfway to Gustave's apartment, several cans fell out of Mr. Quong's bag and rolled
down the sidewalk. Gustave stuffed them back in and ran
a few steps to catch up with September Rose, his schoolbag clanking on his back. As he did, he heard a shout
behind him.

"Hey! Boy! Come back!" It was a burly policeman,
waving something in the air.

Gustave saw the uniform and the dark bulge of a gun,
and his heart leaped in his chest. "Run!" he shouted to
September Rose, and he sprinted down the block. He
darted around the corner and paused to wait for her,
panting. But he didn't hear any running feet. He held his
breath and peered around the corner. The policeman had

turned his back and was walking away, and September Rose was jogging down the block toward him.

"Lose anything?" she called as she got closer, waving her hand in the air. She was holding something in a familiar shade of blue. Gustave reached for his head. His beret wasn't there. September Rose whacked the hat against her leg to get the dirt off it and handed it to Gustave. "What did you run away for?" she asked.

Gustave yanked his beret down over his forehead. "The police . . . ," he said uncertainly. "He had a gun. . . ." His voice trailed off. It was too hard to explain. In his head he had seen the Nazi soldiers with their guns, the border guards hunting for Jews. The French police smashing his family's furniture. His heart was still thudding against his ribs.

"This is America!" Seppie said impatiently. "The police are here to help."

"They used to help in France too."

When they got to Gustave's apartment, neither of his parents was home. He soaked some of the cans in the sink and tried to rub the labels off while September Rose walked around looking at things.

"It's you and your mother and father all in this one room? Where do you sleep? How can you stand not having any privacy?" September Rose burst out. Gustave looked at the dingy room, seeing it the way it must appear to her.

"On the sofa," he said. "It's comfortable enough."

"I like sleeping on our sofa too," September Rose said, sounding embarrassed. "Especially when I'm sick.

My Granma lets me play the radio and snuggle under a blanket there. Sometimes Chiquita jumps up onto my lap, although she's not supposed to. It's cozy on the sofa with her." She picked up Gustave's French Boy Scout manual and flipped through it for a moment before putting it back on the shelf. "Hey, I like your tablecloth! Is that French? Did someone make it?"

Gustave smiled to himself at the way Seppie always jumped from one topic to another. "My mother did." He tugged at the label on a can of vegetable soup, and it slipped off easily. "So, how's your brother?" he asked. "Is his eye better?"

"Yeah, it's lots better." September Rose's face clouded over. "But now he and Granma are fighting all the time."

As Gustave was peeling the labels off the next-to-last batch of cans and September Rose was cutting off the ends and flattening them, a key turned in the lock, and Maman came in.

"Oh!" she said, startled.

Gustave turned around, wiping his soapy hands on his pants. "Hello, Maman. This is September Rose from my school," he explained in slow, clear English. "We're collecting cans for the Victory Rally."

September Rose held out her hand. "Pleased to meet you, Mrs. Becker."

Maman looked confused. "Please to meet you," she repeated in English. She put the bag of groceries she was carrying down on the rickety table. "You and Gustave would like the biscuit?" she asked. "I make some tomorrow."

"You mean 'yesterday,' Maman," Gustave said. "You made them yesterday."

"Yesterday. You like try? We eat them all up tomorrow. Not good for Pesach."

September Rose looked confused. "She made cookies with the last of our flour," Gustave explained. "She wants to know if you'd like to have some. What we don't finish by tomorrow night, we'll throw out anyway, because on Wednesday it is Pesach—Passover. We can't eat flour then."

"Oh, is that like a Jewish Easter or something? It's Easter this Sunday. No, thank you, Mrs. Becker." September Rose fidgeted, twirling a braid between her fingers. "I need to go home now. I'll just take these cans. Gustave, see you tomorrow after the auditions. Meet you at the statue, right? Hey, and decide who you want to do your report on by then!"

September Rose stuffed the cans they had flattened into her schoolbag and left. Maman immediately switched into French.

"That's a new American friend?" she asked, twisting the shopping bag between her fingers. "She's a 'Negro'?" Maman used the American word.

*"Évidemment." Obviously.*

"Ah." Maman's brow furrowed. "She's a nice girl?"

"Of course."

"And well behaved?"

"Yes."

"Respectable? You're sure?"

"*Oui,* Maman! She's the one who gave me that American candy bar you liked so much."

"Oh, that's the girl who gave you the chocolate?" Maman smiled. "It was delicious!"

Gustave took the cans he had been soaking to the table. While Maman started dinner, he worked on the cans and thought about his oral report. He cut the ends off with a can opener and peeled off the labels, trying, just for fun, to get them to come off in one long strip. Underneath, the cans were surprisingly shiny. He held one up and let the light from the bare bulb over the table glitter on its surface. It was one small can, but together with lots and lots of others, it could help end the war. Gustave turned the can in the lightbulb's blunt glare, and for a moment it seemed to gleam with hidden, secret power. Power to defeat the Nazis. Power to win the war. All at once, Gustave knew who he wanted to do his oral report on.

Charles de Gaulle, leader of the Free French.

# ★ 30 ★

"Who is Charles de Gaulle?" Frank asked after history on Tuesday as he and Miles and Gustave left the classroom. Gustave had been a bit worried that Mr. Coolidge wouldn't consider Charles de Gaulle a historical figure, since he was alive, but Mr. Coolidge had nodded and taken down the name. "You're going to need to look at newspapers, Gustave," he had said. "It'll be hard to find information in books."

"He's a general in the French army," Gustave said as the three of them walked past the milk line in the cafeteria. "He's in London now, though. It isn't safe for him in France with the Nazis there. But from London he's organizing the French to fight back against the Nazis."

"Oh. I never heard of him. Hey, look! What are Martha and her friends doing at our lunch table?"

Martha was standing in front of the table where they usually sat, talking to Leo and some other boys, who were already eating lunch.

"We need help," she called as Gustave, Frank, and Miles sat down. She waved a roll of striped red, white, and blue ribbon at them. "Who's got a pocketknife with scissors that I can borrow?"

Frank pulled one out of his pocket and passed it down to her. Martha squeezed into a spot next to Leo and started cutting lengths of ribbon and passing them to the girls. "Tie this around your ponytail," she said, handing one to Caroline. She looked critically at Elsie. "Your hair is too short for a ponytail. But I guess you could wear it like a headband." She handed a piece of ribbon to Leo and turned so that her golden brown ponytail was in his face. "Can you tie this around mine?" she asked.

Leo grabbed the scissors, clicking them at her. "I'll just cut your ponytail off and then you won't have to worry about it!"

Martha ducked, giggling. "You wouldn't dare," she shrieked.

Leo slid the ribbon around her neck, pretending to choke her. "Is this where you wanted it?"

"Do it right, Leo!" she demanded.

After he had tied the ribbon in her hair, she tugged at the bow, smiled with satisfaction, and rolled up the remainder of the ribbon, tucking it into her bag. "Looking patriotic will definitely help us stand out this afternoon," she said.

It was easy to tell who Martha's friends were for the rest of the day. In the hallway Gustave overheard several comments from girls who weren't wearing ribbons.

"Sorry, girls!" replied Martha sweetly. "There just wasn't enough for everybody."

September Rose's braids were unadorned, and Gustave saw her looking at the ribbons. She caught his eye in the corridor and shrugged. "Who cares?" she said. "The auditions are about your voice, not how you look."

As the school day drew to a finish, excitement built. After the final bell rang, many of the students hurried to the auditorium. Gustave went to his cubby first. He wasn't in any hurry, since he was just going to watch. By the time he got to the auditorium, there was a big crowd of kids outside the door. A teacher was walking along the hall with a clipboard.

"Name?" she asked him.

"Gustave Becker," he answered automatically, standing on his toes and trying to see over the heads of the people in front of him, looking for September Rose. There she was, down at the front, near Martha and her crowd. Gustave got through the mob around the door and took one of the seats in the back of the auditorium. They were built on a slant, so he could still see the stage.

As the last of the students sat down, Mrs. Heine walked to the front of the stage. The microphone boomed as she tapped it, and the room quieted. "Welcome to the auditions for the Victory Rally chorus," she said. "When Mrs. Spencer or Mrs. Davis calls your name, come forward. Announce your song, step up to the microphone, and, at the pianist's signal, begin. Briskly, please. We don't want to be here all night."

Mrs. Heine took the center seat ten rows back. The

two teachers who had been asking for names as people came into the auditorium took up positions at the microphones on the sides of the stage. One of them called out the names of the first ten singers and showed them how to line up on the stage steps, and the auditions began.

Each student walked across to the microphone, announced his or her name and the name of a song, and began. Some were pretty good, but some were terrible, Gustave thought—almost as bad as he was. A lot of the students sang "The Star-Spangled Banner." Some sang "You're a Grand Old Flag."

Mrs. Heine stopped most of the singers after just a bar or two. "Thank you!" she called out imperiously, interrupting the song. "That's enough!"

The second group of ten students included Martha and most of her friends. Gustave watched as Martha gave a last tug on her hair ribbon and walked confidently onto the stage, her ponytail swinging. Suddenly everyone in the auditorium was paying close attention. "I'm going to sing 'Over There'" Martha announced. The piano music started, and she sang out, her voice loud and resonant, almost brassy, like a trumpet, Gustave thought.

Mrs. Heine let her sing to the end of the song. "Thank you, Martha," she said. Martha smiled and walked off-stage.

Elsie came out next. "Song?" asked the teacher at the piano.

"'You're a Grand Old Flag,'" she answered, twirling a finger nervously in her short blond hair. The pianist struck the opening notes. When Elsie began to sing, she let her hands drop to her sides and stood straight and confident. Her voice was sweet, birdlike, Gustave thought, and the best he had heard so far. Mrs. Heine let her sing all the way through as well.

One by one the girls with the patriotic ribbons came onstage. Some giggled and sang weakly, others did pretty well, but none of them sang as well as Elsie, or even Martha, Gustave thought. Then came a bunch of boys and some more girls Gustave didn't recognize. The audience was thinning out a little as some of the singers and their friends left, although most of them seemed to be staying to hear the others audition.

Gustave was getting bored. He took out his geography textbook and flipped to the section Mr. Coolidge had assigned. He was reading about crops in East Africa when he heard his name.

"Gustave Becker?" And then the teacher on the right of the stage repeated his name, sounding irritated and impatient. "Gustave BECKER?"

He jumped up, confused. The folding seat slipped up behind him, and his book fell to the floor with a loud bang. Someone giggled. Faces turned toward him.

"I am Gustave," he called, feeling heat rise to his face.

"Pay attention! It's your turn to line up and *sing*!"

*Sing?* His heart throbbed with panic. "Me? No! NO! I did not . . . I don't want to audition!" he stammered. A ripple of laughter went through the auditorium.

"Then why did you waste our time?" the teacher muttered. "Very well. Next?"

As the boy at the head of the line went up to sing, Gustave sat back down, hearing whispered comments and giggles around him. His face gradually cooled, and his heart slowly went back to its normal rhythm. He must have accidentally put his name on the audition list, he realized. That was why the teacher had been taking names at the door. He felt like an idiot. But at least he hadn't been forced to sing.

Suddenly he heard the name he'd been waiting for. "September Rose Walker. 'America the Beautiful,'" Seppie announced, clasping and unclasping her hands in front of her. It was the first time Gustave had ever seen her looking nervous.

The pianist struck up the first notes. September Rose seemed to wait just a beat too long. You can do it, Seppie! Gustave thought, trying to send her confidence. Sing!

*"Oh, beautiful for spacious skies,"* September Rose's voice started out so quietly he could hardly hear her.

Louder, Gustave thought. Louder!

*"For amber waves of grain."*

Her voice expanded, becoming rich and warm as she went on. Now she was singing naturally, singing full throated, the way she did in music class, the way she had in her kitchen, only now she was filling the vast expanse of the auditorium.

*"For purple mountain majesties*
*Above the fruited plain!"*

September Rose's voice soared like an eagle:

*"America! America!*
*God shed his grace on thee"*

235

Everyone was listening now. You couldn't help it. It was impossible not to follow her voice.

*"And crown thy good with brotherhood*
*From sea to shining sea!"*

In the pause as the last note faded away, the room was hushed. A moment later the whole auditorium erupted into applause. Seppie's face lit up with joy.

"Thank you," said Mrs. Heine, scribbling something down on her pad. "Next?"

Four more girls sang, none particularly well, and then the auditions were over.

In the crowded hallway outside the auditorium, Gustave spotted September Rose and squeezed through the crowd toward her. She was surrounded by girls congratulating her. Elsie had said something to September Rose, smiling, and was just moving away as Gustave got there.

"You were great!" he said. "You'll get the solo. I'm sure."

September Rose looked at him, still flushed with triumph, smiling slightly. "Elsie was good too," she said modestly. She lowered her voice slightly, grinning. "Even *Martha* wasn't half bad."

"They weren't as good as you," Gustave said, and he could tell from the excited look on her face that she knew it was true.

"Well, we'll see. Mrs. Heine is going to post the results in a few minutes. I'm going to wait. Then I'll get my stuff and meet you at the statue and we can walk over to the library."

She ran through the crowd to the spot where her friend

Lisa was waiting on the other side of the hall. Gustave got his things from his locker and came back to see if the results had been posted yet, but the students were still milling around, waiting.

"She's coming!" someone near the door called, and a moment later the auditorium door swung open, and Mrs. Heine came out with a list.

"May I have your attention, please!" she said, clapping her hands. The students quieted immediately. "I'll read the names of everyone chosen to sing at the rally," she proclaimed, "and then I'll announce the soloist." She began reading a long, alphabetized list of names. Gustave realized that September Rose was going to have to listen in suspense nearly all the way through before Mrs. Heine got to the "Ws."

Mrs. Heine was reading the letter "S" now. "Rose Sapienti, Martha Teagan—" Here she was interrupted by many loud shrieks from Martha's crowd. "Peter Underhill, Larry Upton," she went on. "And September Rose Walker. Those are all of our singers. And now for the one chosen to sing the solo." She paused dramatically.

"You made it!" Gustave wanted to say to September Rose, but she was on the other side of the hallway with a crowd of people in between them. Still, he caught a glimpse of her excited expression, and he knew that, despite what she had said, she was hoping that her name was coming.

"The soloist for the Joan of Arc Junior High 1942 Victory Rally chorus is . . ." Mrs. Heine paused dramatically. "Elsie James."

## ★ 31 ★

September Rose wasn't at the Joan of Arc statue when Gustave arrived, and she wasn't there five minutes later or ten minutes later. Had she changed her mind about going to the library? Gustave walked around for a while, looking downhill. The sun was out, and the river glinted between the trees, which were covered now with a faint haze of green. He was dipping his finger in a puddle and drawing the Cross of Lorraine in water all over the base of the statue when he heard feet trudging up the stairs to the park.

"Hi, Gustave," said September Rose. "Sorry I'm late. What's that?" Her eyes were red.

"It's the symbol of the French Resistance. It's Joan of Arc's symbol too."

She traced a finger over the double-barred cross. "I like it."

"Mrs. Heine should have picked you," Gustave said awkwardly. "But at least you're in the chorus."

September Rose stamped in a puddle and stared down at the ripples in the water. "I *was* better than Elsie, wasn't I? Or maybe I just wanted to think I was. Maybe you just think so too because you're my friend."

"No! You sang the best. Everybody thought so."

"Not everybody."

"Elsie sings fine. She's nice. But your singing is very . . . I don't know the English word. It makes you feel the music. It makes you think about the words."

*Brotherhood*, Seppie had sung. Brotherhood from sea to sea. Listening to her voice, Gustave had imagined the oceans shining. And he had thought about how brotherhood was a French value too. Liberty, equality, fraternity. There was something about the way September Rose had sung "America the Beautiful"—with such conviction, her voice bringing the words of the song so vividly to life— that was enough to make anyone hearing her believe in those words, or at least think they did, while they were listening.

"That's why everyone clapped for you," he said. "They didn't clap like that for Elsie."

"Mrs. Heine didn't want a soloist who looks like me, I guess. After she announced the results, when mostly everyone was gone, I was coming out of the restroom and I overheard her talking with another teacher. She said that Elsie sings like an angel and looks like one too. Elsie is *so* pretty," September Rose said wistfully. "I love her hair, don't you? It's kind of like a cross between cotton candy and sunshine. I wish I had hair like that."

Gustave shrugged. He watched September Rose

239

tracing the Cross of Lorraine with her finger over and over. "But her hair isn't like Josephine Baker's," he said finally.

September Rose looked up. "True." She rubbed her fingers over her eyes. "I should put on my curls." She took an eyebrow pencil out of a pocket in her schoolbag. Using her reflection in the puddle of water, she traced a curl onto each cheek. Then she pulled her long necklace out of another pocket, looped it twice around her neck, and lifted her chin defiantly, sniffing. "That's better, right?"

"And what Mrs. Heine said about angels . . . that's only true if angels have skinny voices."

September Rose laughed shakily. "Thin voices, you mean? Well, it's Mrs. Heine's loss," she said, blinking hard. "I get to sing solos at my church all the time. Let's go. The library's not that far. It's at Amsterdam and Eighty-First."

She started off, walking quickly and purposefully, not talking. Somewhere in the eighties, they crossed over to Amsterdam Avenue. It was a quiet street, but as they walked down it, an older blond boy suddenly jumped out at them from between two buildings and swung something in their direction. It hit Gustave's right calf, just below the knee. Sharp pain shot up his leg, and it buckled under him. "Hey!" he shouted angrily, doubling over. The boy sprinted down the street, leering over his shoulder and shouting something before vanishing around the corner. Gustave heard the words "Get out!" and "lover."

"Are you all right?" September Rose asked, glaring after the boy.

Gustave's pants leg was covered with white dust, and his leg hurt like crazy. He rubbed it, and it started to feel better. "What was he talking about?" Gustave asked.

"Why can't people just leave us alone?" September Rose burst out furiously.

"It was because we were together? What did it mean?" But he knew she wouldn't say.

"He's just some stupid hoodlum! He had one of those stockings filled with bits of chalk. They're really dangerous. I know a kid who lost an eye when he got hit with one on Halloween. Can you walk all right?"

Gustave nodded. He limped for a few steps, and then his leg was moving normally again. Farther down the block they saw a white patch on a knocked-over garbage can where the boy had whacked it. They walked most of the rest of the way to the library without talking.

Lover? Gustave thought. Had that boy been teasing him and September Rose, saying he was her boyfriend? But his shout hadn't sounded at all like teasing. It had sounded like a threat. It had happened twice now, in two different neighborhoods. This must be the kind of thing September Rose's brother was worried about. The reason he had told her they shouldn't be friends.

# ★ 32 ★

As Gustave and September Rose neared the library, they walked past a synagogue. September Rose looked at the Star of David carved into the pale stone wall. "I wanted to ask you something," she said. "Your friend who's missing. He's Jewish too?"

"Yes."

She played with the zipper on her schoolbag. "So he's in danger, you think? Because the Nazis don't like Jews?"

"Yes."

"He's our age? Is he all by himself?"

"He's with his mother, and maybe an uncle, we're not sure. His mother couldn't leave her job when my family left Paris, so they stayed. Now we don't know where they are."

September Rose twisted one of her braids as they waited for another light to change so they could cross the street. "What's he like?"

"Marcel?" So many memories rushed through Gustave's head that it was hard to know what to say. "He's smart, but not always good in school. He's good at sports, especially *le foot*—I mean, soccer. He's funny. He always plays tricks. On teachers sometime . . ." English was slipping away from Gustave, and his throat was getting thick, but words were tumbling out of him anyway, faster than he had ever spoken in English before. "He was a Boy Scout with me. One time in Paris we had a race to find things on a list. A search . . ."

"A scavenger hunt? Like, find a bottle cap, find a fish-hook, find a magnet, that kind of thing?"

"Yes. But part of it was we couldn't tell what we are doing. We needed a teacher to write his name—"

"A teacher's signature?"

"Right. So Marcel doesn't tell about the scavenger hunt. Instead, he says to the teacher that he collects signatures of famous people. The teacher laughs and says, 'But I am not famous!' Marcel says, very serious, 'Oh, monsieur, I think you will be someday.'"

September Rose smiled. "Smart! I bet your team won the scavenger hunt!"

Gustave shook his head, watching three yellow taxis going by, one right after the other, each one splashing through an enormous puddle and sending up a tall spray of water. "No." The dream about Marcel that he'd had on the ship rushed back at him. "One thing we never got in time. We never found a yellow feather." His throat hurt too much to get any more words out.

"A yellow feather. Hmm. If we wanted a yellow feather, I wonder where we could find one here," September Rose said. Her face was starting to look cheerful again. "I think Lisa's aunt has a parakeet. But parakeets are mostly green, not yellow, right? But I think some of their feathers are yellowish. Or, hey! You could dye a feather yellow the same way you color an Easter egg, with onion skins! Do you do that in France? Well, I guess Jews wouldn't. Here's the library, Saint Agnes."

It was smaller and less intimidating than the main branch, the one he'd visited with Cousin Henri and Jean-Paul back on his first day in New York, but it didn't have the majestic lions on each side of the door. Gustave and September Rose went up the steps together. Inside it was nearly silent, with high ceilings and furniture made of dark wood. September Rose pointed to the circulation desk. "You go there to get a card," she whispered. "If you have any trouble, I'll help you."

A friendly-looking woman with short, curly dark hair was behind the desk. When Gustave had explained what he wanted, she pushed some papers toward him.

"Fill these forms out in triplicate, please."

Gustave took them and went to the large wooden table where September Rose was sitting. The top form asked for his name, age, address, school, and parents' names. That was easy. But something the librarian had said was bewildering. He flipped through the papers looking for an envelope with a sticky flap.

"What am I supposed to lick?" he whispered to September Rose.

"What? Nothing!"

"She said, 'Lick it.'"

"I don't see anywhere to lick." September Rose flipped through the papers. "You just fill out that form three times."

"She said, 'In trip,' and then, 'Lick it.' Is something getting mailed somewhere?"

September Rose suddenly laughed out loud, and a man at the next table turned around and scowled at her. "Fill this out '*in triplicate*'! Is that what she said? That means fill out the same form three times! I'm going to go find some books on Abraham Lincoln for my report."

Gustave filled out his information three times and brought the completed forms back to the desk. As the librarian typed out his library card, September Rose returned and dropped a stack of books on the table with a loud thud.

"There!" The librarian handed him the small rectangle. "Don't mark up the books. And return them on time. Is it your first library card?" She smiled at him.

"My first library card in America," he said, fingering it.

"You're from France, aren't you? Well, have fun! Read lots of good books. Do you need help finding anything?"

"For school, I need to find three things about Charles de Gaulle. My teacher said probably newspaper articles, not books."

"That's ambitious! Well, let's see what we can find."

When she was finished helping him, he had several newspapers and two magazines. "And if you need a

French-English dictionary you can use this." She handed him a thick book, much bigger than their dictionary at home.

Gustave thanked her, then joined Seppie at the table. Even with the dictionary, the newspaper articles were hard to read, so Gustave was glad they were short. He had to look up lots of words. But an hour later he had taken notes and was starting to write his report. He looked over at September Rose, noticing that she had already written two pages. He worked hard for another hour, and with lots of erasing, checking the dictionary, and rewriting, he had written a short paragraph by the time a bell sounded and the lights flicked on and off three times. "They're closing!" September Rose slammed a book shut. "I'm almost done memorizing mine. How's yours going?"

"I wrote it. It's going to be short. I don't want a lot to memorize."

"Makes sense." She peeked at his paragraph. "*'Charles de Gaulle is a French hero,'*" she read out loud. "That's a good way to start. It'll make people pay attention."

When they walked past the circulation desk, the librarian was putting on her own coat.

"Did you see that?" September Rose whispered as they went out the front door of the library.

"What?"

"Her hat. It had a yellow feather in it. Like the one you and your friend Marcel couldn't find. Maybe it's a sign. Maybe it means that your friend's all right."

Outside, the buildings on the opposite side of the

street were silhouetted against a dusky blue sky. Gustave looked behind him. The librarian was coming down the steps, the yellow feather in her hat illuminated by the streetlight overhead. He didn't think that he believed in signs. "Maybe," he said.

September Rose looked unhappy, as if going outside had made her think about the auditions again. "Do you think Elsie James will stand in front for the whole performance at the Victory Rally?" she asked. "Do you think she's going to wear something special? She has the prettiest dresses. Remember that peach-colored one with the lace collar? She wears it to school sometimes. Maybe she'll wear that."

Gustave shrugged. "I never noticed it. At least Mrs. Heine didn't pick Martha."

"True—that would have been a lot worse." September Rose paused at the street corner. "I don't feel like going home and telling Granma about the auditions. She'll say it's all for the best or that everything happens in God's own time or something like that, and I don't want to hear it." She fidgeted, tightening the straps on her schoolbag. "My brother's Negro Youth Group is meeting at five-fifteen in back of a furniture store near here. Do you want to go with me?"

"He said you could come this time?"

"Not exactly." September Rose twirled a braid around her finger and let it go. "They're planning something. I want to go spy on them and see if I can find out what's going on and how he got that black eye. He wouldn't ever tell us what happened. I just want to hear what they say."

Her voice was nervous, but her eyes were gleaming with excitement.

"Won't they see us?"

"Not this time, they won't. They usually meet at people's apartments, but Alan's friend Willie works at the furniture store, and he has to get right back to work after the meeting, so they're gathering behind the building. I've been there once before with Alan when he was getting together with his friend. There's a shed. We could hide behind it. Come on—it'll be exciting!"

Gustave hesitated. His parents knew he was at the library, but he was supposed to be home soon, and he didn't want to get punished again. But spying did sound like fun. "As long as it won't take too long."

"I'm sure it won't—it's almost nighttime. Come on!"

The furniture store was squeezed between two larger businesses. September Rose looked about furtively and led the way around the side. "There's the shed," she whispered. "They should be here any minute. They're meeting on the back steps."

Gustave and September Rose crouched behind the shed in the shadows. It was a cool night, but not cold, and even in the heart of the city, the evening air smelled like warming earth and spring. A light above the back entry to the building lit up a set of concrete steps, a rectangle of cement, and a garbage bin.

Two Negro boys who looked as if they were high school age came out of the back door together.

"The one in the blue shirt is Alan's friend Willie," September Rose whispered.

A minute later two girls of about the same age walked down the alleyway and up the steps to join them. The four of them stood there talking quietly, their faces illuminated by the electric light.

September Rose nudged Gustave. "Alan," she mouthed. Gustave saw him approaching. His eye was still slightly bruised. Two other boys came around the side of the building right behind him.

"Thanks for coming on time," Willie said. "My break's over in fifteen minutes, so let's get right to it. I guess what we need to talk about is, do we stop picketing Baumhauer's because of the"—he grinned sarcastically—"shall we say, *unwanted attention* last time? We could move on to another department store for our Don't Buy Where You Can't Work campaign. There are a lot of other places Negroes shop where they won't hire any of us."

"We could picket Lindeman's instead," one of the girls said. She was wearing a gauzy green scarf over her hair.

"Yes!" The other girl nodded enthusiastically. "They were really rude to my sister there one day when she went in looking for a pair of gloves. They treated her like a thief."

"NO!" Alan said. "I mean, we can picket Lindeman's later, sure. But why take the pressure off Baumhauer's now, when they're really feeling it?"

"Um . . . because we don't want to get beat up again?" said another boy, who was built like a football player. "It could be much worse next time." September Rose drew in her breath sharply. The girl in the green scarf and the girl standing next to her both looked toward the shed. It felt as if they were staring directly at Gustave and September Rose.

"But that means it's working!" Alan said. "They're feeling the pinch."

"Did you hear something?" the girl in the green scarf asked. "Over there." Seppie put her hand over her mouth. Gustave's elbow suddenly felt unbearably itchy, but he bit down on his lip and stayed absolutely still, willing himself not to scratch it.

"Probably an alley cat. There are a lot of them around here," Willie said.

"I agree with Alan about this," said a tall, serious-looking boy who had been standing silently next to Willie. Everybody turned to look at him, as if they had all been waiting for him to speak. "Baumhauer's is losing sales. They hate losing money. That's what's going to make them change their mind about hiring Negroes. I say we keep it up. Let's vote. Everyone in favor of continuing the pickets at Baumhauer's?"

Six of the seven hands went up immediately, and then the boy who looked like a football player looked around and slowly raised his hand too.

"Good," said the boy with the serious face. "We're all agreed. So I'll let you know when we should meet there. Roberta, you're going to try to get us some attention from the newspapers? You'll talk to your cousin?"

The girl with the green scarf nodded. "Absolutely."

"Double V for Victory!" the tall, serious boy said, holding up his hand in a V and flashing it twice.

The others did the same. "Double V for Victory," th chorused quietly.

Willie glanced at his watch. "My break's over. I'v gotta go," he said, pulling open the back door of the fur niture store. The rest of the group stood talking quietly for a minute before leaving.

When footsteps were no longer audible, September Rose looked at Gustave. "So they *did* get attacked by someone. That's how Alan got that black eye. And he's going to go on picketing anyway," she whispered with a mixture of pride and fear in her voice. "Granma will hate that. But I don't get it: if people are beating them up, why don't they just tell the police?"

She chewed on her lip nervously as the two of them crept around the building and out to the street. Alan and his friends were gone. Across the way the door of a bar opened, and light and cigarette smoke spilled out as three American sailors emerged, singing loudly and off-key. Suddenly the street felt deserted and dangerous.

"It's late. We should take the bus," Gustave said. Seppie nodded. A moment later a bus came around the corner and they ran down the block and got on.

"Do you think I should tell Granma about Alan?" September Rose asked after the bus had gone a few blocks. "I don't think so. She'd just worry. Alan knows what he's doing."

"Yeah, he does." Gustave nodded. "And there are a lot of them in his group. They'll be together."

Gustave's stop came first. He jumped up as the bus

slowed. It lurched, startling him, and he dropped his bag. He leaned down to pick it up as the door hissed open in front of him.

"Careful, butterfingers!" September Rose said, grinning, as he went down the steps. Gustave waved from the sidewalk. "Butterfinger—Rich in dextrose! The sugar your body needs for energy!" she called.

"You sang best, Seppie!" Gustave called back.

She smiled at him through the window as the bus pulled away.

# ★ 33 ★

At Boy Scouts that week, Gustave was surprised to hear more talk about the Victory Rally. Everybody's school seemed to be going. The Lycée Français was sending a chorus, just like Joan of Arc Junior High, but none of the French Boy Scouts were in it.

"I have an exciting announcement!" Father René said as the meeting began. "Several Manhattan Boy Scout troops are going to lead the flag salute at the rally. So for today's activity, we're going to practice the flag ceremony."

"Is someone from our troop going to present the American flag, Father?" Xavier called out immediately. "Can I do it?"

"No, a different troop is leading the salute. But all the Boy Scouts will gather round and salute the flag, so we need to rehearse the ceremony. We'll also all say the Pledge of Allegiance in unison."

Gustave's homeroom class said the Pledge of Allegiance every morning. It worried Gustave every time.

"Father René, if we say the Pledge of Allegiance, are we saying we are more loyal to the United States than to France?" he asked.

Several of the boys started talking at once.

*"Mais non!"*

*"Jamais!"*

*No! Never!*

"France will always be my home," said Xavier.

"I agree with the boys," Father René said. "The pledge can mean that you are loyal to both countries."

They rehearsed the ceremony several times, and then Father René called for a break. "So I know that we've been very relaxed about coming to meetings in Boy Scout uniform, what with clothing shortages and new members and so on. But wear what you have of the uniform to the rally, boys. *Viens ici,* Gustave. I need to talk to you for a minute," he said, leading Gustave aside. "I have a hand-me-down Boy Scout sweater and a kerchief that you can wear for the ceremony," he said, handing him a bag. "You can keep them."

"Thanks." Gustave felt his face getting hot.

"It's nothing. I found them lying around in the storeroom. It'll be fun, this rally. You'll see!" The priest smiled his infectious smile. "Lots of kids, lots of music, rollerskating! Go on—join the others."

The rest of the troop was gathered around the snack table eating Passover almond macaroons that the rabbi's wife had made for them.

"These are so delicious!" Guy said, taking two more. "Why wasn't I born Jewish?"

"And you haven't even had matzoh ball soup yet," Bernard said. "Passover is the best holiday for food."

"I wonder if there's going to be good food at the rally," Xavier said.

"Food! Who cares about that? There are going to be so many girls there!" said André.

"Ooh, are you going to bring a date?" asked Xavier.

"Are you?" André asked ironically. "I'm going to meet girls there!"

"I might bring a date," said Maurice.

"Really? Who?" asked Jean-Paul.

"Her name's Jacqueline. She goes to my school."

"Is she pretty?" Xavier asked eagerly, reaching for another macaroon.

"Well, I guess you can decide for yourself when you see her, Tenacious Sponge!"

When the scout meeting was over, Gustave went to the church bathroom and, with the door latched securely behind him, tried on the sweater. It was dark blue wool, like the sweaters he had seen the other boys wearing, and it was thick and warm and scratchy. The cuffs were a bit ragged, and the name Mathieu was written on the tag on the back of the neck, but he could cut that off when he got home and no one would ever know that it hadn't always been his. He tied the bandana around his neck. It felt stiff and new. Maybe it wasn't really secondhand. Maybe Father René had actually bought it for him and fibbed about it, he thought, flushing. He quickly took the bandana and the sweater off and shoved them back into the bag.

Jean-Paul started banging on the door just as he opened it. "What took you so long? Come on!"

None of the other scouts were around. Gustave opened the bag and showed him as they left the church. "Father René gave me these, so I could wear the uniform at the rally," he whispered. "He said they used to belong to some other Boy Scout. But I think this kerchief is new. Do you think so?"

Jean-Paul reached in and fingered it. "It does feel new. But maybe that other scout quit before wearing it much."

"Or maybe Father René bought it for me and just said it was secondhand. He's a priest—he shouldn't fib!" Gustave kicked angrily at a piece of newspaper on the sidewalk.

"He might have bought it, I guess. Or maybe Rabbi Blum did."

Somehow that was a little less embarrassing. "Maybe."

"So are you going to invite a girl you know to skate with you at the rally?" Jean-Paul asked him, grinning. "Someone from your school?"

"I don't know. What about you?" Gustave asked his cousin.

Jean-Paul laughed. "Remember, they still have me in fourth grade! If I went with a girl from my class, it would be like skating with my baby sister!"

# ★ 34 ★

That evening Gustave heard Papa bounding up the steps to the apartment. "Great news!" he called, bursting in, carrying a bag full of food, and smiling in a way Gustave hadn't seen him smile in a long time. "I got a promotion! Tonight we celebrate!" He was in a great mood, and he listened to Gustave reciting his paragraph about Charles de Gaulle out loud over and over again as Maman roasted the whole chicken he had bought. After they'd feasted on it, as Maman cleared the plates and boiled water for tea, Gustave put his notes away and recited his speech again for both his parents. "Bravo!" Papa applauded. "Listen to you! Giving a speech in English!"

"Maybe you should show them the Cross of Lorraine," Maman said. "Don't just say 'a double-barred cross.' You could draw one on the blackboard."

"Good idea. But what if I forget my whole report?"

"Oh, how could that happen?" Papa scoffed. "You could say it in your sleep. And when you've given it, we should have a big celebration for your speech and my new job! What do you say—ready to move into a new apartment, Lili?" He squeezed out his tea bag and laid it on a saucer.

Maman put the used tea bag in her cup and poured hot water over it. Gustave watched as tea seeped out of the bag in a paler shade of brown, swirling into her cup. "Maybe when our year in this apartment is up," she said. "Meanwhile, we'll keep saving."

Gustave bit into an apple. "Congratulations, Papa!" he said with his mouth full. "Aunt Geraldine was wrong about you not being able to get a better job."

"Well, I'll only be supervising the janitors," Papa said. "I'd still like to get a position as a fabric buyer. But with a son who can give speeches in English—with you helping me, soon I'll be able to speak enough English to do some more interesting work. It's all happening! I told you things would work out for us in America!"

Gustave thought Papa was probably right that he could give his oral report in his sleep. Still, he practiced it many times over the weekend, and on his way to school on Monday morning, he repeated it again and again in his head. He waited nervously for history class, which was last period. As he went into the classroom, he caught September Rose's eye, and she gave him a quick thumbs-up sign.

"So, oral presentations today!" Mr. Coolidge beamed at the class as if he couldn't possibly think of anything more exciting. "Who wants to go first?"

September Rose raised her hand.

"September Rose Walker! Wonderful." He consulted his list. "September Rose is going to tell us all about Abraham Lincoln."

September Rose stood calmly in front of the class, looking elegant in a plaid skirt and shiny brown shoes, telling them about Abraham Lincoln's early days in a log cabin, about his family, his opposition to slavery, the Civil War, and his assassination. "Abraham Lincoln was a very important president," she concluded, "because he put an end to slavery."

The class applauded politely as she sat down. "Excellent!" Mr. Coolidge said. "Now—what about you, Leo? Ready to tell us about Lou Gehrig?"

Gustave found it hard to listen to the oral reports that followed, because his heart was pounding so loudly. Instead, he ran the words of his own oral report over and over in his head.

"Gustave Becker," Mr. Coolidge said finally. "Your turn. Are you ready to present?"

Gustave took a deep breath, nodded, and made it to the front of the room. He drew the Cross of Lorraine on the blackboard, his sweaty fingers damp against the piece of chalk. When he turned to face the other students, he realized how big the classroom was. Row after row of faces looked at him, all of them native English speakers, some of them kids who had laughed at his accent before, all of them waiting to hear him speak. At least he looked all right, because he was wearing his new pants and tie. He took a deep breath, and his mouth went dry. Mr. Coolidge nodded at him warmly.

Gustave swallowed. His mind was completely blank. Suddenly he couldn't remember a single word of his oral report. "Charles de Gaulle . . . ," he said desperately. He couldn't remember what came next. Somebody yawned loudly. Feet shuffled.

"Why don't you start by telling us about what you've drawn on the board?" Mr. Coolidge said encouragingly. "Why is this symbol important?"

But if he didn't say his report exactly the way he had memorized it, he was sure he wouldn't remember anything. "Ch-Charles de Gaulle . . . ," he stammered again. "Charles de Gaulle . . ."

Leo smirked in the front row. The boy next to him groaned softly. Gustave's armpits prickled with sweat.

A chair scraped in the rear of the classroom, and heads turned. September Rose stood up and looked into Gustave's eyes. "*Charles de Gaulle is a French hero,*'" she quoted, and then she sat down.

Relief flooded over Gustave. "Charles de Gaulle is a French hero," he said, and all the other words from his report rushed back into his head. He started to speak, telling the class about the Free French; about the Cross of Lorraine, Joan of Arc's symbol; about the French Resistance and the French people fighting back against the Nazis. "Charles de Gaulle is an important historical figure because he is trying to save France," he concluded.

Gustave heard roaring in his ears as the class applauded. He had done it. He had given a speech in English. A short one, but still a speech. In front of lots of people. He felt dizzy with relief and happiness as he walked back to his seat.

As he sat down, he heard a voice murmur, "How did *she* know his oral report?"

Gustave looked at Seppie, and she grinned at him.

As he went down the school steps that afternoon, he heard feet running behind him. "Gustave!" September Rose called, catching up with him. "I guess the cat's out of the bag now."

"The cat . . . ?" He looked to see if there was one nearby.

She laughed. "It's a saying. I mean, everybody will know we're friends now, after history class. They'll probably say we're boyfriend and girlfriend and tease us. Do you care? I don't. Anyhow, something bigger is going on. Today's the day," she said, dropping her voice to a whisper. "I heard Alan talking to Willie on the phone. They're going back to Baumhauer's department store to picket this afternoon. There's a big sale today, because it's the Monday after Easter, so they thought it was a good day to get attention."

"Are they picketing right now?"

"Some of them might be there already. Alan won't be. He doesn't get out of work until five p.m. He's going over right afterward. I heard him tell Willie. And you know what? I'm going too. I know where Baumhauer's is, so what's to stop me? Somebody needs to keep an eye on Alan and make sure he's safe."

"You're going all by yourself? What if something bad *does* happen?"

"I'm not going to picket. Alan would never let me. I'm just going to hide and watch."

Gustave looked at her. Her face was fierce and brave and just a little bit scared. "I'm coming with you," he said.

"Really? It might get dangerous."

"That's what I was telling *you*!"

"He's my brother. I have to be sure he's all right."

"Then I'm coming too."

"Well, okay. But don't come to my apartment. I don't want Granma to get wind of what we're doing. She'd never let me go. Baumhauer's is on West One Hundred and Twenty-Fifth Street. Let's meet at the corner of One Hundred and Twenty-Fifth and Seventh Avenue at five-fifteen."

"All right. I'll see you there."

"And, Gustave?" Her voice was tense again. "Wear dark clothes. So we'll be hard to see."

# ★ 35 ★

It was funny, really, that September Rose hadn't noticed how few clothes he had, Gustave thought that evening as he walked uptown. Girls were supposed to care about that kind of thing. Luckily, the clothes he did have were dark in color.

As the street numbers got higher, Gustave saw more and more Negro faces on the street. He hadn't been so far north before. By the time Gustave got to 125th Street, he hadn't seen any white faces for several blocks, and he was feeling self-conscious about his own skin color. It was uncomfortable to stand out in that way. September Rose must have that feeling all the time at school, he realized.

She was at the corner, waiting in the dusk. She didn't have on her usual bright red coat. An old navy blue men's jacket hung, massive and shapeless, around her slender body, but she had drawn her elegant curls on her cheeks, and under the jacket he spotted the gleam of her long necklace. Something darted toward Gustave, yipping, as he approached.

"You brought Chiquita?" He squatted down to pat her behind the ears. "How are we going to hide if we have a dog with us?"

September Rose's face was pale. "I know! I couldn't help it! I told Granma I was going over to Lisa's to study, and just as I was going out the door, she said to bring Chiquita, because she's been barking all afternoon. She didn't get a long enough walk today. I didn't know what to say to get out of it. Then Chiquita gave me so much trouble at One Hundred and Third Street. There's a sweet-potato vendor there, and you know how she loves those. I had to pull and pull to get her to go past."

Gustave nodded, remembering the buried orange potato Chiquita had dug up from the snow in the park that day.

"I haven't fed her dinner yet, and she just pulled and whined like crazy. It was murder getting her past there."

"Let's find her something to chew on. That'll keep her quiet." Gustave looked around. Big, brightly lit stores lined the wide street. Shoppers were going in and out of them carrying bags. A few trees overhung an alleyway. He ran toward them, and under one he found a fallen branch. He ran back to September Rose. "Here, Chiquita," he said, giving it to her. "That should work."

"Thanks! Smart thinking." September Rose was gazing apprehensively down the street. "Look. I see them gathering. Down there. That's Alan with the tan band on his hat."

A cluster of young Negro men and women was forming outside one of the brightly lit stores. Gustave recognized Roberta from the meeting behind the furniture store, because she was wearing the same green scarf over her head, and Willie, as well as the serious boy who seemed to be the leader. Alan was handing out picket signs. When everyone had one, Willie said something, and they all held up a hand and flashed the double V at each other. Then they formed a loose oval on the sidewalk in front of the store and began to walk, holding the signs high. "Don't buy where you can't work!" Willie started the chant, and the others picked it up. "Don't buy where you can't work!"

Shoppers coming out of the store looked at them before walking away. Others who had been about to go in paused on the sidewalk. One Negro woman began talking to Roberta, walking with her while she marched.

"Come on!" September Rose whispered. "I want to get closer. I can't hear what's going on."

They crept down the street, staying out of the light spilling from the buildings.

"There!" September Rose hissed, pointing at a mailbox. "Let's hide behind that."

They squatted in the shadows. Chiquita flopped down by them, contentedly gnawing on the stick. Gustave and Seppie peered around the side of the mailbox together. A supercilious-looking white man strode out of the store and said something to the protestors. Willie stopped marching to talk to him.

"What's he saying? I can't hear!" September Rose hissed.

"I can't either."

The man turned abruptly and went back into the store. Willie rejoined the marchers. Another chant began. "Victory abroad, victory at home! Victory abroad, victory at home!"

Alan put down his sign and moved to a spot on the sidewalk in front of the picketers. He began handing out leaflets to the people going by. "I can carry a gun for Uncle Sam, but I can't carry a crate for Baumhauer's," he called. "Baumhauer's discriminates against Negroes."

September Rose watched him, entranced.

A crowd of people was beginning to gather, reading the leaflets, murmuring in agreement, and watching the marchers.

Suddenly one of the marching girls gave a shrill cry, and a rock clattered against the sidewalk. Blood streamed down the girl's face. "Shana!" Roberta cried out, dropping her sign and running to her friend.

More rocks flew through the air. Three burly white men advanced on the group. Several more appeared on the sidewalk behind them. "Go home! Get outta here!" a thick voice shouted, and an empty can hit the sidewalk.

"Oh, no! Oh, no! Those rotten skunks!" September Rose moaned. "Why aren't there any police around?"

The crowd that had gathered quickly dispersed, and the picketers clustered together. Somebody stepped on a dropped picket sign, and Gustave heard a sharp crack. The white men remained a few yards away, jeering and occasionally hurling something. And then a broad-chested white man wearing a red-checked shirt ran forward and shoved Willie in the chest with both hands, knocking him to the pavement. The other white men closed in around the Negro teenagers, shouting and punching.

"Alan!" September Rose screamed, jumping to her feet. Gustave grabbed her arm, holding her back.

Down the street a siren wailed and lights flashed. Chiquita stopped gnawing and lifted her head, her ears alert.

"Finally, the police are coming!" September Rose cried in relief, shaking her arm free.

Three police cars wailed to a stop. Six policemen ran toward the chaos, shouting and wielding clubs. But something was wrong. In the blur of bodies and fists in front of him, Gustave saw that the police weren't pushing back the white attackers. They were hitting the Negro teens. September Rose darted forward, and Gustave grabbed her shoulder again. Chiquita tugged frantically on the leash. Alan emerged from the chaos of bodies, and a cop tackled him, slamming him against the sidewalk. September Rose screamed. Another cop closed in and raised his club. The white man in the red-checked shirt came out of the crowd, spat at Alan, and kicked him in the side.

"Alan!" September Rose shrieked. She struggled out of Gustave's grip and ran toward her brother, dropping Chiquita's leash. "Stop!" she shouted at the policemen. "He didn't do anything wrong!"

Gustave grabbed for the leash, missed, then ran after Seppie, trying to catch her and pull her back. With her thin hands September Rose grabbed at the policeman who was holding her brother, and the policeman swung around. She fell hard to the sidewalk, and her long necklace broke, beads spilling all over the cement.

Gustave knelt down by her, and someone stepped on his foot. Hot red pain shot up his leg.

"Seppie!" Alan's voice was shouting through the din. "Get out of here! Go home!"

Seppie's eyes were closed. "Are you all right?" Gustave asked, grabbing her hand. Her eyes opened. Out of the corner of his eye, he saw the policeman lifting his club. "Stop!" Gustave shouted up at him. "She's his little sister!"

The policeman stepped backward and fell on the beads, landing heavily on his side and swearing as he pushed himself back up. Gustave and September Rose scrambled up from the sidewalk. Chiquita circled the scene, snarling and yipping at the police. A shot rang out. Chiquita's ears went back, and she bolted down the block, her leash dragging. The cop who had knocked September Rose down pulled at her arms and yanked them together behind her back.

"We were over there!" Gustave shouted to the cop, pointing at the mailbox. "She's thirteen! She didn't do anything!"

"Get Chiquita!" September Rose shrieked at him.

"What are *you* doing here?" A red-faced cop grabbed Gustave's collar and stared down at him. "Why are you mixed up in this? Let the girl go, Riley," he called. "These two are just kids."

He blew his whistle shrilly. The thudding stopped,

but somewhere Shana was crying, a thin, high wail that went on and on.

The policeman holding September Rose let go of her, and she ran to Gustave. "You kids get out of here," the red-faced cop said. He turned to the other policeman. "Take the rest down to the station. Book 'em. Assault. Disturbing the peace."

"No!" September Rose cried. "They didn't do anything! My brother's hurt! He needs help!"

The red-faced cop turned. "You brats get out of here before I change my mind," he snarled.

"Come on." Gustave pulled her arm. He got her across the street and helped her sit down on a bench at a bus stop. She was breathing raggedly.

"I'll tell Granma where you're at!" she screamed as Alan was handcuffed and pushed into a police car. "Don't worry!"

The three police cars pulled away from the curb, and the sidewalk, littered with broken picket signs, was dark and empty.

September Rose took a deep, gasping breath.

"Are you hurt?" Gustave asked her.

"I'm fine," she said. "But Alan isn't! And where's Chiquita?"

# ★ 36 ★

September Rose wasn't fine, not really. Her face was scratched, and a trickle of blood ran down her cheek, blurring one of her spit curls. But she insisted on walking down 125th Street in the direction Chiquita had gone, calling her.

Soon September Rose started to limp, and the limp got worse and worse. Finally she stopped, leaning against a lamppost.

"My ankle's twisted, and it really hurts," she said. "Poor Chiquita. The loud sounds must have terrified her, like that time in Maryland with the fireworks."

"You have to go home. Lean on me," Gustave said. September Rose was in too much pain to argue. "Anyway, maybe Chiquita ran home," Gustave added.

September Rose brightened. "Oh—maybe!"

With her arm around Gustave's shoulders, Seppie hobbled, wincing, down the long blocks back to 99th

Street. "Chiquita!" she called as they went. "Cheeky! Come!"

No little feet came pattering toward them.

"Maybe somebody let her into the building," Gustave said as they got to 99th Street.

"Cheeky! Cheeky!" September Rose called on each floor as they went up the stairs. When they got to the fourth floor, Miss Noelle's door opened.

"Have you seen Chiquita, Miss Noelle?" September Rose asked.

"No, honey child, I sure haven't. Oh, you're hurt?"

Just then Mrs. Walker opened the apartment door.

"Is Chiquita home, Granma?" September Rose cried, hobbling forward into the light.

"Chiquita? Oh, Lord have mercy! What happened to you? Gustave, what happened to her? Oh, my baby girl!" She ran toward her.

"Alan . . . ," September Rose started to say as Mrs. Walker reached her.

"You hurt your ankle? Oh, Seppie!" she moaned. "I might have known it had something to do with your fool brother. Noelle, can you come help me tend to this child?"

"I have to go back out and find Chiquita!" September Rose cried.

"You're staying right here. Oh, my Lord, your poor face too!"

September Rose turned as the two elderly ladies hustled her in the door. "Please find Chiquita!" she called as Gustave started down the steps.

But where in this vast city did you look for one little dog? Gustave walked the blocks around 99th Street, calling into the night. He retraced their route all the way back up to 125th Street, calling and calling, peering into every dark alley. At 125th Street he turned around. His feet were getting sore, and he couldn't bear to look at his watch to see what time it was. His parents must be going crazy. Maybe the question he should be asking was, where would a small dog who didn't like loud sounds go for comfort in this enormous, noisy city? Somewhere small and dark and safe? Or somewhere warm with good food?

*Sweet potatoes!* That was it. Where had September Rose said Chiquita had stopped and pulled, whining for a roasted sweet potato? One Hundred and Third Street.

Gustave headed south again. Would the vendor still be there? "Chiquita!" he called as he got closer. "Chiquita!"

He saw a cart with an umbrella a block away and smelled roasting potatoes. And then, as he ran toward the cart, calling, a bedraggled little dog emerged from under it, chewing on something orange.

"There you are! Silly dog!" Gustave grabbed the dangling leash jubilantly.

"Is she yours?" The sweet potato vendor smiled at Gustave, showing two missing front teeth. "What a sweetheart. She's been hanging around here for an hour or so. She won't need any dinner now. She's eaten so many potatoes!"

"Thanks!" Just to be sure the little dog couldn't get

away again, Gustave gathered her up into his arms and ran all the way back to 99th Street. He panted up the stairs with Chiquita wriggling in his arms and rang the doorbell. Mrs. Walker answered it, her face drawn and worried.

Gustave saw September Rose on the sofa behind her. At the window brightly colored tin-can birds swayed and jingled in the gust of air from the open door.

"Chiquita!" September Rose cried out joyfully. "You found her!"

Gustave put the little dog down, and she darted across the room and leaped on top of September Rose. "I thought I'd never see you again!" September Rose said. She put her face into the little dog's fur and started to cry in great, gasping sobs.

# ★ 37 ★

After that, things were a bit of a blur. Gustave's parents were upset when he got home, but after he told them the whole story, their anger turned to concern. "Their poor grandmother," Maman said. "What's she going to do now, with her grandson hurt and in jail? Still, I thought it wasn't such a good idea for you to spend so much time with that girl, Gustave."

Papa nodded. "The way things are in this country, it's just asking for trouble, being friends with Negroes. It's tough enough being in a new country. Why make things harder on yourself?"

Hot anger washed over Gustave. "Her name's September Rose, not 'that girl'! And we *are* friends! It's not her fault that Negroes are treated badly here. And what you're both saying about not being friends with Negroes—people said the exact same thing about Jews in France!"

Gustave felt shaky and sick. He had never felt so different from his parents before. "And anyway, it isn't supposed to *be* like that here in America!" he added miserably.

Maman looked at him worriedly. Papa set down his cup of tea, and it clattered against the saucer. "Gustave, this is something you know as well as we do by now, I'm afraid. The grand proclamations countries make and what really happens, how people really behave—those are often two very different things."

September Rose wasn't in school the next two days. On the second day she was out, Mrs. McAdams asked in homeroom if anyone could bring September Rose her homework assignments. Gustave immediately raised his hand to volunteer, ignoring the comments and giggles coming from the back of the classroom.

After he rang the Walkers' doorbell, he waited longer than usual, and then he heard a thumping sound. September Rose opened the door, standing on one foot. Her face was still scratched, and she looked tired. "I'm supposed to keep my foot up," she said, hopping back to the sofa. "Come on in."

Gustave perched on the armchair across from her, watching her prop her bandaged foot up on a stack of pillows. "I brought your homework," he said. "Does your ankle hurt a lot?"

"No, it's much better today. I'll be able to walk tomorrow." The swinging door to the kitchen opened slightly. Chiquita's nose poked through, and then she pattered in, wagging her tail. September Rose brightened. "Look who's here, Cheeky! Your rescuer!"

Chiquita licked Gustave's hand, stayed to be patted for a moment, and then jumped up next to September Rose. Seppie lifted her up and rubbed her face against Chiquita's. "Thanks so much for finding her," she said. "I was so worried that maybe she'd gotten hit by a car." Her voice turned hard. "Or kicked by one of the cops, and that she was curled up wounded in an alley somewhere and I'd never see her again."

Now that she had mentioned what had happened with the police, Gustave thought it was all right to talk about it. "Do the cops still have your brother?" he asked hesitantly.

"No. Alan's home now. He's sleeping."

"Is he all right?"

"The doctor said he had a lot of bruising and two cracked ribs. It hurts when he takes a deep breath." Her voice turned angry. "And the police charged *him* with assault and disrupting the peace. Him and the others in his Negro Youth Group."

Gustave stared at her, confused. "Wait—who is charged with assault? Alan and his friends? Not those men who attacked them?"

"Yes. It's so unfair!" September Rose was almost crying. "Only Alan and his group are being charged. And they didn't do anything wrong. But the men who attacked them—not a single thing is happening to them. That man who kicked Alan and broke his ribs—the cops just let him go! It's so unfair, Gustave. Alan's court date is next month. We're going to have to hire a lawyer, and lawyers are really expensive. Granma is so upset. She's off talking to some ladies from the church now."

Gustave stared at her. "I'm really sorry," he said finally.

"I know. Can you believe this is happening?" Her voice was loud and shaky. "Remember that song I sang at the audition? 'Crown thy good with brotherhood!'" she quoted bitterly. "I mean, I knew about bad things a few stupid white people did, of course. Calling Negroes dumb names. Not letting us in some restaurants and theaters and stuff. Looking at us suspiciously in stores. But in school, at Joan of Arc and back in elementary school, the teachers always said, 'The police are your friends.' 'If you get in trouble, go to the police.' I was so dumb, I believed it!" She pounded the sofa cushion, almost crying. "They beat up Alan, and now *he* has to go to court!"

"Seppie! Settle down!" Alan was standing in the doorway of the living room. He nodded at Gustave, to Gustave's surprise. Moving carefully, he eased himself down onto the sofa next to his sister, patting her on the back. "It's not so bad, String Bean."

"How can you say that?" She wiped her eyes roughly with the back of her hand.

"What happened was lousy, of course, you're right. But it's actually good, in a way, because now people are going to hear about our protest."

"What do you mean? How?"

"Roberta's cousin was there. He got some photographs

of us all being attacked by the police. He's taking them to the *Amsterdam News* and then some other Negro newspapers."

"You think they'll write about what happened?" Seppie's face brightened slightly.

"The store not hiring Negroes, the protest, and the attack by the cops—all of it. It's big news. Didn't you hear the phone ring earlier today? That was Willie, telling me that one of the ministers at our church wrote a letter to the editor of the *New York Times* about 'respectable Negro teens being attacked during a peaceful protest.' He just heard that it's going to be printed tomorrow!"

"Really? The *Times*? That's good. . . ." Her voice trailed off.

Alan cuffed her in a friendly way. "It's better than good, you moron! That's what we're doing it all for! People paying attention is what's going to make things change."

"And I expect sales aren't so good at Baumhauer's right now," Gustave added.

Alan looked at him as if he had forgotten he was there, then grinned. "You're right, Frenchie! No Negroes are shopping there now, and their profits are *way* down."

"His name is Gustave!" September Rose protested, swatting her brother.

"Goose-tav." Alan made a face. "If you insist, Seppie, but that name's a real tongue twister. Anyway, listen, Goose-tav. Sorry about when we met. I guess I was wrong about you. You're all right. You two just be careful when you're together, hear? But thanks for getting my sister home that night. And thanks for finding her dog.

She wouldn't know what to do with herself without that mangy mutt, would you, Sep?"

"Who you calling a mangy mutt? *You're* a mangy mutt!" September Rose jumped up and tossed Chiquita's ball at her brother. The ball bounced off his shoulder and hit the tin-can birds dangling in front of the window, making them jingle against each other.

"Ooh, you're in for it now!" Alan snatched up the rubber ball and hurled it back at her as she held a pillow in front of her face as a shield, giggling madly.

September Rose was back in school the next day, on crutches. Gustave hardly got a chance to speak to her, because she was suddenly so popular. At lunch and recess, lots of kids asked for a turn on her crutches, swinging around the cafeteria and the blacktop, yelling and laughing and lining up for extra turns. But the next week September Rose was walking again, so things were back to normal, except that, now that it was the week before the Victory Rally, the chorus members got out of all their afternoon classes to rehearse.

"No geography for me today!" September Rose exulted to Gustave one day after lunch. "Don't you wish you were in the chorus now?"

Gustave shuddered. "Absolutely not!"

When the day of the rally came, excitement in the school was so high that most of the teachers gave up on getting the students to do any real work. School ended early, right before lunch, and Gustave hurried home. He had to change into his scout uniform and his new American pants and get his bag of flattened cans. Jean-Paul was coming over, and then the two of them were going to take the subway down to Battery Park together for the rally.

Gustave checked his family's mailbox in the lobby, as he did every day. His fingers felt only the cool metal. Nothing. He felt his usual stab of disappointment, but he shoved it away, slamming the door of the mailbox shut and running up the stairs. Today was a day for celebration.

The apartment was empty. Papa was at work, of course, and Maman was off delivering her completed piecework to the factory. But on the white tablecloth was a pale blue airmail envelope. N.M., La Chaise, Saint-Georges, he read.

*This is it,* a voice inside him said. *This letter has the information about Marcel.* A shiver ran through him. He picked up the envelope. So thin, so light. But what was in it might be the most important thing in the world.

As always the envelope had been cut open at each end by the censors and resealed. Gustave took a deep breath, ran a shaky finger under the flap, and tore it open. A flimsy sheet of pale blue paper fell out.

*28 March, 1942*

*Cher Gustave,*

*Finally your letters came—two of them on the same day. Weird. They must have gotten held up somewhere. So how's*

*it going? Do you like life in America more now that you are
getting used to it? Not much is new here in sleepy Saint-
Georges, and that's the way we like it.*

*You wanted to hear more of my rutabaga recipes, but
we've run out of rutabagas. Lately we've been eating Jerusalem
artichokes for every meal. And believe me, I am thoroughly
sick of them! At this point I would jump up and down if I saw
a rutabaga. Jerusalem artichokes for breakfast, lunch, and
dinner—mashed, boiled, and in soup. And then yesterday I
tried to make a quiche. But with only two eggs and gritty flour,
it was mostly a paste of mashed Jerusalem artichoke. Papa ate
it, but he looked a little green!*

*By the way, I'm glad you enjoyed my colorful letter. I had
to look really closely because your handwriting was faint at
times in your last letter. Thanks for sending greetings from our
friend Lorraine—what a surprise!*

*I am writing this at recess. Sylvaine is racing Yvonne
around the school yard. I can see that Sylvaine will win. Jean
and Henri are kicking a ball. It just rolled over a game of
marbles. Philippe won Armand's best green glass shooter and
then the ball rolled over the game and destroyed it. I think Jean
and Henri kicked the ball over the game on purpose!*

Gustave laughed. Philippe was awful. He was the one
who had put that note saying "Hitler was right" on Gustave's desk last year.

*I think we'll be called in for history class soon. Simone is
standing next to me. She wants to talk about her mother's new
baby all the time. Alice is listening to her, but I'm so bored*

*hearing her going on and on about how cute the baby is! I'm watching the little kids playing tag instead. Some of the others are using sticks to play swords. I go into so much detail because I know you miss us and want to know everything that is going on here. Our friend, you know who I mean, he is playing hide-and-seek. He is very good at hiding. Robert is drawing something on the pavement. Eloise and Monique are whacking at a tree with sticks. I have no idea why.*

*So are you ever going to meet any movie stars? Write and tell me more about life in the US when you can.*

*Je t'embrasse,*
*Nicole*


Gustave's mouth felt dry with disappointment. There was nothing about Marcel. Nothing at all. Not even a sentence saying there was no news. It was as if she had forgotten what Gustave was most worried about. And she had put in all that meaningless stuff about the other kids at school. Who cares what they're all doing on the playground so far away? Gustave thought angrily. What a waste. Why had she even bothered spending the money to send it?

Still, it was news from France. He read it over again carefully. And then he sucked in his breath.

"Our friend, you know who I mean, *il joue à cache-cache." He is playing hide-and-seek.*

All at once, as if those words had turned red, Gustave knew that they were a secret message, hidden from the

Nazi censors, from the prying eyes that would look over the letter before it left Occupied France. "He is very good at hiding." She was telling him that Marcel was in hiding! Marcel was alive!

The air in the apartment shimmered, and Gustave let out a deep, shuddering breath. Wherever Marcel was—the letter didn't say, maybe because Nicole didn't know—he was alive. Hiding and alive.

Some time later Gustave realized that he could hear an insistent banging at the door, and that it had been going on for a while. Still in a daze, and still holding the letter, Gustave opened the apartment door. It was Jean-Paul, looking impatient, with a bag full of cans. "What's wrong?" he asked immediately. "What took you so long? What's going on?"

"Marcel is alive," Gustave said.

"She wrote it in code? You're sure that's what it means?" Jean-Paul was asking in disbelief, sitting at the table next to Gustave and bending over the letter. "You're absolutely sure?"

"Positive. We always write some stuff in code so the censors don't understand it. She couldn't mean anyone else by 'our friend, you know who I mean.' And right before that she says, 'I know you want to know everything that is going on here.' She knows I want to know what happened to Marcel more than anything! And why would I care what everyone else is doing on the playground? She just put that stuff in so she could disguise that she was talking about Marcel when she said he was playing hide-and-seek!"

"You might be right. But are you really sure? What does this mean, at the end?" Jean-Paul pointed at something written in tiny handwriting along the side of the letter. "PS. On the other side, you will see that our friend sends you a little gift. He says you've wanted it for a long time."

Gustave flipped the letter over, but there was nothing on the back. Nothing but a slightly greasy mark. "What's that? Where's the gift?" Jean-Paul demanded. "It looks like something was stuck there."

Gustave stared at the greasy mark, baffled, and then at almost the same moment, he and Jean-Paul both reached for the envelope. Gustave grabbed it first. He opened it, turned it upside down, and shook it. A small yellow feather fell out and fluttered down onto the table.

# ★ 38 ★

"*Il joue à cache-cache! Il joue à cache-cache!*" *He's playing hide-and-seek!* Jean-Paul couldn't stop saying it as they rode the subway down to Battery Park. "How did you know? All that time, how did you *know* that he was alive, Gustave?"

"I didn't know. I just hoped."

"How do you think your friend Nicole got that feather? She couldn't have seen him, could she?"

"I don't think so. Maybe her father's Resistance connections got it to her somehow. It must be through them that she found out that Marcel is in hiding."

Gustave still felt as if he were in a dream as they left the subway, found Battery Park, and got into a long line of kids carrying crates and bags full of flattened cans.

Guy and André, in Boy Scout uniform, were up ahead in the line. Jean-Paul shouted to them. Guy heard and nudged André, and they both turned around and waved. There were a lot more Negro kids around than there were

285

at Joan of Arc Junior High. Ahead in the line, Gustave saw younger boys who looked Chinese, and immediately behind him and Jean-Paul was a group of kids speaking rapidly in Spanish. A warm breeze blew, making a cluster of daffodils by a park bench bob up and down. It was finally April, and after the long, cold New York winter, spring was really here.

"Gustave!" September Rose appeared to Gustave's left. "He's my friend," she said to the girl behind Gustave. "Can I cut in line?" The girl nodded and stepped back, letting her in.

"Who's that?" Jean-Paul whispered, nudging him.

"That's September Rose," Gustave whispered. Then, speaking in English, but slowly, so Jean-Paul would understand, he said to Seppie, "This is my cousin, Jean-Paul."

"Hi," she said.

*"September Rose?"* Jean-Paul said the name with emphasis as the line moved forward, nudging Gustave and smirking. "Pleased to meet you!"

"You've got a lot of cans," Seppie said as they got near the front, glancing in Jean-Paul's bag and Gustave's. "But look at mine!" She held up not one shopping bag but two, both of them heavy with flattened metal.

"Where did you get all of those?" Gustave asked. "I thought you weren't going to be able to get any besides what we collected."

"That's what I thought too. Some of these are the ones we got that day. But look what my Granma did." She held up an irregularly shaped, flattened piece of blue metal.

It took Gustave a minute to figure it out. "Is that one of your grandmother's birds?"

September Rose looked at him with a peculiar expression, partly proud and partly mournful. "She took them all down, smashed them, and gave them to me to donate. Every single one. She said that it was the best way to bring Dad home. But the apartment is so empty now, and quiet."

He could see it, how it must look to her and Alan and her grandmother, the blankness of the rooms without the delicate, brilliant birds, the silence of the fire escape without the chimes. The April wind would blow through the apartment as the days grew warm, and there would be no sound.

They had moved forward, and they were almost at the head of the line. "Pour them in here," a cheerful man was saying, pointing to a bin. "Support our boys overseas!"

They tipped their shopping bags into the bin, first Jean-Paul, then Gustave, and then September Rose. The colors of the flattened birds flashed and then slid down among hundreds of other pieces of metal, disappearing into the silvery-gray heap as if they had never been.

September Rose hurried off to find the chorus, and Gustave and Jean-Paul looked for the flagpole where they were meeting up with the Boy Scouts. Battery Park was at the very southern end of Manhattan, overlooking New York Harbor. Beyond the grounds and walkways of the park, the sun moved out from behind the clouds, glittering on the blue-green water. The park was getting crowded with groups of students talking and laughing.

"There's the flagpole!" Jean-Paul shouted. "I see them!" They ran to the base of the pole to join their group of scouts.

"Ah, good. There you are!" Father René said. "Our whole group is here now, François!" he called to Rabbi Blum. "Let's go, everyone. The ceremony will begin soon." There wasn't time to tell Rabbi Blum the good news about Marcel now, Gustave thought. He didn't want to talk about it in front of a lot of people. But he'd tell the rabbi at his next bar mitzvah lesson. Just the thought of having the good news to tell made him feel buoyant with joy again.

The troop found their places on the temporary stage.

"Post the Colors. Scouts salute!" It was an Eagle Scout, an older boy from troop 2332. With his fingers at his forehead, Gustave watched the colors of the American flag ripple in the wind. The Pledge of Allegiance began, and he was saying it too, with the others, in English. The final words were the best ones, even if they weren't always true: "With Liberty and Justice for all."

After the flag salute, the Boy Scouts left the stage. Men in suits made speeches about supporting the soldiers and pulling together for the country. And then came the singing. Choruses from school after school filed onto the stage, sang, and filed off. Finally the familiar faces from Joan of Arc Junior High were in front of them. September Rose was in the back and not very visible, but Gustave heard her voice, confident and powerful, mingling with the others yet distinct, soaring out into the open air.

By the time the concert was over, the sun was setting,

and it was getting chilly. Two policemen were tending a bonfire, and a lot of the crowd moved in that direction. The bonfire had a high barrier on one side, and Gustave was relieved that the barrier did seem high enough to keep the light from shining out to sea, keeping the ships along the coast safe from Nazi U-boats.

"Bonfire or roller-skating?" asked Bernard.

"Roller-skating," said Maurice. "I'm meeting Jacqueline there."

"Ooh, Jacqueline! Let's all go see *Jacqueline*!" said Xavier.

"Don't you dare embarrass her," said Maurice, scowling at him.

They all went together. The line to rent roller skates was long. The rink, which was a large expanse of plywood a foot or so off the ground with rough wooden railings and entrances at each end, was already full of skaters circling. A small group of musicians stood to the side, playing patriotic music, and vendors were selling food and drink. The smell of hot chocolate and frankfurters wafted through the air.

Gustave waited in line with the others. When he got to the front, he pulled a dime out of his pocket, and the man behind the counter handed him a pair of scuffed roller skates. The laces were in a snarl. By the time he had untangled them, the other Boy Scouts were up on their feet and skating. Gustave buttoned his coat and tied his roller skates with cold fingers. He saw that Xavier had fallen, and André was laughing at him and pulling him up. Maurice was skating next to a tall, willowy girl with a shy smile. Martha and Leo glided by, holding hands. Toward the center Gustave caught a glimpse of September Rose's blue hat with the pom-pom. He jumped up from the bench and hurried to the rink, impatiently waiting in line to step up onto the platform. He wobbled once, then got his balance. Gracelessly but quickly, he pushed his way across the skating surface to the spot where she was. Seppie seemed especially tall today in her roller skates—a good three inches or so taller than he was.

"Hi!" he gasped, catching up with her. "You sang in front of your first big audience! Congratulations!"

Her eyes were bright in the evening air as she looked over at him. "Thanks!"

"I have news," he said. "My friend Marcel. He's alive."

She stared at him, gliding forward, and nearly fell when her skate hit a bump in the rough plywood. "You got a letter?"

"Yes. From my friend Nicole. Her father knows people. Marcel is alive, but hiding."

September Rose shrieked and jumped, and then she did fall. Gustave swirled to a messy stop just beyond her and then circled back and helped her to her feet. "I'm so, so glad," she said.

*"Clear the rink!"* boomed a voice over the sound system after they had circled a few times.

"But we just started!" Gustave protested.

"They're doing specials," said September Rose as they

skated to the exit, filed down, and stepped off onto the damp grass. "Wait and see—it'll be fun."

"*Salut,* Gustave!" Jean-Paul, Guy, and Xavier materialized, holding cups of hot chocolate.

"This is Guy and Xavier from my Boy Scout troop," he said to Seppie. "You know my cousin Jean-Paul. Fellows, this is my friend September Rose."

"Hello, *September Rose!*" Xavier emphasized her name, grinning, but the others just said hello and smiled in a knowing way.

"Now in the rink," the announcer called, "let's have *girls only!*"

"So long, boys!" September Rose said tauntingly, and she went back up the stairs and skated off. The rink filled quickly.

"Look at all those girls!" Bernard marveled as bright coats and hats and hair flashed by.

The musicians struck up a familiar tune. "'Don't Sit Under the Apple Tree with Anyone Else but Me!'" several of the girls shrieked at once.

"Let's do the movements we do to this song in physical education," Martha called.

Girls' voices started singing the song, September Rose among them. Many girls were doing hand movements in unison while they were skating. September Rose whizzed by. "No, no, no!" she sang, one hand on her hip, the other arm straight out, shaking a finger toward the other laughing girls who were doing the same thing.

"Clear the rink!" the announcer called again as the

song came to an end. The girls moaned good-naturedly and rolled toward the stairs. The boys lined up, ready to go on, sure it was their turn. Leo, who was at the front of the line, had already started skating when the announcer laughed at him and said, "Now let's have *couples only!*"

Amid lots of shrieking and giggling and people pushing and pulling each other, three or four couples got onto the rink and skated around the open space as slow, dreamy music played. Then a few pairs of girls joined hands and jumped in. "A couple just means two people!" one of the girls shouted as she skated by.

"That's a very poor showing, boys!" the announcer chided. "Come on, *couples only.*"

By now, many more couples had formed. Maurice and Jacqueline went by, and then Gustave saw Martha and Leo. A Negro boy and girl who looked like high school students skated by, moving very expertly, swirling around, one skating backward while the other skated forward. Gustave's heart pounded. Should he ask September Rose? He caught her eye across the rink, and she very distinctly shook her head. He felt disappointed and relieved at the same time. Then he noticed an older Negro boy making his way over to her and saying something. September Rose nodded hesitantly, took his hand, and stepped onto the rink. Hand in hand they glided along the rink, curving around the end and skating past the other Boy Scouts. Gustave felt a burning in his chest as he watched them go by.

"That's more like it!" the announcer boomed. "Clear

the rink. And now, everybody's favorite special: *crack the whip!*"

Long, screaming chains of kids crowded onto the rink, and as they came to a curve, the ones inside slowed almost to a standstill and pulled until the ones on the outer end whizzed around the bend. Gustave joined a chain with Xavier, Jean-Paul, and Bernard and skated around dizzily.

On the far end of the platform, several people crashed into each other and fell. A whistle blew. A rowdy group of boys zipped by. They seemed to be slamming into people on purpose. Suddenly their chain smashed into the Boy Scouts. An older boy in a gray cap crashed heavily into Jean-Paul. "Ooh, sor-ry!" he said mockingly as Jean-Paul went down hard.

Jean-Paul got up slowly. His lip was bleeding where his teeth had cut it. "I'm going to go get a soda," he said to Gustave and got off the platform.

"I'm getting off too." Gustave skated behind him, catching up. "But I don't want anything to drink. You go."

The whistle blew again. "Clear the rink!" the announcer boomed. "And now let's have a few quieter numbers. *Couples only!*"

The rowdy boys got off the platform in a pack and gathered near the spot at the end of the rink where Gustave and the other French Boy Scouts were standing, near the hot-chocolate line. Maurice went off to join Jacqueline again. In the crowd around the edges of the rink, Gustave caught sight of Seppie's hat with the pom-pom.

She was standing with her friend Lisa and a tall Negro boy, somebody Gustave didn't recognize.

He found his feet moving before he knew what he was planning to do. He stumbled over the damp grass in his heavy skates, heading around the rink toward Seppie. She looked up and saw him coming. When he was still at a distance from her, he held up his hand, flashing a double "V," and then he held out his other hand toward her. She hesitated. But then she smiled and flashed the sign back. A moment later they were stepping onto the rink together, their hands clasped, and then they had joined the coupled skaters.

Gustave and September Rose soon got into sync with each other, pushing and gliding, pushing and gliding. The wind rushed against his face, cool now after the brief, deceptive warmth of the April day. The sky was starting to darken, and he could smell the ocean and the smoke from the bonfire. Seppie looked over at him and laughed. *Marcel is alive!* Gustave thought, with a rush of joy.

The rink was wide open ahead of them, much less crowded than it had been when he'd been skating before. As they turned at the curved end of the rink and headed back, he saw the dusky harbor and in it the Statue of Liberty, tall, majestic, holding up her glowing lamp. The light of her lamp was dimmed now, because of the war, but it was still faintly shining.

As Gustave and September Rose passed the spot at the edge of the rink where the other scouts were standing, Guy waved. Up ahead a boy was skating with a much taller girl, and Gustave heard the group of rowdy older boys taunting the pair as they went by. "Hey, Shorty! You're skating with a skyscraper. What's it like skating with *the Empire State Building*?" The couple turned, heading around the bend, and as they came back Gustave saw that the girl's face had gone a painful red and that there were tears in her eyes.

Noticing again how tall September Rose looked in her skates, Gustave veered toward the center of the rink, pulling her along with him. "Hey, where are we going?" she shouted, laughing.

Several other couples glided by on the outer edge. He heard another couple made up of a short boy and a taller girl getting jeered at. "Skyscraper alert! Hey, Shorty! What's it like skating with *the Woolworth Building*?"

But that couple was quick and fearless. They were both really good skaters. The boy swirled the tall girl around showily, ignoring the taunt. Her black curls floated through the air.

Gustave and September Rose glided along the length of the platform, away from the rowdy group. Gustave could feel the bumps in the plywood as he skated methodically, push, glide, push, glide. Some of the pleasure had gone out of it. They rounded the far end and headed back down the rink. Gustave saw the Statue of Liberty again dimly in the distance. They were approaching the end where the rowdy boys were, and both of them were skating stiffly now, bracing themselves. September Rose's hand inside his was taut, clenched. *What's another skyscraper?* Gustave thought frantically. The Empire State Building, the Woolworth Building . . .

"Skyscraper alert!" one of the rowdies jeered, his voice low and insinuating.

Another voice shouted, "Hey! That Boy Scout kid's skating with a Negro!"

"Hey, Boy Scout!" several voices jeered. "What's it like skating with a n—"

But before they could finish the insult, Gustave was yelling in English, as loudly as he could, drowning them out, *"Yeah, yeah! I know I'm short! I'm skating with the Statue of Liberty!"*

September Rose looked at him, startled, then smiled, and as they turned at the rink's end, she lifted her hand in a regal gesture just like the statue's, holding up a beacon of light.

The music was ending. *"Everybody skate!"* the announcer boomed. Soon the rink was mobbed with people. September Rose kept her hand in Gustave's, but they had to slow down, maneuvering their way through the crowd.

Several kids from Joan of Arc Junior High went by. Leo and Martha skated up, arm in arm. "Hey, good one, Gus, September Rose," Leo said, looking over at them. "We saw that."

"Yeah, you showed them!" Martha giggled. She was a tiny bit taller than Leo, Gustave noticed. "I was afraid of what they were going to say when we went by, but you shut them up!"

Suddenly someone crashed into Gustave hard from behind. He let go of September Rose's hand and fell, slamming against the rough plywood.

"Are you okay?" Seppie reached down and pulled him up.

As he got unsteadily to his feet, the boy with the gray cap zoomed at him from the right, and he went down heavily again, landing on his elbow. He heard jeers. "Why are you skating with a n—"

"Get lost, you creeps!" André shouted. He and Jean-Paul were suddenly on the rink to Gustave's right, and Maurice and Xavier circled around to the left of September Rose. September Rose pulled Gustave up again, her face determined, and the two of them stood still before starting off again slowly, not holding hands this time. The French Boy Scouts stayed on either side of them.

"I've got your back!" Leo called, and, glancing over his shoulder, Gustave saw him and Martha, hand in hand, gliding behind them. Lisa and the tall Negro boy she'd been skating with came up and joined Maurice and Xavier on the left.

Gustave and September Rose looked at each other and clasped hands again.

Surrounded by the others, they skated through the dusk. This is what America is *supposed* to be like, Gustave thought, everyone equal, everyone free. But it isn't! Off to his left, Xavier laughed. Gustave looked over at him.

"We're still right behind you, Gus!" Leo shouted.

September Rose's hand was warm in his. "This is great!" she said, her eyes shining.

And suddenly happiness flooded over Gustave. Maybe America wasn't always like this. Not always the way it was supposed to be. But at this very moment, it was. He would write back to Nicole tonight and tell her about how this moment felt. America wasn't perfect. No place was perfect. But America had saved his life and the lives of his family. Gustave's new life was going to be here, in this country. He knew that now, and his future stretched out ahead of him, unknowable, unimaginable, but full of promise and hope.

Gustave would always be partly French in his heart. But he was on his way to becoming an American. He had friends in this strange new country. Despite everything that made it difficult, he and September Rose were really friends. And Gustave was right here, right now, alive on this particular April evening in New York, as dusk fell over the Statue of Liberty, with his friends around him, skating with September Rose.

# ★ AUTHOR'S NOTE ★

*Skating with the Statue of Liberty* is a work of fiction. But like *Black Radishes*, my earlier novel about Gustave in France, it was inspired by my father's experiences during the war. Like Gustave, my father, Jean-Pierre Meyer, came to the United States as a French Jewish refugee in 1942. Along with his mother and sister, he sailed from Lisbon into Baltimore Harbor on the *Carvalho Araujo*. From there they took a train to New York and settled in Manhattan. My father attended Joan of Arc Junior High, as Gustave does, and my grandmother learned English in night classes at the same school. Many of the events in this novel were inspired by my father's experiences, including the incident on the train involving the jeweler's suitcase, Gustave's first encounter with the German music teacher, and the winter camping trip with the Boy Scouts. The Franco-American Scout troops were very important to my father and my aunt Eliane Norman (the original *Méhari Pondéré* and *Éponge Tenace*!) as they adjusted to life in the United States.

In one way, my father's arrival was even more dramatic than Gustave's. For reasons having to do with the plot of *Black Radishes*, I had Gustave and his family arrive in the United States in January of 1942. But when the *Carvalho Araujo* actually sailed from Lisbon carrying my father, my aunt, and my grandmother, it docked in Baltimore on November 2, 1942. Nine days later, on November 11, 1942, Nazi forces occupied what had been the Unoccupied Zone of France, the safer part of the country, where my father's family had been living. So they and the other passengers on this ship were among the last French Jews to escape. In fact, a Portuguese ship, which may have been the *Carvalho Araujo*, left Baltimore on November 7, on its way back to Europe, on a mission to bring five hundred more French Jewish children to safety. But it was too late. Those children were refused exit permits and were not able to escape from France.

As Gustave does, my father worried about the fate of his family and friends left behind in France as he adjusted to life in America, and like Gustave, he found that his English improved from listening intently to the war news on the radio on WQXR. Little was known in the early war years about the fate of the Jews in Europe, but it was clear that they were in grave danger. The American news media devoted much more attention at the time to what was going on in the Pacific than to the war news from Europe, although a few newsreels did mention German internment camps.

The Double V Campaign is no longer widely remembered, but it was an early campaign against racial segregation. In February of 1942, the *Pittsburgh Courier*, a prominent black newspaper, published the letter by James G. Thompson that started the campaign, in which he urged blacks to fight for victory abroad but also for victory at home, to fight their second-class status in America. The *Courier* used a double V insignia on its front page for the duration of the war. Other newspapers picked it up, and the double V became a popular antisegregation rallying cry. The racial terms used in the novel—"Colored" and "Negro"—are of course the terms that were used in the 1940s, which the characters would have been familiar with, not those used in the present day.

To get a feeling for life in New York in the 1940s, and in particular for race and interethnic relations as they were experienced on a daily basis, I talked to a number of people who could either recall that period or who could recall family stories told about life in New York in that period. I'm grateful to Rita Howard, Anthony Pazzanita, Charlotte Winkler, Margery Sabin, Jim Sabin, and Eric Velasquez for sharing stories about all aspects of life in New York and life in the 1940s. Memoirs of the period also proved useful in allowing me to envision various aspects of my characters' lives in the 1940s, particularly Faith Ringgold's *We Flew Over the Bridge,* Althea Gibson's *I Always Wanted to Be Somebody,* Charles B. Rangel's *And I Haven't Had a Bad Day Since,* James McBride's *The Color of Water,* Madeleine L'Engle's *Two-Part Invention,* Gerd Korman's *Nightmare's Fairy Tale: A Young Refugee's Home Fronts 1938–1948,* Sophie Freud's *Living in the Shadow of the Freud Family,* Edith Kurzweil's *Full Circle: A Memoir,* and Livia Bitton-Jackson's *Hello, America.*

I read widely while researching the novel, and the following works of history and primary sources were particularly helpful. For information on race relations: *Harlem at War: The Black Experience in World War II* (1996) by Nat Brandt; *This Was Harlem: A Cultural Portrait, 1900–1950* (1981) by Jervis Anderson; *The Double V Campaign* (1998) by Michael L. Cooper; *To Stand and Fight: The Struggle for Civil Rights in Postwar New York City* (2003) by Martha Biondi; and *Fog of War: The Second World War and the Civil Rights Movement* (2012), edited by Kevin M. Kruse and Stephen Tuck. For information about daily life: the *New York Times* historical archive online and *Don't You Know There's a War On? The American Home Front,*

*1941–1945* (1970) by Richard R. Lingeman. For information about the demographics of New York: *The WPA Guide to New York City* (1939), published by the Federal Writers' Project, and "1943 New York City Market Analysis," scanned by the CUNY Graduate Center's Center for Urban Research and online at 1940snewyork.com. For information about Jewish refugees: *Flight from the Reich: Refugee Jews 1933–1946* (2009) by Debórah Dwork and Robert Jan van Pelt and *Visas to Freedom: The History of HIAS* (1956) by Mark Wischnitzer. For information about the postal system, letters from France, and censors: "United States Mail to France in World War II, Part II" by Lawrence Sherman in *American Philatelist* 127 (February 2013) and *Je vous écris de France: Lettres inédites à la BBC 1940–1944* (2014) by Aurélie Luneau. I'm also grateful to my aunt for giving me letters that had been opened by censors during the war.

For those readers who may be wondering, Rabbi Blum has been reading William James's "The Will to Believe" (1896).

In some small ways, I adjusted minor historical events for the purposes of the novel. The Chiquita Banana jingle, designed to teach Americans how to ripen this exotic fruit, actually hit the airwaves two years after the events in the novel. And I pushed back the major construction on the Brooklyn-Battery Tunnel by a few months to allow the schools to gather in Battery Park for the Victory Rally in the spring of 1942.

That spring, New York was in a partial dim-out, and the only lights burning at the Statue of Liberty were two 200-watt lamps in the torch, illuminated at night to guide US aircraft.

Like Gustave, my father enjoyed eating at Nedick's as a boy and at the Automat, where he especially loved the cheesecake!

# ★ ACKNOWLEDGMENTS ★

My father, Jean-Pierre Meyer, and my aunt Eliane Norman shared with me memories of their childhood in France and their early years in New York. This book would not have come into being without those stories, and I am deeply grateful to them. I am also thankful to others who shared stories and memories: Margery Sabin, Jim Sabin, Rita Howard, Anthony Pazzanita, Charlotte Winkler, and Eric Velasquez. Susan Elia MacNeal related to me an anecdote about Edna MacNeal that found its way into this novel. Abigail Samoun shared intriguing anecdotes about her own childhood immigration, many years after Gustave's, from France to the United States. Phyllis Brooks Schafer, who has an extraordinarily precise memory, helped me with details about daily life in early 1940s America.

I am grateful to Misha Mitsel, senior archivist at the American Jewish Joint Distribution Committee, and to Deb Weiner, family history coordinator at the Jewish Museum of Maryland, for locating helpful and inspirational documents from my family history.

My Wellesley colleague, economist Ann Velenchik, helped me make sense of the arcane regulations violated by the real-life jeweler on whom my character Monsieur Benoit is based, leading to his arrest on the train from Baltimore to New York.

Thank you to my Wellesley College French Department colleagues Venita Datta, Michèle Respaut, Jim Petterson, Marie-Paule Tranvouez, Sylvaine Egron-Sparrow, and Hélène Bilis, as well as to Michel Bilis and Alice Kaplan, and particularly to Catherine Masson, Barry Lydgate, and Claude Beauclair for helping me with arcane questions about French usage and French expressions from the 1940s.

Laura Reiner, research and instruction librarian at Wellesley College, has been an extraordinary help to me, enthusiastically and energetically assisting me in finding just about anything I could think of: subway maps of New York in this period; a demographic survey of the city indicating, block by block, the ethnicity and the income range of the people who lived there; even detailed information about the international postal situation during World War II.

Jacqueline Davies read an early draft of the first chapters and gave thought-provoking advice. The members of my writing group, Susan Lubner, Patty Bovie, and Anna Staniszewski, read draft after draft of this manuscript, giving astute commentary as well as encouragement and support. My thanks to Erin Murphy, my agent, for believing in this book before it existed and for moral support as it came into being.

Alison Meyer gave me the moon at a time when I really needed it. Thank you.

Rebecca Weston, my wonderful editor, waited with patience and understanding for this novel and responded to early drafts with both rigor and enthusiasm, helping me see what the book could and should become. Without her intensity, her confidence in me, and her insight, this novel would not be what it is.

And thank you, as always, to Ken Winkler and to Hannah Meyer-Winkler for their daily love, encouragement, and belief.

# READ ABOUT GUSTAVE'S ADVENTURES IN FRANCE!

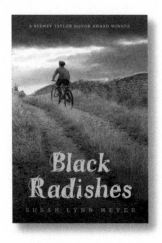

Gustave doesn't want to move from the exciting city to the boring countryside, far from his cousin Jean-Paul and his best friend, the mischievous Marcel. But he has no choice. It is March of 1940, and Paris is not a safe place for Jews.

When Paris is captured by the Nazis, Gustave knows that Marcel, Jean-Paul, and their families *must* make it out of the occupied zone. And when he learns that his new friend Nicole works for the French Resistance, he comes up with a plan that just might work.

But going into Occupied France is a risky thing to do when you are Jewish. And coming back alive? *That* is nearly impossible.

## PRAISE FOR
## *BLACK RADISHES*

A Sydney Taylor Honor Award Winner

A Bank Street College of Education
Best Children's Book of the Year

An *Instructor* Magazine Best Kids' Book: Historical Fiction

A Massachusetts Book Award Must-Read Book

A Boston Authors Club Highly Recommended Book

An Illinois Rebecca Caudill
Young Readers Book Award Finalist

A Pennsylvania School Librarians Association Top 40 Book

———

"More than an account of Jewish survival in Nazi-occupied France, *Black Radishes* is an empowering, suspenseful story of a unique young boy with cunning, patience, and courage."
—Francisco X. Stork, winner of the Schneider
Family Book Award for *Marcelo in the Real World*

"A fascinating, deftly gripping tale that reminds readers, young or old, of events we must never forget."
—Zilpha Keatley Snyder,
three-time Newbery Honor winner and author of *The Egypt Game*

"*Black Radishes* is a vivid and moving story about a Jewish family's efforts to escape the Nazis, seen through the eyes of a clear-sighted and sensitive young boy. Susan Lynn Meyer manages to capture the reader's interest from the start and keeps up the suspense until the last pages." —Annika Thor, winner of the Mildred L. Batchelder Award for *A Faraway Island*

"*Black Radishes* transforms the past into a gripping story. Gustave's growing maturity and loss of innocence perfectly mirror the mounting horrors he and his family experience."
—Kit Pearson, winner of the
Governor General's Literary Award for *Awake and Dreaming*

"This debut novel, loosely based on the author's father's experiences . . . raises important questions about nationalism, equality and identity and fills a void in Holocaust literature for this age group." —*Kirkus Reviews*

"[Depicts] vivid details of daily life and the . . . changes slowly taking place within Gustave. This fine first novel could be read in conjunction with *The Good Liar.*" —*Booklist*

"Meyer builds the tension by using real-life events (detailed in an author's note), creating in Gustave a very believable boy struggling to learn to cover up his emotions, who behaves bravely when he must."
—*The Bulletin of the Center for Children's Books*

"A dramatic tale of courage and determination."
—*School Library Journal*

"Meyer delivers a rich, well-written tale of lost innocence and newfound courage." —*Association of Jewish Libraries Reviews*

"This story will not disappoint children looking for a safe entry into the subject of the Holocaust. . . . Children will enjoy this well-told story about the day-to-day struggles of a French family." —*Jewish Book World*

"Full of tension, this coming-of-age story presents a picture of life during the early days of World War II."
—*Children's Literature: Independent Information and Reviews*

"Meyer offers up a colourful, intelligent story that is true to the child's perspective and told in a deft, natural prose that makes it eminently involving on school scenes, breath-stopping encounters with Nazi guards and family conversations." —*Toronto Star*

"Meyer provides a fresh take on the experiences of World War II with Gustave's story of survival in Occupied France. . . . A successful blend of history and adventure that is sure to appeal to middle-grade readers." —*The Edmond Sun*

# ★ ABOUT THE AUTHOR ★

SUSAN LYNN MEYER'S *Skating with the Statue of Liberty* is the companion to her debut novel, *Black Radishes,* which won a Sydney Taylor Honor Award and was named a Massachusetts Book Award finalist and a Bank Street College of Education Best Book of the Year. Both books were inspired by stories she grew up hearing about her father's childhood escape from Nazi-occupied France and his early years in New York City. She lives with her family in Massachusetts and teaches literature and creative writing at Wellesley College. Visit her online at susanlynnmeyer.com.